THERE

ONLY ZUUL.

ENJOY

Fire on the Water

A Companion to Mary Shelley's *Frankenstein*

By
P.J. Parker

First published by The Writer's Coffee Shop, 2013

Copyright © P.J. Parker, 2013

The right of -P.J. Parker- to be identified as the author of this work has been asserted by her under the *Copyright Amendment (Moral Rights) Act 2000*

This work is copyrighted. All rights are reserved. Apart from any use as permitted under the Copyright Act 1968, no part may be reproduced, copied, scanned, stored in a retrieval system, recorded or transmitted, in any form or by any means, without the prior written permission of the publisher.

All characters and events in this Book – even those sharing the same name as (or based upon) real people – are entirely fictional. Any resemblance to real persons, living or dead ... *or undead* ... is purely coincidental. No person, brand or corporation mentioned in this Book should be taken to have endorsed this Book nor should the events surrounding them be considered in any way factual.
This Book is a work of fiction and should be read as such.

The Writer's Coffee Shop
(Australia)   PO Box 447 Cherrybrook NSW 2126
(USA)   PO Box 2116 Waxahachie TX 75168

Paperback ISBN- 978-1-61213-196-2
E-book ISBN- 978-1-61213-197-9

A CIP catalogue record for this book is available from the US Congress Library.

Cover design by L.J. Anderson

www.thewriterscoffeeshop.com/pjparker

This one is for Jack.

"Did I request thee, Maker, from my clay to mould me Man? Did I solicit thee from darkness to promote me?"

Paradise Lost, X, 743-5 (Milton)

"Sometimes it is so easy to believe in things that we know may not be true. Perhaps it is belief more than truth that helps us survive."

Adam

Fire on the Water

Prologue

To: Margaret.Saville@newyork.com
From: WaltonRachel@freemail.ch
Date: December 11

Dear Margie,
 Arrived in Montreux early this evening on the 7:05 from Geneva.
 I was reticent to leave Geneva's cobbled passageways, its chic restaurants and unexpected bars hidden in dark subterranean basements. The blaring techno, filling clubs no bigger than my tiny Manhattan apartment, always promised a good night surrounded by sexy French-Swiss sailors, invariably with their shirts off by midnight.
 You'll be glad to hear the months I spent researching Mary in the Université de Genève archives have allowed me to complete the first draft of the bio. Methodical review of several scores of tomes and essays, thousands of paper scraps, notes and ledger entries, as well as personal documents belonging to Byron and a number of Geneva households of the time period, have created a broader view of my subject than would have been possible back in Manhattan—or even during my time spent in the reading rooms of the London Literary Museums. But it has been without a doubt the days and nights wandering the twisting streets and quiet squares of Geneva's medieval Vieille Ville that have heavily influenced the style of the work. I can picture Mary at eighteen, exuberant and full of life, self-exiled from the strictures of Mother England with Percy and Lord Byron, taking tea and croissants in the cafes surrounding the Pice du Bourg-de-Four, or walking hand-in-hand along the Promenade des Orpailleurs as it hugs the churning current of the Arve toward the Rhone—and always with the majesty of Mont Blanc in the distance.
 How it must have excited their imaginations!
 I could have daydreamed on the ferry for the full length of the lake from

Geneva to Montreux, but decided to make the journey by train instead so I might spend the afternoon in Lausanne with the subtle ambience of Quai d' Ouchy, the exhilarating sumptuousness of the Beau-Rivage Palace.

I've yet to find permanent accommodation here in Montreux. Meanwhile, I have booked into the Suisse Majestic Grand Hotel for the week, hoping to locate a small studio to call home for the next several months while I complete the research and writing.

You may think me strange, but I'm certain there is more to Mary Shelley connected with this beautiful, idyllic town than the archives would suggest. There's something that keeps nagging at me. While her husband, Percy, and friend Lord Byron crisscrossed the lake and Swiss Alps on their own adventures, did she really stay within the confines of her suite to write *Frankenstein*? This magnificent village calls for afternoon constitutionals, beckons to be explored, demands visitors be awed by its simple beauty and mystery. I see her sitting at her graceful Maggiolini desk, her pen lying dormant in its well of ink, yet to write the horrors filling her head as she stares out the window. Would she dare step out alone into the crooked and convoluted laneways? Did she make her own discoveries in the primordial apothecaries, decaying bookshops, and intimate cafes and salons?

Something must have occurred here to jolt the monster into existence.

Something occurred while she was here on her own.

Alone.

This evening, I spoiled myself with a magnificent steak tartare at the Confiserie Zurcher on Avenue du Casino. The *maître d'hôtel* assured me the onions, capers, and raw egg were all from the chef's own garden. The rye bread was unbelievable. It was dark by the time I walked the several blocks along Avenue des Alpes back to the hotel. Grand apartment buildings rise on either side to cast the street into an almost pitch blackness, lit only by the glow of light seeping through closed shutters. Mansions in the Belle Époque style loom like whitewashed specters from secretive walled gardens that make the imagination wander. A chilling December breeze promised snowfall, however I stopped awhile in the dark, listening to the tones of a saxophone drifting from somewhere up above me. The somber, haunting melody transported me to another time when Mary may have strolled unaccompanied along this very avenue. I pressed my back against a cold, stone façade among voluminous reams of ivy, and took in a vista of an ancient streetscape altered little since she was here.

There was not another soul to be seen.

Just me, the intriguing, forbidding avenue, the first flakes of snow, and my thoughts of Mary . . .

I promise to e-mail the initial draft of the biography by the end of this week. I'm certain you'll agree with what I'm feeling. But for now, my dear editor and friend, it's time to crawl up into my oversized bed with its quilt almost two feet thick with duck and goose feathers.

Rachel

Fire on the Water

To: Margaret.Saville@newyork.com
From: WaltonRachel@freemail.ch
Date: March 28

Dear Margie,
Time passes so slowly here. But with the passage of the landscape into a beautiful spring, I'm becoming more and more enamored by its beauty. The last few months of research have been revealing as I trawl through the documents and parchments stored in Château de Chillon and the private libraries of families who have resided along this placid shoreline since before the time of the Savoys. One family, who live in a wonderful Tyrolean Chalet hidden up in the forested mountainside of Hauts-de-Montreux, have entrusted me with a chest full of letters and diaries that hasn't been opened for generations. My heart leaps whenever I touch its burnished silver latch, but methodology demands I complete my study of the Chillon papers before delving into its depths.

I acquired a lovely little studio in the outer buildings of Le Château du Châtelard—a massive fortress, now converted into apartments, that dominates the ridge above the villages of Montreux and Clarens. I suspect my small space was once a stable, and I love it even more for that possibility. It has its own private courtyard and a terrace with a view of local vineyards and across the rooftops of Montreux to the lake and mountains beyond. The rent is quite inexpensive, which I'm very glad of, as my meager savings will need to stretch much further than I had originally anticipated in finishing this project.

The true purpose of this e-mail, however, is to tell you something I never could have dreamed possible in this quest. His name is Jack and he's from Chicago. I saw him at Harry's Bar in the Montreux Palace Hotel and in no time found out he's a literature teacher at the nearby American school. At twenty-three, just a few days older than me, he's all blond, tussled hair, ridiculous smile, and powerful, tattooed arms. We hit it off right away and there's not a day we don't see each other. Honestly, I haven't felt like this since college days. I spend weekends riding passenger on his Harley, my cheek pressed hard against the soft, brown leather of his jacket, which does nothing but enhance his physique. Together we've discovered the Valais, the myriad walled laneways that snake through the countryside among dormant vineyards, and the isolated hiking trails of Foret de Jor. In late January we rode up through rain and sleet on snow-covered roads via Les Diablerettes to view the hot-air balloon festival at Château-d'Oex. We were frozen by the time we were sipping hot chocolate *densa* on Le Petit Pre. The festival was canceled due to the miserable weather, but I didn't care. It was the most wonderful day of my life.
Love, Rachel

To: Margaret.Saville@newyork.com
From: WaltonRachel@freemail.ch
Date: July 7

I'm glad we got to talk on the phone last night. It was good to hear your voice.

I still can't fathom what's happened.

Officers from the Direction de la Sécurité Publique knocked on my studio door just after sunrise. I had barely finished my breakfast and was staring across the room at the unopened trunk—for the time had come to open it. The knock startled me, as Jack and I had already made plans to meet that evening, and I wasn't expecting any other company. As soon as they entered, my heart sank. I knew from the gray pallor of their faces before they mustered even one word.

A terrible, terrible accident, they said.

His motorbike a mangled mess, they said.

Dead, they said.

RW

To: Margaret.Saville@newyork.com
From: WaltonRachel@freemail.ch
Date: August 5

M,

I'm afraid I've done nothing these past weeks other than sit in my courtyard and gaze at the ivy that creeps and spills around its confines.

Dark clouds have rolled over the mountains to engulf the lake and town.

The chest remains unopened.

R

CHAPTER ONE

Château de Chillon sits plumply in the shallows of Lake Geneva, connected to the shore by a slim drawbridge and covered walkway. Dominant and foreboding in its isolation, it's the only building positioned where the forested Swiss Alps press in hard against the broad expanse of lake. Water laps all around the base of the ancient fortress; mollusks cling tight to the lowest blocks of chiseled, battle-worn stone.

From where Rachel sat, on a wall beside the lake's edge, the looming fortifications and turrets blocked any view of Montreux further to the west. The sun was setting, the sky a deep orange hue, and the last rays of light pierced through the heavy layer of storm clouds that had lain dormant above the lake for many days and nights. The eerie luminosity of waning daylight made the tiles on the château's conical and slanted roofs, and the thin slivers of glass in the highest windows, shine in defiance as they must have done for more than eight hundred years.

Rachel's gaze fell to the farthest edge of the structure where the water surged and eddied into the barred lake entrance of the dungeon. She could easily imagine being trapped in there, surrounded by raw rock face and stone columns graffitied by men and women who never left its miserable confinement alive. The thought made her own heart clench tight, an ache that had refused to leave her since Jack had been . . . since Jack had been sent back to Chicago.

She opened her laptop to review the paragraphs she'd typed the previous evening. She read them over and over again. The sentences seemed sad, depressing, not representative of her subject at all. They left her cold. Word by word she deleted the offending passages until only one line remained in the chapter. She stared at the few residual words without seeing them and then pressed the backspace button to wipe them from existence, one letter at a time.

The blank page seemed even more disconcerting. She reverted her gaze to the ancient building in front of her.

The château was abruptly lit up by a brilliant sheet of lightning that stretched the full width of the lake before snaking back on itself to plunge into the highest turret. The clap of thunder was immediate. It reverberated off the Alps, echoing back and forth across the lake, making the water ripple. The air vibrated and rumbled, and Rachel's skin crawled and shivered electric. A second streak followed the same course as the first and hit the same point, and the rolling crash of thunder filled the entire valley. Then came a third strike and its churning, suffocating rumble.

Rachel stared, horrified, as the fire staccatoed across the water and appeared to embrace, to lick, to caress the château with a mesmerizing glow, giving it unexpected life. The air tasted metallic, her hair lifted and cracked with static, and the heat drained from her body to dissipate out into the thickening darkness of approaching night. She closed her laptop and gathered her papers together before stuffing them into the duffel bag beneath her trench coat—not too soon, as the sky fractured and haphazardly split open with torrential rain and a battering, gusting wind flung down from the Alps.

The storm clouds tumbled and dropped to seize both earth and water in a crumpled, disorienting shroud. Rachel conceded it would be a long, wet, and uncomfortable hike back to Montreux and her studio.

Hurrying along Quai Alfred Chatelanant, Rachel squeezed between the whipping waters of the lake and a walled-off pasture, attempting to leave the unbearable thoughts of Jack behind her in the shifting shadows of Chillon's dungeon. She was submerged in a complete, foggy obscurity. The lake offered an iridescent glow, but still she had to feel her way along the gravel walkway, ensuring she stayed on its central ridge and not trip down into the ditches on either side that now ran fast with water.

Further streaks of electricity cut across the sky. They purged the night and illuminated the precipitation, their momentary intensity making perception even more difficult as Rachel stumbled through the downpour. The hollow clatter of bells echoed around her—unseen cattle in a nearby field, no doubt huddling under the protective canopies of trees. She could just detect the gleam of their eyes but was unsure; instead, she pulled her soaked coat tight about her shoulders, head held low, and continued moving one tentative step at a time toward Montreux.

It was several minutes before the opulent mansions of Quai Ami Chessex and Quai des Fleurs emerged out of the mist ahead of her. They forced her to continue along the water's edge, but at least the illumination from their manicured gardens and terraces made the route distinguishable. The Casino Barrière de Montreux was still many minutes' walk around the bay. It sparkled in the distance.

The storm intensified until she couldn't bear it. The sky itself was tormented and deafening. Rachel hunched her shoulders against the battering force, held her hands over her nose and mouth so she could breathe within the deluge, and concentrated on her feet as they sloshed through the rising depths of water now cascading across the walkway. Every droplet of water around her suddenly pulsed a gangrenous yellow-green, and she realized she was at the marina, near its beacon. She could just make out the shadow of the Rue de Bon-Port ferry terminal behind the insipid, repetitive glow. She ran toward it as fast as she dared, skirting the curve of the small harbor, wary of the waves that crashed and sprayed against the lakeside wall of the boardwalk.

The weight of the assault lifted as she passed the wrought iron columns holding the terracotta-tiled roof high above the open pier. The shriek of the wind skipped and dropped lower. It took several moments for her to catch her breath, and she took in the damp odor of the refuge as she threw off her waterlogged coat and attempted to shake the misery from it. Her blouse and jeans were saturated right through, clinging to her skin, offering no protection or humility. Thankfully her laptop, diary, and notes were dry inside her duffel.

She wiped at the moisture on her face and attempted to wring it from her hair as she studied her surroundings. The terminal was deserted. A small flotilla of pleasure craft bobbed behind its quay. The yachts were all pristine white, glistening in the rain, emblazoned with names in French that declared love and beauty: *Beau, Magnifique, Mon Ami, Amour.* Rachel was thoughtful of their message, her eyes stinging at the thought of love, not knowing what it meant to her anymore.

At the end of the terminal sat a lonely bench, and she knew she should keep it company—should wait out the worst of the tempest. She started toward it, her footsteps echoing against the concrete, making her stop now and then to ensure the echo was her own. Less than halfway there, she hesitated, standing motionless for several moments in the dim light. She listened to the wind and rain, to her own heartbeat, for anyone who might be sharing this refuge and gone unnoticed. The wind had begun to pick up again and now howled all around her and the space, through the exposed rafters of the roof, through the incessant, quickening thoughts of Jack that refused to leave her be.

In the several weeks since his death she'd been able to think of little else. All her life she'd been methodical, disciplined, and analytical—able to classify and place any aspect of her research, or existence, neatly and precisely into the correct box. But with Jack it had been different. And now that he was . . . now that he was gone, she was left confused and heartbroken. What they'd shared was something she couldn't label or categorize, something that seemed unreal and incredible. The warmth of his hand against the small of her back. The beguiling or serious conversations whispered into her ear, each thought punctuated by the touch of lips or caress of fingertips. The smell of his skin, his hair, his clothes. The excruciating excitement of his tongue pressed against her own, in between sips of Chardonnay and discussions of Mary and what her creation of the wretch represented . . .

Lightning struck through the night; thunder rumbled in its jagged wake.

As she peered around at the rain-splashed concourse, at the rattling downpipes that somehow clung to their wrought iron columns, her attention settled on the shutters of what she presumed must be the port master's office. She imagined the slightest movement of shadow and so called out toward it, her voice insignificant beneath the hammering torrent on the tiles above. She approached and knocked on the office door, but there was no answer. The large brass knob turned under her grip, but the door would not open, even with a push of her shoulder.

Again she thought she saw movement in the darkened ticket window. She called out a second time and peered through the grate into the office. The space was pitch black, but she stared into it until she resolved it was indeed empty, that she was alone, that Jack was not there . . .

She looked down at her hands on the ticket counter. Unease nudged at the back of her mind, scratched amongst her deepest fears. Her hands rested on the ledge, her fingers extending into the shadow. At first she dared not move them, then, slowly, she pulled them from the darkness. Unexpected relief caused her breath to catch in her throat as she confirmed they were intact. She clenched her hands tight and pressed them to her chest as she moved to the end of the ferry terminal, as far from the shadows as she could get.

Rachel slumped onto the bench and focused on the cold, hard concrete at her feet.

Uncomfortable, wet, and shivering beneath the flicker of fluorescent light, Rachel sank further than she had previously allowed herself. But she didn't care. She could suppress her emotions no longer, could hold back her feelings for what had happened to Jack no more. The first sob cut deep, exposing her heart to the full brunt of the turmoil that surrounded her. Somehow she felt glad for the pain, knowing it had to be confronted to be understood—even if only in some small way. The agonizing emotions and memories slashed into her and, one by one, were mangled by thoughts of metal, leather, and flesh, skidding, twisting, and disintegrating across the tar of an unknown Alpine road.

Shadows and puddles flowed and seeped about her as she pulled her feet up onto the bench and bent down until she was lying awkwardly on her side. Wet, trembling hands melded against her face so she could see only the pulsating darkness behind her eyelids, could feel only the painful throb of memories throughout her body, could continue to sob without the past weeks of numbness and restraint. The noise of the night dominated and drowned her anguish, sucking it from her until she was spent.

For the longest time she didn't move—her body and thoughts lying dormant, tending toward little more than a decayed loneliness, mixed, perhaps, with fragments of relief.

When she again became aware of the wet and cold discomfort, the gusting wind and downpour appeared even more harsh than it had before.

Tentatively she lifted her face from her hands to stare out into the darkness —to gaze past the dull ache she thought would never leave her. She rubbed at her eyes. Quick and sharp, the night, the rain, the hack of lightning and reverberating clamor of thunder came back into focus. In the distance, Chillon fluoresced behind the vacillating curtain of precipitation. The lake roiled, waves whipping up to six feet high, their surface broken and spotted by the weather, which refused to halt its attack. The medieval sea wall jutted out into the lake and curved around to a sheltered entrance to protect the small ferry harbor. Waves crashed and broke across it.

And then she saw *him*.

He stood in the downpour at the end of the breakwater. He was strongly built, his silhouette over seven and a half feet tall, maybe eight, his massive arms hanging lifelessly at his sides. He was wearing dark clothing. Thick, long, dark hair, sodden and miserable, whipped about his shoulders in the storm. Was he barefooted?

At first, Rachel thought he was looking out across the waters toward Chillon, but a swift vein of lightning revealed he was staring in her direction.

He was staring right at her.

It made her feel even more uncomfortable and alone. She looked around the ferry terminal, toward the bobbing yachts, to the mansions several minutes' run back along the walkway, and then back toward the lone figure at the end of the causeway. He continued to stare, motionless.

The rain cut down upon him.

He clenched his hand into a fist, a slight movement, but one that made his entire body straighten to his full height and give more bearing to his true immensity and conspicuous strength. Rachel stood, wiping at her eyes and her nose, and pulled her wet coat over her shoulders, not daring to look away from him.

He took a step toward her . . . or did he? Her heart pounded and, despite herself, despite the rain, despite what he on the causeway may or may not have done or intended to do, she turned and she ran.

She ran from that wretched bench and her memories of Jack.

She ran toward the lights of the casino.

She ran away from him.

CHAPTER TWO

The back shelves in the Librairie Rue de la Rouvenettaz had become a favorite afternoon haunt. Mary touched her gloveless hands to manuscripts written on fine vellum and caressed the dust away from words that had not been read in decades. She pursed her lips and blew on the book she held, watching as the fine motes lifted into the air to sparkle in the light from the lanterns above, then settle on the disintegrating digests and novels on the highest ledge. The bookseller had begged her to not venture into this part of the store, lest her beautiful afternoon dress become soiled. She humbly assured him, however, that the treasures she sought would not be in the front window with the picture books. She pulled her gown tight about her, compressing her empire silhouette further that she might squeeze between the walls filled with ancient tomes. Her neat little pile of volumes was growing higher: Cornelius Agrippa, Paracelsus, and two by Albertus Magnus. She hoped to find at least one essay by Newton.

Mary was exhilarated by her newly acquired independence in Montreux—something she had never before experienced, something her mother had long championed, something her father would approve of, though he'd still be reticent toward the possible dangers of a young lady left to her own devices, even if only for a few days. She had bade farewell to Percy and George under the grand *porte cochère* of Villa Eden Au Lac that morning, long before the sun had made its appearance, and definitely before any other guests at the residence had stirred in their bedchambers or commenced their morning *toilette*.

Several donkeys from the livery, burdened with trunks and supplies for the long and arduous journey through the Alps to Chamonix, had stood amongst the pristine white columns of the villa's entrance. Their large, dark eyes blinked in the blazing light from the lanterns about them. Her darling Percy had leaned against his animal, ensuring his packs were secured, and promised to write to Mary every day. He'd implored her to do the same and brushed his lips against the back of her hand, held tight in his own, before climbing up onto the frayed remains of a well-worn saddle. He'd patted his buttock and grimaced at the days of pain he was about to endure. Mary laughed at his antics before placing young William into his arms for one last cuddle before the journey.

"Be good for your mummy, Willmouse," he'd said before returning the babe to the nursemaid and leaning down to brush the back of his fingers against Mary's cheek. The team had moved off into the first rays of morning light. George, Lord Byron, had turned on his mount to give an overly dramatic wave to Mary as he called out his goodbyes.

"Keep us apprised of how your ghost story evolves, Mrs. Shelley. Your concept has me intrigued and excited."

The bell above the *librairie's* front door rattled, and Mary peered through the shelves toward the dashing man who entered.

"Doctor Frankenstein, *bonjour*," the keeper said before making several apologetic noises. "Just one moment, sir, I certainly have the book you requested."

Mary caught a glimpse of the few wisps of hair on the top of the storekeeper's balding head as he shuffled his short, tubby body down the aisle. Several feet away, he pushed against a decrepit wooden door. It scraped open in uneasy jerks, hindered by the defiant, hidden literary detritus of the merchant's private existence. "Won't be just a minute, Doctor," he called.

Mary continued observing the gentleman at the counter. She removed one of the tablets from the shelf before her, to afford a better view, and lowered her gaze to one of her books when he stared in her direction. She read a few words, the occult esoteric meanderings of Agrippa, and then turned the page before again peering through overhanging tresses toward the stranger. He was staunch, mature, not old enough to be her father but perhaps a much younger debonair uncle. He wore a blue riding coat and cape spattered with mud and with . . . something much darker. His hair glistened, lush and brown, as were his eyes. Distinguished streaks of gray hair lightened his otherwise ominous appearance. *Quite the handsome mystery*, thought Mary, unable to contain a gentle chuckle. The doctor turned in her direction and gave a slight bow before placing both hands on the counter and awaiting the storekeeper's return.

Mary selected several more books for her own library, determined to ignore the doctor and any conversation he may have with the merchant, as she did not want to appear impertinent or rude for, indeed, she was not. By the time she returned to the front of the store, the doctor had already departed. The merchant, flecks of ancient parchment scattered in his wisps of hair from the excursion into the back room, took the pile of books from her arms. He seemed happy by the number. Mary stood patiently as he placed them side by side along his counter, then rearranged their order by some unknown configuration.

"May I ask what book the doctor purchased?" Mary asked, as off-the-cuff as she was able.

"Of course, *Madame* Shelley," the storekeeper said. "Milton. *Paradise Lost*."

Mary looked out the front door of the *librarie* at the bustle of horse-drawn cabs and summer tourists on their afternoon constitutionals, and then back toward the merchant who was writing her purchases into his ledger.

"Do you have another copy?"

CHAPTER THREE

The red-and-white-checkered tabletops outside the cafe Rue du Sacre du Printemps were almost always bathed in sunshine. Only wide enough to hold a latte and a small bowl of muesli, it gave Rachel the excuse to leave her laptop at home and empty her head of thoughts as she watched the streetscape around her. Two young men sped around the corner on a scooter, singing boisterously above the hum of their electric bike. Rachel noted the emblazoned red and white of their T-shirts and guessed they were on their way to a football match. A well-dressed family ambled down the opposite sidewalk, stepping toward church bells that pealed in the village below. Sundays were quiet and lazy for Rachel. She'd have had no plans to make it otherwise, but the ornate key in her jacket now distracted her and made her bite her lower lip in renewed excitement and consternation.

She'd woken before dawn that morning. The incessant rain of the past week had stopped overnight and, though everything outside her windows was still wet, she could see by the crisp glow of moonlight that it would be a sunny day. She'd stood for almost forty minutes staring out the multi-paned French doors to the terrace, across the vineyards, sipping at her coffee. An old vintner wandered up and down the long rows of vines, inspecting them, sampling a grape here and there, his tricolored Swissy bounding around his legs and back and forth between the fruit-laden plants. The great dog ran to the farthest end of the walled-off terrace, where it barked at something still shrouded by morning darkness. The vintner let out a whistle, but the dog continued to bark and growl into the grove of twisted trees.

Rachel watched, intrigued, as the Swissy held its ground, its growls eventually trailing off into silence. It remained very still for a full minute before taking tentative steps backward away from the trees and sinking lower to the ground. The vintner whistled a second time, and the Swissy backed under the vines into the fifth row of the field. Rising to its full height, it barked once then sprinted back toward its owner. Rachel continued to stare at the grove of trees but could see no hint of movement, even as the sun began to rise above the Valais, to skim along the lake and up the dew-laden terraces before her.

She was glad for the sunshine. The days of sodden weather and moping around the studio had almost been enough to make her give in and return to Manhattan. But of course that was unthinkable. It had taken years to catch the eye of an agent, two more to get an editor interested in the biography, and several months to finalize the commission. What was once simply a passion had become a contractual obligation. But she was glad of it. Rachel loved Mary and her creation and, somehow, she needed Mary to be with her as she resurrected her own purpose, as she jolted her own passion back into the world of the living, to resume her search for the truth of what occurred.

Rachel pondered what words Mary would have used. *Ah, yes*, she thought as she took another sip of coffee. *The flints are sparking, the torches doused in oil and ready to flame for the continued hunt.*

She pushed open the doors to the terrace, allowing an invigorating chill to enter the room, and caught the reflection of the trunk in the glass. It made her heart jump as its silver emblem shone in a slim beam of reflected light that arced around the studio. Discarding her coffee cup on the counter of the kitchenette, she hunkered down in front of the trunk and hitched up the striped pant legs of her pajamas to sit cross-legged before it.

The box was a sumptuous construction of burr walnut and worked silver. The streaking, swirling colors of the wood were emphasized by a high polish of wax and an intricate inlay of light walnut in a pattern of leaves and flowers across the surface. Rachel ran her hands over the wood, feeling its warmth and beauty against her palms. It was smooth, almost silky to the touch, the luster of gloss giving no indication it had ever been handled by anyone. It wasn't heavy—she could easily lift it with two hands. She gently tipped it to and fro, its contents scraping and jostling, and surmised most of the trunk's moderate weight came from whatever lay inside.

The skeleton key was already in the lock, its decorative bow larger and shinier than a silver dollar. Rachel grasped it and turned the shaft clockwise, but it wouldn't budge. She rattled the key, slipping it out of the keyhole and back in without effort. Still it wouldn't turn. She tried counterclockwise. Nothing. After removing the key a second time, she turned the trunk to catch more light from the windows and peered into the hole. The wooden sides of the key chamber were heavily scarred, but she saw no corresponding groove for the key's teeth to turn through. She pushed the key in again, trying to turn it any which way, and wondered if it was even the right key. She pulled it out and scrutinized the design that spiraled up its shaft and around its bow: delicate fig leaves interspersed with what appeared to be bolts of energy or electricity. The same pattern was scrolled about the emblem on the front of the trunk and was stamped into its metal corners.

Rachel leaned back against the base of her bed, tapping the key upon her chin and staring at the trunk. She'd completed her research and documentation of the papers held at Chillon, and they had confirmed Mary had resided in Montreux for several weeks but gave no indication of any occurrence that might have contributed to her novel. There was nothing more to be discovered in the museums and archives of either Switzerland or England that she was aware of. And if there was nothing in this box, then that was it. The biography could be finalized in Manhattan with the data she'd already gathered.

But still Rachel felt there must be more. There was something she was missing. She placed her hand upon the box and gazed at the pattern of flowers in the walnut. She tried the key again, but again it would not budge.

Outside a cockerel crowed.

She placed the skeleton key on top of the trunk and walked to the French doors and out onto the terrace. The sun had risen above the jagged line of perennially snow-covered peaks and now cast itself across the pavement so the stone was warming beneath her bare feet. The vintner and his dog had disappeared. The shadows of the grove were cut by shards of light, but the darker recesses still camouflaged any sign of movement. From the edge of the terrace she could see smoke climbing from the chimney of her favorite cafe, the waiter already wiping down the red-and-white-checkered tables out in front for breakfast service.

She turned back to stare in through the terrace doors toward the trunk, glad she was again at least thinking on how to move forward. The trunk appeared extraordinary within the whitewashed plainness of her studio—an elaborate thing of the past that belonged where it had come from and not where it now sat.

Rachel took her time readying herself for the new day. She sunk into the bath in her tiny tiled bathroom, the refreshing scent of the vineyards blowing in though the open terrace doors and causing the bathroom door to creak gently. There was a shower head above the cast iron tub and, although it always dripped, she had never used it. Instead, she'd become accustomed to the extravagance of a bath as her calming morning ritual.

The water steaming about her was luxuriant, eddying back and forth with her every breath, with her every deliberation of the days ahead, and those behind. She gazed at the antique, enameled wall tiles closest to her face, a pattern of fine lines and scars she could happily lose herself in.

Her ears pricked at a dull thump out in the main room.

"Hello?" she called, but of course there was no answer because there was no one there.

She reached for the soap and skimmed it along her upper arms and around her shoulders before sinking low within the temperate water.

Outside, the cockerel's crows were replaced by the milder song of a lark.

Rachel rose from the tub and wrapped a large bath sheet about her as she walked out into the main room. The summer breeze blew in to caress her as she wiped the water from her body and pulled on jeans, sweater, jacket, and hiking boots. Her stomach growled and she could already taste the Rue du Sacre muesli on her tongue. Before leaving the studio, she plucked the key from the keyhole, instead of from the top of the trunk where she'd left it. She turned it over in her hands, thoughtful, then shrugged and looked around the studio as if there was something else she needed to remember before leaving.

CHAPTER FOUR

Despite very modern suspension, the cabriolet tilted back at a threatening angle as the stallion pulled it through the squelching mud of Avenue Rambert, past the Cimetiere de Clarens, and on toward Le Château du Châtelard on the crest of the hill. Mary had often admired the fortress from the windows of her own suite down in Montreux. Now she was quite excited to be attending an evening lecture on galvanism in the château's grand salon. Her cab climbed further up the hill, past rustic farm buildings and terraced vineyards, all still glimmering with remnants of the late afternoon rainfall.

The livery came to an unexpected halt, and the whole carriage lurched sideways through the mud until it and the horse were turned askew across the laneway. Mary was thrown against the shoulder of the villa's driver. He apologized profusely, but there was no time to be alarmed before a *gendarme* appeared, holding up his blue lantern to shine under the hood of the carriage.

"*Excusez-moi, madame.*" The *gendarme's* light was before them only a moment before it bobbed off again into the darkness ahead.

"Driver?" Mary asked.

The driver pushed open the cabriolet's hood and stood upon the apron. "There are several carriages in disarray ahead of us, *Madame* Shelley. There appears to have been an accident."

Mary craned her neck to see the disruption as the valet jumped from the rear of the cabriolet. He said something to the driver in an indistinguishable Vaud accent and then ran past them and their horse toward those ahead. Mary watched as blue lanterns moved to and fro in the darkening twilight.

Above them, high on the hill, the lights of Châtelard blazed.

Several minutes passed before the valet came running back toward them. Again he spoke to the driver in his thick inflection before jumping up onto the board, between the large springs behind the cabriolet's hood. The carriages ahead staggered and pitched back into motion.

The driver urged the hood over their heads and flicked the reins once, and the stallion trod slowly forward, pulling the carriage back into the well worn, but sludgy, ruts of the lane. Mary clenched her gloved hand around the side rail, intent on observing the *gendarmes* and their activities. As the cabriolet pulled alongside the blue transport of the authorities, her driver begged her not to look.

"Please, *Madame* Shelley, please look at the night sky. See how bright the stars are beginning to shine."

But Mary's gaze was held to the ditch on the edge of the road. A blanket covered what appeared to be a motionless body, but nearby, a forearm and hand with its index finger pointed toward her intended destination, lay dismembered and alone. A *gendarme* stepped between Mary and her view, but it was already burned into her mind. There was no evidence of carriage accident—indeed, there was no carriage—just the remnants of a poor soul who had been scattered irreverently along the gutter.

The cabriolet passed a grove of trees, effectively blocking all view of the scene behind them. Mary fell back into the cushions and could do little but ensure her breathing continued at a normal cadence and her mind did not descend into the depths of horror—horror she knew flowed just under the porcelain skin of her awareness.

There certainly was horror behind her, and also hidden in her deepest creative thoughts.

It appalled her, but it also . . .

The final sweeping curve of Sentier du Châtelard almost circumnavigated the impressive château on the top of the hill, passing copses of mature magnolias and along the gravel drive to the medieval gatehouse and portico. The cab pulled into the cobbled internal courtyard, where at least two dozen cabriolets, horses, and larger carriages were being attended to by the men and boys of the livery. Mary was assisted from her cab and walked quickly into the reception, as she knew she must surely be late. The manager took her mantle and escorted her into the salon. He located an empty chair and ensured it was to her satisfaction before giving a courteous bow and returning to his station.

For many minutes, Mary sat with little recognition of the lecture and people about her until she was able to push the scene on the roadside deep into her subconscious for later analysis—later dissection and critique on how it might affect her. Perhaps she might use the sadness of truth to infuse sentiment into her ghost story.

The high-pitched scrape of chalk on a board brought her attention to the man at the front of the salon.

She listened to the words of *Monsieur* Aldini, who conversed in both English and French, albeit with a heavy Italian accent. He spoke of the experiments of his uncle, Luigi Galvani, which documented the "animal electricity" that made muscles spasm and jerk, that allowed people to move their limbs. Mary looked down at her own hand and rotated it back and forth. She touched her thumb to each of her fingertips, imagining the course of current through it to make it do her will.

Monsieur Aldini continued on with the counter arguments of Volta and the eventual creation of the galvanic cell. The discourse continued, covering ideas and concepts Mary was already well versed in, punctuated by the further screech of chalk upon the drawing board. She could not see the speaker well from the rear of the salon, so she allowed her eyes to wander around the magnificent murals that covered almost every inch of the space. Brightly painted stone archways disguised one wall, framing mountainous green vistas with skies full of fat summer clouds. Another wall displayed a delicately drawn minstrel entertaining a refined lady. Mary imagined the tune being played on the minstrel's mandolin, noting the quaint, old-fashioned couture of the woman as she admired the minstrel's fingers strumming across his instrument.

"What a pity Galvani's 'animal electricity' could not bring them to life."

Mary tilted her head from side to side to reassure herself the minstrel and lady were indeed part of the mural. From the corner of her eye, she caught a glimpse of a familiar debonair gentleman. He sat rigid in his chair, his hands in his lap, craning his neck to view the speaker on the platform at the front. Doctor Frankenstein appeared to be taking copious notes, hanging on every word that echoed about the salon. For a moment, Mary contemplated moving to sit closer to him, as he was situated in a row of otherwise empty seats, but then decided it would be unseemly and so stayed put.

The orator's discourse turned to the Newgate Prison exhibition of 1803, and there was a sudden murmur of excitement throughout the room. Mary herself felt an unexpected surge of adrenaline at hearing the words from the very man who had performed the experiments. In between the beating of her own heart, the shocked whispers of the other audience members, and the magnetic distraction of the doctor taking his notes, Mary's eye was once more caught by the perceptive gaze of the colorful immortals painted on the wall. The minstrel stared in Mary's direction, his brow furrowed as if he were cross that a woman of her means should be involved in this address, that she could so easily relegate the horror she had witnessed to the back of her mind. Likewise, the refined lady, who Mary could have sworn had been admiring the minstrel's mandolin, now looked at her in abject consternation. Mary held their gaze as their admonishment of her seemed to increase.

Mary felt suddenly flushed and in need of air. Thinking she might be ill, she rose from her seat and dashed from the salon out into the main reception, then toward the draped doors leading out to the Terrasse d'Honneur. A member of the château personnel was soon at her side, offering Mary her mantle, followed by a second who held a silver platter in white-gloved hands. Mary pulled the cloak about her shoulders and accepted a Bitter Sling from the waiter. She smiled at each of the staff as she sipped at the cognac, savoring the bitters and sugar that tempered its sharpness. It warmed her as she crossed the terrace and sat on a lounge to take in the air and nighttime view of Montreux twinkling far below. It was refreshing after the closeness of the salon—and after the shock of the body in the ditch.

She listened to the ambient noises of night and the distant neigh of animals in the château stables. She thought she could just distinguish a lantern halfway down the hillside, perhaps a night watchman doing his rounds through the headstones and tombs of Cimetiere de Clarens. Further up the hill she noted the blue lanterns of the *gendarmerie* still bobbing through the dark lanes, fields and, perhaps, stables. They were looking for something.

The remainder of the lecture's congregation soon spilled out onto the flagstones for cocktails, scenery, and discussions of the evening. *Monsieur* Aldini was one of the last to step from the lobby out into the torchlit night. He turned up his collar against the fresh night air and positioned himself beneath a broad pergola set against the wall of the château, where ivy and berried vines crept over the ancient wooden beams and clung to the massive blocks of stone. As Mary rose and walked toward him to be a part of his group's conversation, Doctor Frankenstein appeared from the main reception, accepted a cocktail, and stepped directly in front of her without recognition or courtesy. He walked to the farthest end of the terrace and stood alone under an enormous tree, one foot upon the stone balustrade separating them from the steep embankment that dropped to the vineyards below. He balanced his cognac and notebook on his knee, reviewing his notes and making adjustments.

"Did you enjoy my lecture, *Madame* Shelley?" *Monsieur* Aldini asked. He indicated with his hand for her to join his circle and recline on the chair he had just vacated.

"Oh, very much, sir; in particular your observations at Newgate. Unfortunately I was required to leave the salon before your finish. May I request you reiterate the last few minutes for my convenience and knowledge?" The surrounding gentlemen murmured in agreement. The wait staff recharged everyone's glasses, and the *Monsieur*, after taking a sip from his cocktail, recounted the episode. Mary sat beside him, intrigued, his congenial and animated face no more than a whisper from her own. Yet she looked beyond him toward the lone figure of the doctor who now sat at the terrace edge, attentive to their conversation.

"Mr. George Foster had been executed not more than an hour previous to my experimentation. The medical staff of Newgate Prison had confirmed and reconfirmed he was indeed dead. His corpse had been drained of blood, hauled onto a trolley, and brought into the auditorium. He was a large man, Mr. Foster, heavily muscled but also with much fatty tissue that softened his appearance, especially in death. For the first part of the experimentation, I inserted into his mouth and ear metal rods that were connected to my machine by cables. I turned the control knob by less than a few degrees, and almost immediately Mr. Foster's jaw began to quiver. There was a gasp from the doctors who had pronounced him dead, but I held up my hand for them to stay back as I turned the control further. The muscles adjoining Mr. Foster's jaw became horribly contorted, as if he wished to sneer at those who had executed him. His eye opened, causing all in the room to scuttle back and the Warden of Newgate to call for his guards to subdue the criminal. I, too, had been quite shocked, but had the right of mind to remove the metal rods from Mr. Foster, causing the quivering to stop and the eye to close.

"Without hesitation, the prison doctors were upon the corpse, prodding and poking and testing to ensure he was still dead. In the end, they stepped back dumbfounded, proclaiming yet again that there was no evidence of life."

Mary was intent on the dialogue, however she also studied the doctor who was now in deep conversation with a young man who was exceedingly large, perhaps two feet taller than the doctor himself and of a muscular disposition, cloaked in ill-fitting and ill-made couture. His features were hidden by shadow and an upturned collar, and he appeared somewhat hunched, his torso twisted. His hand—of a dull, yellow pallor—hung loose from the sleeve of his frock coat. Though Mary could not discern their words, their slight gestures seemed urgent—perhaps angry, perhaps afraid —flicking from one emotion to another, each movement seeming to bring the two closer in an intimate debate. The doctor looked momentarily toward the main group on the terrace, as if aware that his interaction was being monitored. He placed his arm around his companion's waist and continued to converse as he urged him behind the trunk of a great tree that sprouted from the stones of the terrace.

"I continued my experimentation, inserting the metal rods into various parts of the body. After several attempts, I was able to make the right hand rise and clench at my command." *Monsieur* Aldini demonstrated with his hand, and all stared at it in amazement. "Reapplication of the rods into the lower extremities caused the legs and thighs to come alive and thrash violently upon the gurney. The prison doctors felt comfortable enough that they approached the body even as the legs and thighs kept up their odd motion. It should be noted that four guards now stood around the room, their batons at the ready. Two interns held the legs down, subduing the corpse beneath them as one of the doctors pricked the skin to see if it would bleed, then deftly thrust his scalpel deep into the gluteus maximus to determine any reaction. There was none, however the interns were adamant they could feel the life within."

The audience sat in silence. Some stared into their cocktail glasses, swirling the contents before taking thoughtful sips. Mary, too, thought about what the experiment proved, but she was distracted by the two at the far end of the terrace, almost entranced by their quiet and urgent solicitude.

Doctor Frankenstein looked after the young man as the latter walked from the tree to the darkened edge of the château terrace and down a metal balustraded stair that led to the gardens and vineyards below. Mary felt a tinge of sadness when she saw the man's movements, for they were cumbersome, naïve, as if wreaked by pain and uncertainty. He passed down the stair and glanced toward the guests on the terrace. Torchlight illuminated his face for but a moment behind the bars of the balustrade, and Mary's breath caught in her throat. She set down her cocktail and pressed her hands into her lap to stop them from shaking.

"Would you like me to introduce you to the good doctor?" *Monsieur* Aldini asked her.

Again Mary's heart jumped and she felt quite breathless. "Perhaps another time, *monsieur*. Will you be in Montreux for any extended period?"

"I will not be leaving for Bologna until the beginning of next week. I will have my secretary contact your residence to establish a date for a dinner perhaps. Will Mr. Shelley and Lord Byron be joining us?"

Mary smiled at the mere mention of her husband's name. "No, Percy and George are gallivanting around the countryside, as is their way. I don't expect to see them for several weeks yet."

"Very well, it would more than please me to chaperone you to the wonderful gastronomy I have discovered here. I will also enquire into the doctor's schedule that he may join us."

CHAPTER FIVE

Rachel locked her studio door and walked across the internal courtyard of Le Château du Châtelard toward the portico leading to the Terrasse d'Honneur. The building was massive when viewed from such close quarters, rising several stories above the manicured and graveled grounds. Its opulent suites and apartments were all very grand compared to her humble but comfortable studio in the outbuildings. One of the papers at Chillon indicated Mary had visited the château, but it was unclear why. Rachel made a mental note to check if the château maintained its own records of visitors and events.

The view from the Terrasse was stunning. Though Rachel's private studio terrace had a similar orientation, it couldn't compare to the broad vista commanded by this flag-stoned space. Vineyards toppled down the hillside from it. The lake spread before it. The snow-covered Alps surrounded it. The very air, fresh and vital, emanated from this magnificent point of view. Rachel walked over the cobbles, past the ancient ivy-covered pergola to the metal balustraded stair that led to the lower gardens.

During her first months at Châtelard, she would walk the two and a half kilometers down to Montreux via the main route. Now, however, having made acquaintance with many of the locals, she felt accepted enough to take the shortcuts across private land, down through the vineyards and cow-filled pastures, amongst the ornate headstones of the Cimetiere de Clarens.

She followed a track that led almost directly to the cafe Rue du Sacre du Printemps, where she sat and leisured over her muesli and latte before resuming her walk through the cemetery toward town.

The streets and alleys of Montreux were bustling by the time she reached the town center. The ornate trunk key was secure in her pocket, and she hoped to come across a locksmith who could assist her. By one o'clock she'd shown the key to several smiths, but none were of any help.

"Why don't you ask the owners of the trunk?" one obliging smith suggested. He was young, with a clipped beard—well versed in modern deadbolts and electronic locks but not in two-hundred-year-old trunks and their skeleton keys. Rachel had, of course, already contacted the owners, but they didn't know how to open the trunk and that was why it hadn't been opened in generations. All they had was rumor of its contents from the long-dead matriarch of their family. She'd been certain it contained papers and drawings by Lord Byron himself, and perhaps by those who accompanied him on his self-imposed exile to Lake Geneva. The matriarch had seen them herself when she was a child. She'd never been allowed to touch them—only look. They were too fragile and important, her father had said.

Rachel stood despondent in the locksmith shop, running her fingernail along the grooved design of the key's shaft. She held it up close to her eye to study the intricate motif and turned it in the light, wondering if it offered a solution to its workings. There was no way she was going to force or break the trunk, its hinges, or its latch, as it was without doubt a historic relic. If it contained what she hoped it contained, then it was even more important to keep intact and in original condition. She may need to ship it to Geneva or London to have it opened.

Placing the key into her pocket, she turned to leave.

He was at the door.

His fingers gripped the handle, but his face was turned to stare along the street, as if he were going to enter but had changed his mind.

Less than a foot away, separated only by a corroded metal grille securing scratched, beveled glass, Rachel was struck by how tall and massive he was. His structure filled the entire doorframe—he would need to duck if he were to enter. His hair was a glossy black and flowed about his shoulders, and the skin of his face was very white, etched by thick, dark eyebrows and stubble that accentuated his defined jawline. Again he wore black—cotton and denim—just as he had that night at the marina. She couldn't tell through the mottled glass whether his clothing was dirty or just very, very dull.

He looked into the shop, into Rachel's eyes.

Rachel held his gaze for an instant, wondering if the minor flick of his eyelids determined recognition, and noting the slightest of sneers by his upturned lip before he turned to walk off into the crowded backstreet. She looked over her shoulder at the locksmith who held his head low over his key-lathe, unaware she was even still there, his key sparking as it was worked.

She pulled at the door and its bell clattered above her head as she opened and rushed out onto the sidewalk. She caught a glimpse of him turning right on Rue d'Etraz. Walking as fast as she was able, Rachel pushed through the crowd that hovered at the *patisserie*—their arms full of baguettes and tarts—and stepped into the gutter to bypass an elderly man distracted by puff pastry and sugar. Hurrying into the *rue*, she saw him turn into Sentier d'Etraz. She could have sworn he'd waited on the corner for a moment until she saw his broad shoulders and swaggering gait, but of course that was nonsense. His route led under the railway line. Grand shopping streets full of people and commerce gave way to deserted lanes and alleys as he strode toward his own unknown destination. BMWs and Mercedes-Benzes gave way to Skodas and rusty bicycles. Warehouses and garages yawned to expose gaping black interiors better left unexplored.

And then she lost him.

Rachel stopped a block from the train station and dropped onto the grassy curb that sloped up to the raised railway line. She felt stupid for the way she'd reacted. It wasn't like her at all—following a stranger just because he looked at her through the door of a shop, just because he might have been the silhouette on a rainy night that had scared her, just because his sheer size intrigued her, made her wonder.

Stupid.

And yet she couldn't erase the image of his face from her mind: the way his lashes brushed against the top of his stark white cheeks, the impossible straightness of his nose, the gentle upturning curl of his lips—had it been a sneer or an attempt to smile?

She imagined his lips parting to reveal strong white teeth.

She pondered him for many minutes before realizing she was sitting opposite another locksmith shop. She stood from the grass and made her way across the road, careful of a Skoda that chugged and smoked along the asphalt and a gang of corroded bicycles that chimed and honked as they skidded past. She stepped up onto the sidewalk in front of the shop, zipping her jacket against a chill that had crept along the avenue.

The building was of soot-blackened stone, with a roof shingled by immense shards of flat rock. A wooden key hung swinging from the eave, notwithstanding the lack of any real breeze. The windows had gone uncleaned for many decades, conceivably longer. Indeed, it was impossible for Rachel to see through them even with her nose pressed up against the brittle glass. A sign by the door said *Sonnerie sonnette*—"ring the bell," Rachel guessed with her college French, but she knocked on the glass anyway. When there was no response, she reached for the chain above the sign and gave it a tug.

A bell tinkled inside the door, no louder than her knock. The latch clicked and the door swung ajar, scraping against the floor as Rachel pushed it further open to gain entrance. The walls of the shop were covered with thousands of keys of different dimensions and metals, from ancient skeleton keys to modern plastic key cards, all tacked onto the wooden planks that lined the space from floor to ceiling. Shelves held boxes filled with key blanks and what looked like machinery parts: large cogs, saw-toothed wheels, pistons, and metal and wooden blocks of various shapes and sizes. Every ledge, every key, everything appeared covered in a dark, greasy soot. Little appeared to have been touched or disturbed for a very long time. A slice of quiche sat on a cracked plate. It, too, had been there a very long time.

"*Bonjour.*" A thin, bespectacled man stood behind the counter. He definitely belonged here.

"*Bonjour.*" The smell of metal shavings and oil crept into Rachel's nose. "*Pourriez-vous aider* . . . Could you help me with this key? It's supposed to open a trunk . . . *un tronc* . . . but I can't make it work."

The locksmith took the key and studied it. He scratched at his scalp, and his entire head of hair moved as one from left to right and back. Slipping his monocle magnifier from his forehead onto his left eye, he considered the fine filigree work of the bow and the engraving of leaves and lightning —or was it electricity?—down the shaft. He turned to the shelf behind him and extracted a large, well-worn book. He flipped through the pages, then back one, two, three. He stared at the page in silence for several moments then thrust his finger against it with a thud.

"*Non* . . . no . . . I am afraid I am unable to assist you, *mademoiselle.*"

Rachel peered at his book. His sooty finger left a mark on the parchment.

"Are you certain?"

The reflection of her own face in the lens of his monocle distracted her.

"Absolutely, *mademoiselle*. This key was made for a specific trunk that is no longer manufactured. It is useless unless you already have the trunk it was made for. No other key will fit the trunk and no other trunk will fit the key."

His words seemed naïve, as if Rachel missed something in the translation from French to English.

"But I do have the trunk. It is just that the key won't unlock it"

"Ah . . ." The smith nodded. He shuffled his book around on the counter so she could see the engraving in the center of the page. "That, *mademoiselle*, is because this key does not unlock the trunk. The trunk unlocks this key."

Rachel stared at the engraving, bewildered.

CHAPTER SIX

Even with gloved hands, Mary was able to manipulate the tongs to securely hold the escargot. She urged her petite fork into the opening, felt as it dug into the succulent meat, and twisted and dragged the delicacy from its helix to place it upon her tongue. She savored the flesh until it all but dissolved, and gave *Monsieur* Aldini a knowing smile as he took his first bite. After reaching for a small chunk of torn bread, Mary dipped it into the buttery, garlic concoction and popped it into her mouth.

"You must forgive my manners, *monsieur*."

"Oh, no, no, no, *madame*, it is the only way to enjoy this treat. Every last morsel demands to be devoured with gusto." *Monsieur* Aldini nodded and smoothed his moustache with his fingers as Mary selected her last chunk of bread.

"I can only agree." Mary looked out through the windows of the salon's conservatory. "It is such a shame the weather is so miserable. Dining in the gardens outside would have been a joy if the sun were shining."

"I am afraid, my dear *Madame* Shelley, this is not the best year for your grand tour."

"How so?"

"It is expected there will be no summer at all this year. Scientific articles attribute the unseasonal conditions to a volcanic eruption in the Dutch East Indies."

"So far away? The other side of the world?"

"Most definitely, *madame*. Volcanic clouds of ash drifting in the upper atmosphere. An enormous amount, unheard of in recorded history."

Mary stared at the rain splashing against the glass. "Incessant rainfall. Such a wet, ungenial summer it has been so far. We've had but a handful of days and nights when I could venture out without use of an umbrella, though the evening of your lecture was fine—following the afternoon shower." She thought for a moment of the body in the ditch. Then, pushing it from her mind, she thought of her Percy in the higher reaches of the Alps where, instead of rain, he might be enjoying snowfall. "Tell me, *monsieur*, has the snow on the Italian side of Mont Blanc, *Monte Bianco*, really been red this past winter? Is that also due to the ash from the antipodes?"

"These are strange times, that is for certain."

Turning back from the windows, Mary saw the table had been cleared of the hors d'oeuvres and her water glass refilled. Even the crumbs had disappeared from the pristine white tablecloth.

"I am disappointed Doctor Frankenstein was not able to join us today," she said.

"As am I, for I am rarely able to meet with him in a social setting."

Mary hoped her host would continue his discussion, but he said no more.

"This is a fine salon you have discovered, *monsieur*. The papering on the wall is magnificent. It must have taken the artisans months to carve the blocks and stamp the portions of the landscape scene. The detail is breathtaking."

Monsieur Aldini nodded once and peered around the room and up at the ornate ceiling. Mary followed his gaze. White plaster filigree surrounded an oval panel, painted the brightest of summer blues. From its center hung a chandelier twice the size of any of the salon tables. Even in the dull light of the afternoon rain, it shimmered and sparkled. "Just delightful."

A waiter set the *salade frisées* before them on the table, and the aroma of Dijon and sherry vinaigrette tantalized Mary's tastebuds before she could even lift her fork to her mouth.

Monsieur Aldini took but one mouthful of his salad before slouching back into his lounge, his fork absently pricking the egg yolk to let it ooze over the luscious chunks of bacon. "May I confide in you, *Madame* Shelley?"

"But of course, *monsieur*." Mary dared to hope for the subject of his intended discourse.

"You are a well-traveled and educated woman, singularly bold and, without doubt, more versed in the social niceties and etiquette of our current society than I. Hence, I do feel at ease to discuss my concerns about an acquaintance, that you might offer me some advice."

"I would gladly and humbly supply any of my knowledge that may assist you."

"Thank you. I have concern over the health of my friend, Doctor Frankenstein, and am uncertain how to approach him regarding my anxiety. I have known of him for a number of years, having been introduced at the University of Ingolstadt by a mutual friend, Mr. Henry Clerval. At first we corresponded regularly by letter, discussing both his work and mine in the areas you are acquainted with. And then the communication ceased. I became worried and inquired after his health among others I knew at the University, but they also saw him very infrequently and, when they did, he looked pale and drawn as though he had not slept for many days and nights.

"He had been working on his project, locked away in his rooms, and eventually Mr. Clerval visited to find our friend a wretched shadow of his former self. On the very night of their reunion, the doctor had seemed overjoyed at meeting with his dear friend and invited him back to his rooms. But afterward, his joy and laughter took on a maniacal pitch, and ended when he apparently saw a specter from the corner of his eye and yelled, 'Oh, save me! Save me! The wretch has returned to destroy me!' He struggled before falling down in a fit, and dear Clerval nursed our friend through a nervous fever that lasted several months."

"Oh dear, I never could have imagined. How terrible for you all. But the doctor has appeared well on the two occasions I have seen him here in Montreux."

"I had thought so, too, until I honored an appointment to meet him at his summer residence up in Hauts-de-Montreux. I arrived at his chalet and waited in the library for over an hour. His servants assured me he would be down momentarily, and yet he did not come. A note was delivered to me that I should enjoy his library and service, and that he was to join me for dinner. I accepted his hospitality, as several manuscripts had caught my attention as I'd paced around the dark, wood-paneled room with its low ceiling. I settled into Book III of Ovid's *Metamorphoses* near the squat fireplace for a number of hours, and when supper came, I ate alone at Frankenstein's table. I could hear him shuffling around upstairs and inquired whether my host would be joining me at all. I was finally appeased that he would be with me for brandy and cigars."

Mary noted that they were now the only guests remaining in the salon. The waiter removed their salads and set their entrees before them as *Monsieur* Aldini continued.

"I saw nothing of the doctor on that evening." He dug his fork into a fat dill Spaetzel on the plate that showcased his *filet de saumon au beurre rouge*.

"May I inquire as to the night of this strange hospitality?"

"*Certamente*, it was the night after the Châtelard conference. The doctor made the appointment before leaving the château and I was most pleased to accept, intrigued to discover the progress of his line of work and also to inquire about our friend, Mr. Clerval."

Mary peered out the windows of the conservatory, the distant snow-covered Alps shimmering like a hallucination, a waking dream, as the rain splashed down the panes of glass. "It would seem the doctor has once again thrown himself into his work to the detriment of his relationships." Mary pulled with her fork at the moist flesh of the lamb *Noisette*, releasing an invigorating perfume of fennel and lavender. "Perhaps it would be wise to contact Mr. Clerval. The doctor seems to have a trust with your mutual friend that may be beneficial at this time."

"Yes, yes. I agree and am glad you came to that conclusion also, for this very morning I sent a messenger to Ingolstadt University where Mr. Clerval continues to study the languages of the East."

Mary nodded, satisfied she had been of some reassurance at least, before a watery memory distracted her. "What of the young man who accompanies the doctor? Might he assist in your intervention?"

"Young man?"

"On the château's grand terrace, Doctor Frankenstein appeared possessed by a young man." Still the *monsieur* showed no recognition. "A tall, robust, well-muscled youth of strikingly large stature, in fact . . . I saw his countenance for but a moment and, though another's perspective might differ, I would, without a doubt, classify him as truly beautiful."

Monsieur Aldini went white and set his forkful of sauerkraut back down onto his plate beside the half-eaten salmon. "I saw no such man on the terrace. He was walking, you say? He was alive?"

Surprised by the *monsieur's* response, Mary also rested her knife and fork on her plate—the sweetbread and roasted shallot stuffing to remain untasted for a while yet. "What an odd question. He was perhaps nineteen or twenty —a ward of the doctor?"

Monsieur Aldini took several gulps from his water and two from his wine. He pulled a handkerchief from his pocket and wiped at beads of sweat that had appeared on his forehead.

"Are you all right, *monsieur*?"

The *maître d'hôtel* was immediately at their table but the *monsieur* waved him away before taking another gulp of wine.

CHAPTER SEVEN

It was a balmy evening, and the terrace doors were wide open to allow the breeze from the lake to fill the studio with the rustic smells of the vineyards below. Gauzy sheer curtains fluttered gracefully into the room, taking on an incandescent glow from the overhead lighting, their whiteness echoing the ardor of moonlight bouncing off the flagstones.

Rachel had undone the buttons of her blouse, intending to bathe before eating dinner and setting to work that night, but the trunk had sat there, beckoning. She couldn't take her eyes from it as she'd pulled off her boots and jeans. There was no way she'd be able to relax in the bath while the trunk lie there unopened and the key burned in her hand.

Rachel lifted the trunk up onto her bed. It sank elegantly into the thick comforter as she climbed up to sit cross-legged before it. With the skeleton key secure in her hand, she studied the carved filigree surrounding the trunk's emblem. Above the elaborate silver plate, flush with the metal work, was a precise gap in the walnut, just as the locksmith predicted. It was too thin for the shaft of the key, but the exact dimension as the decorative bow used to grip and turn the key itself. Rachel pursed her lips and blew into the gap; particles of aromatic dust puffed back into her face—lilac.

She pulled the trunk toward her and pushed the head of the key into the gap until she heard a click. As she turned the key, she sensed the head itself was not turning, but the shaft was unscrewing from its connection to the decorative bow. The shaft pulled free from the trunk to reveal two thinner shanks that had been hidden within. Rachel wiggled them free from the gap. The decorative bow had separated so that half remained attached to each of the minor keys she now held. Small teeth covered the length of each.

Holding them up to the light, Rachel detected the same engraving of fig leaves and electricity. The filigree at the two top front corners of the trunk cut deep into the silver, the lowest indent on each corner revealing an otherwise unnoticeable opening. Rachel inserted the two keys into these holes and turned them in opposite directions to feel the click-click-click of the lock's inner workings.

And then both keys would turn no more.

Rachel placed her fingers on either side of the trunk lid and slowly urged it up and back.

It moved without a sound.

The inside of the lid was covered in brilliant red raw silk.

In the mouth of the trunk, a similarly swathed tray hid the contents that had remained unseen for generations and that gave the trunk its intriguing weight.

In the tray itself lay a yellowed envelope, a fragile blond ribbon tied loose around it. It was sealed with an embossed globule of red wax across the opening flap. The seal had been broken long ago.

Rachel stared at the envelope for many minutes, still holding the lid of the trunk with both hands. She could sense the blood draining from her face and felt giddy, lightheaded.

The seal was that of Mary Wollstonecraft Godwin Shelley.

Rachel lowered the lid of the trunk and swung her legs over the side of the bed. She went to the kitchenette, removed a glass from the shelf, and pulled an open bottle of sauvignon blanc from the fridge. After pouring an ample portion, she walked across the studio, without looking at the trunk, and out onto the moonlit terrace.

The breeze was soft against her naked legs and arms, and her blouse blossomed about her. She swirled the wine around her mouth and swallowed with delight. *No*, Rachel thought, the writer in her coming to the forefront, *with* unbridled *delight*. Yes, that was the word. Of all the papers, dossiers, and letters she'd reviewed for her biography on the author of *Frankenstein*, not one had been in the handwriting of Mary herself. And yet here, perhaps, were personal thoughts and musings unknown to the literary world.

Rachel took another gulp of wine, knowing she should wear gloves with the letters just as she did with the ancient papers in Château de Chillon and the Université de Genève. She should photograph and document the contents of the box to record their sequence before she disturbed them. She had a lot of work to do.

She walked to the edge of the terrace to take in the full evening view of Montreux. She caught the glow of eyes in the undergrowth beneath her. Though she heard no clatter of cowbell, she thought it must surely be one of the château's herd. She stared down at the eyes and raised her glass with a smile. The eyes blinked out and she saw them no more.

Rachel took her time returning to the trunk. She savored the glass of wine in the steamy confines of her bathroom, pulled on her summer pajama shorts and matching tank top, grilled some Gruyère cheese in her kitchenette, and then sat at her dining table to finish off the toast and sauvignon. She opened her laptop and created a spreadsheet to document her actions and findings before taking several pictures of the trunk and then putting on gloves to open it for a second time.

She took several photos of the yellowed envelope from different angles, made notes on her spreadsheet, and then picked up the envelope between two gloved fingertips. The ribbon fell free with a gentle nudge, and the flap of the envelope pushed up easily, nowhere as brittle as she'd thought it might be. She pulled out the letter contained within—a single piece of paper, folded once— and opened it, her glance flicking immediately to the signatory: *M. Shelley.*

Rachel's heart skipped a beat.

CHAPTER EIGHT

Doctor John Polidori
Villa Diodoti, Cologny
Geneva   *July 1816*

Doctor Polidori, Darling John,
How I wish you were here with me in Montreux. Percy and Lord Byron have left me stranded once more while they proceed on their own adventures. Do you miss George as much as I miss Percy? I had initially wanted to visit Chamonix with them, to be close to that most beautiful Mont Blanc, but the thought of several hours, if not days, on donkey and then horseback over the singularly bad trails to that wonderland left me for naught. And of course I could never subject Willmouse to such a horrid journey. Instead I am in the comfort of this beautiful little gem on the easternmost reaches of the lake. But, oh, how the summer weather eludes us.
I read with much horror the excerpt you sent me entitled "Vampyre." Undeniably I shivered throughout the night after reading but a few pages. Your story is exciting indeed, however I am certain I am on the cusp of writing something comparable for our ghost story competition. While our . . . while my husband and your "patient" gadabout the wilderness, I trust we shall show them we also have some small literary talent.
If you are able, my darling John, please join me here in Montreux. The residence where I am situated has several spare rooms befitting a man of your means, and my suite is large enough to accommodate my sister Claire —if she wishes to leave the bright lights of Geneva to visit her sister and nephew. And I do expect Percy and George to return within the next month. They would be as overjoyed as I to see you here.

M. Shelley

CHAPTER NINE

Rachel was electric with excitement. She'd read the letter several times before e-mailing a photo to Margaret in New York. Almost immediately she'd received a congratulatory reply from across the time zones. The more than perfunctory exclamation marks assured Rachel her editor recognized the importance of the find.

Below the letter, below the red-silk-covered tray, were perhaps three or four dozen similar envelopes of correspondence and cards, plus two smaller wooden document boxes. At the very bottom of the trunk was a shawl—cashmere woven in the French style, a golden thread with emblems of empire braided throughout in the same burnished color. It was neatly folded and remained so, though Rachel did dare stroke it with the tips of her ungloved fingers.

Working through the night, she photographed, documented, and read six more of Mary's letters. All were addressed to either Doctor John Polidori, her husband, Percy, or her sister, Claire. They covered varying aspects and descriptions of three events: an excursion to a bookshop, a lecture on Galvanism held here at Châtelard, and an extravagant luncheon she attended with *Monsieur* Aldini. The letters surprised and delighted Rachel —though they offered more questions than they answered. She'd never read documentation that linked Mary with *Monsieur* Aldini and his theories, but it made sense that a woman of her scientific thought and application should have such a connection. Perhaps the Università di Bologna could confirm the *monsieur's* schedule during 1816. She'd check with the owner of Châtelard to ratify any possible conferences and lectures of the time.

But what had her intrigued more than any other intricacy of the rich shorthand was the repeated reference to a Doctor F.

Rachel's thoughts lingered on the trunk and its documents as she slid the handful of letters back into their correct sequence and position amongst the plush, red silk.

"*Doctor F.,*" she mused to herself, knowing who it couldn't possibly refer to, but wondering who it did. "I suspect even you will continue to keep some secrets from me." She caressed the polished top of the trunk. The pungent smell of antique parchment and shawl lingered in her nostrils long after she'd closed and locked the walnut lid with its dual silver keys and placed it respectfully upon the sideboard. An unframed watercolor of Mont Blanc hung above it—appropriate and sublime—but it was the trunk and its contents that continued to arrest Rachel's thoughts as she retired to the terrace to await the rising sun.

The first rays of light struck up the valley, filling her with exhilaration and eclipsing any need for sleep long lost. Her stomach grumbled, the fondue of the previous night forgotten as she basked in the warmth of the arriving day. The cafe Rue du Sacre du Printemps wouldn't be open for another half hour, but she pulled on her jeans, slipped on her boots, stuffed a few francs into her pocket, locked the doors and windows of the studio, and headed toward the steps that led down to the vineyard. As she took the first step, she turned to look back at the terrace doors. Normally she'd have left them unlocked and open. The château staff were observant, the farmers and vintners surrounding the area were all aware of those who belonged and those who didn't, and there'd been no incidence of theft in the months she'd resided in the hills above Montreux.

But now the contents of her tiny space were too important to be lax with. She strode back across the terrace to recheck and rattle the doors to ensure they were solidly locked. She peered in to reconfirm the position of the trunk upon the sideboard. It sat—almost smug—beneath the chilled blue and white painting. Maybe she should hide it under her bed, she thought, but knew the security of the door would suffice. Satisfied, she jogged across the terrace and took the ancient stone steps two at a time through the several levels of ornamental garden. She jumped onto the rich, black soil of the vineyard and took the trail between the rows of fruit-laden trees.

For the first time since Jack died, she felt some true sense of happiness and purpose.

She pulled a printout from her pocket—an image of the first letter she'd opened—and reread it with unabated enthusiasm: the magnificent copperplate, the curling serifs, the invariable slant of each letter. Her attention was glued to it as she passed through the vineyard, across pastures, and onto the cobbled laneway between two pastoral buildings that opened onto the *rue* directly across from the cafe. Folding the printout and pushing it into her pocket, she raised her gaze to the far side of the *rue*.

There he was.

Sitting at her table.

His gigantic legs spread lazily across the sidewalk.

A book held close to his face.

He reached up with his great hand to turn the page and held it down against the morning breeze.

Rachel felt suddenly naked, wishing she'd bathed and better dressed before venturing out. She pulled her hair back and attempted to brush the creases out of her pajama top. The skimpy cotton would be okay as long as the breeze remained warm and the sun shone as promised during her walk through the fields. She crossed the *rue* and took a seat at the table farthest from him. The cafe hadn't opened yet, but she was comforted by the readying clatter and movement emanating from inside. She pulled the copy of the letter from her pocket once more, spread it out onto the checkered tabletop, and pretended to read it for the one-hundredth time.

He wore scuffed boots and slim-cut, dark-blue jeans. His thighs were thick with muscle and his T-shirt was tight with sleeves that nearly covered the tattoos on his immense upper arms. His solid forearms were covered by a translucent layer of golden hair, contrary to the inky hair of his head. He wore broad leather bracelets around his wrists and held his book securely in his enormous hands. Rachel turned her head to see the title: *Paradise Lost*.

She held the printout up off the table between herself and her true point of interest and watched as he flicked his lengthy hair over the back of his shoulder. The movement made his bicep squeeze out the end of the sleeve, exposing more of the tattoo, but he quickly pulled at the cotton and stretched it down to cover his upper arm. His face was kind, though his features were thick. Luscious was the word Rachel was searching for: generous cheeks and lips, his chin now cleanly shaven, an Adam's apple that continually moved up and down as he read.

Above the neck of his T-shirt was a scar that crossed the top of his collarbone, pale pink against his white skin. Rachel slowly lowered her paper without realizing she now stared openly at him. She was leaning forward slightly when he turned to look at her, shifted in his chair, and pulled the neck of his T-shirt higher to cover the scarring. Again, he stretched his sleeves over his upper arms and then twisted the leather bracelet at each wrist.

"*Bonjour*," Rachel said, embarrassed at her rudeness.

"Hello." He, too, seemed hesitant. His tongue was Swiss, possibly more German-Swiss than French. Rachel had never heard a more masculine voice.

"I'm Rachel," she said, wanting to distract herself from her own thoughts.

"Yes, I know. You're the American."

Rachel stiffened in her chair and looked through the windows of the cafe to ensure the chef and waiter were within earshot.

"I mean to say, I've heard the local *providores* mention your name. You are the writer who resides up in the château. You're researching Shelley."

"Oh." The response barely left Rachel's lips.

They were silent for many minutes as the waiter came out to wipe down the tabletops and ensure all the chairs and tables were evenly spaced along the walk. He gave a generous smile and a high-pitched "*bonjour*" to Rachel and a nod to his other customer before heading back into the cafe. He soon returned with Rachel's café latte and a bowl of muesli. Turning to the other patron, he asked, "Latte, *monsieur*?"

"Café express. Double. *Merci*."

Rachel sipped her latte and stared up into the vine-covered hills and the Alps beyond, well aware he was facing her, his book held less than half open, as he waited for his café. She placed her cup onto the table, then dug her spoon into the muesli before daring to look directly at him.

He was staring at her; pitch-black irises set in pure, unnaturally white orbs, surrounded by dark, thick lashes—a profound contrast to the starkness of his flesh. His wide, dark brows arched across his blemish-free skin, almost meeting above the strong ridge of his nose. His hair curled and swept back vigorously from the top of a broad, creaseless forehead. His lips, full and soft, spread genially to expose a double row of perfect, straight teeth. He was more than just good-looking.

"Are you enjoying your breakfast?" he asked.

Rachel blushed. "I'm sorry. I didn't mean to stare. It's just that I thought I knew you from somewhere and was trying to think where."

His smile became even more broad, though with the slightest glimmer of underlying apprehension. "Perhaps you'll remember and let me know, huh?"

"Are you enjoying Milton?" she asked, wanting to change the subject.

"Yes, I think I am. It's, um, teaching me something about myself and why I'm here."

"Really?" Rachel thought perhaps she should read the manuscript again to know what he meant.

The waiter returned to the sidewalk with the double espresso, placed it on the table beside the book, and strode back into the cafe. Rachel ate her muesli in silence as he sipped his espresso and read the words of Milton. The book was enormous even in his large hands, over one-thousand lines of blank verse, the epic poem of Adam and Eve and their temptation. Rachel recalled the details of the story in her mind, attempting to determine their probable fit to the man who sat before her. Every possibility made her blush. She watched as he continued to read, his Adam's apple jumping and his brow furrowing. Slowly, he lowered the book down onto his lap, and his attention shifted from the pages to higher reaches of the Alps that dominated the vista surrounding them.

"Do you think it's possible?" His words were almost inaudible. "Could it be real?"

Rachel wondered if he was talking to her. She moved uneasily in her chair.

"The temptation?"

He turned to look at her, puzzled. "No." He shook his head. "Shelley's wretch . . . her Frankenstein's monster."

Rachel couldn't suppress a truncated laugh of surprise. "Well, of course not—it's fiction!" And then, to reinforce her academic integrity, she added,

"Don't be stupid."

She regretted her response immediately. He tensed, their curious dialogue destroyed almost as soon as it had begun. He averted his eyes and lifted *Paradise Lost* before his face once more, though his attention flicked from the page to the Alps, down to his jeans, and then settled on his feet, which rested askew in the gutter. With his right hand, he rubbed at the side of his head and grimaced at what appeared to be an escalating ache.

He slammed the book shut and thudded it onto the table. His grip on its spine increased, his knuckles turning from white to red as his thumb and fingers pressed into the vellum in palpable pain. No, anger. No . . . pain. He stood, pulling at his T-shirt collar and sleeves, and threw several francs onto the table. He glared in Rachel's direction, then left down the *rue* without a word.

CHAPTER TEN

It was a rare but welcome dry summer morning that Mary strolled along the waterfront with Mr. Henry Clerval. Still, she had her umbrella ready, should the weather turn.

"You must stay as long as you are able, Mr. Clerval. George, when he returns, would be much appreciative of any conversation in the languages you study. He often speaks of the East and the romance of their culture and history."

"A pleasure, Mrs. Shelley. It would be an honor to make acquaintance with Lord Byron and your husband, Mr. Shelley."

They took a seat on a bench to enjoy the vista of the lake and the elegance of the swans in the shallows. Clerval had removed his top hat and it now rested on his lap. Mary was pleased to be escorted by such a charming young gentleman with faultless personal cleanliness, snug pantaloons tucked into his boots, immaculate linen shirt with high collar, and double-breasted frockcoat in dark blue, topped off by a perfectly tied cravat, clipped curls, and fashionable long sideburns.

"How fares your friend, Doctor Frankenstein? I have held much concern since being made aware of his sad history by *Monsieur* Aldini. I was much relieved upon hearing of your expedient arrival in Montreux to assist him."

Clerval nodded. "It is true he had not slept soundly in several weeks and, per his housekeeper, also refused to eat more than a slice of bread and lard at her urging. When I arrived with *Monsieur* Aldini at the Frankenstein residence, we climbed the main lobby stair past dark-stained wood-paneling and even darker portraits whose oil had tarnished ancestral faces into a blackness well beyond recognition. We entered Victor's private rooms without invitation—though, of course, his housekeeper supplied the key, as she was as much concerned as us all. I was aghast at the state of the spaces. You must understand, Mrs. Shelley, his downstairs staff were not permitted in the rooms to do their duties, so what I am about to reveal is not to bear on their good character or diligence."

"Of course." Mary raised her umbrella to afford some shade.

"The first vestibule and corridor of his rooms were quite pitch-black, the candles having long burnt out. We carried two lit chamber sticks, but they did not paint a handsome picture of our friend's abode. His sitting room was in disarray, the bedchamber unkempt. Please, you will forgive me if my narrative is slim, as there are facets of my account I am loath to utter in the presence of a lady such as yourself."

Mary nodded, her imagination filling in the missing details.

"We lit fresh candles and opened the windows and shutters to the night air but, even so, the atmosphere continued very stale with a subtle stench of unknown origin. Perhaps decay or—please forgive me, Mrs. Shelley—death. Light seeped from under the door of the final room. Victor's housekeeper said the doctor referred to the chamber as his laboratory. There was a shuffling followed by silence, then further shuffling and clattering. 'Victor!' I called out, 'It is Henry Clerval, come to visit.' Footsteps crossed rapidly back and forth, followed by the opening and closing of cupboard doors and glass instruments clanking against one another. There was a shattering crash, followed by words a gentleman seldom requires. I tapped on the door. 'May I enter, Victor?' No sooner had I uttered my request than the door opened, and Victor exited and closed the door behind him. I caught but a glance of the laboratory within."

Mary noted how Mr. Clerval's pupils dilated and his face flashed white before taking on a gray hue. He held a shaking, clenched fist tight against his thigh, staring in earnest at the Alps on the far side of the lake.

"Victor . . . er . . . well, well then, where was I? Oh, yes. Victor closed his laboratory door behind him. He was indeed very pale, his eyes slack and rimmed red. He said he was excited to see me, but I could tell he was distracted by his unfinished work in the laboratory. We sat for over an hour on a settee, talking, or at least I talked at first and eventually Victor seemed to become enthused and joined me in conversation. Suddenly he appeared to come to his senses, as if just realizing I was with him in the room. He looked up, surprised, to see *Monsieur* Aldini. '*Monsieur*!' he exclaimed. 'You have come for supper at last.' He begged us to follow him from his private rooms to the comfort of the study, almost running down the staircase as he called to his housekeeper for sherry and a light supper.

"He was animated for some time but finally conceded that he was, indeed, exhausted. Our friend fell fast asleep in his great chair by the study fire, the attentive housekeeper extracting the sherry glass from his hand before it might fall. We thought it best to leave him as he was, rather than disturb him to retire to his chamber. *Monsieur* Aldini proposed to spend the night in the study, keeping watch over Victor as he slept, but I retired to my lodging to prepare for the new day of assisting Victor as might be required. By the time I left the Frankenstein residence, most of the street lanterns had been put out and I had only a few stars to light my journey back to the centre of town."

Mary took Mr. Clerval's hand in hers. Even through her gloves and on this sunny morning, his skin felt cold to the touch. "Mr. Clerval, Doctor Frankenstein is fortunate indeed to have both yourself and *Monsieur* Aldini as acquaintances. Your untiring friendship is admirable. I trust the doctor is regaining his strength and sensibilities?"

"Yes, he most certainly is—though I will stay several weeks more in Montreux to ensure he keeps his schedule intact and is more conservative in the hours spent on his work." Uncertainty passed across the young man's face.

Mary could see she needed to change the subject. "Come. The public salon at my residence has a most wonderful afternoon luncheon. There we may talk of happier times, a more amiable conversation. Perhaps you would wish to hear a portion of the ghost story I am writing . . ."

CHAPTER ELEVEN

Doctor John Polidori
Villa Diodoti, Cologny
Geneva   July 1816

Darling John,
The details of my waking dreams become more vivid with each falling of night. This evening just past I was seated at my desk, watching the horrid rain splash so hard against the panes they were more mirror than window to the outside world. The reflection was transmuted, but I could clearly make out my own image and the larger furnishings in the parlor behind me. All shimmered, and I had to touch my face to assure myself I was not undergoing metamorphosis. My eye caught the play of shadow reflected from behind me. Was it a specter or some person of criminal intent secreted into my rooms? The shadow crouched beside the bureau, but even as I spied upon it, it rose to its full height. I surmised the demon be at almost eight feet tall. I was not in the least part scared as I watched the creature's reflected silhouette form within the watery shadows, for I knew if I turned toward him he would not be there. He stared at me from the darkened corner, his face not unkind, but perhaps tinged by a sadness that he himself could not explain. He held out his hand to me and quivered as his fist slowly and purposefully clenched.
The floorboards creaked as his weight switched to his forward foot.
The smell of decaying cadaver seeped throughout the room.
I do not know what overtook me, but I was frozen upon the odor reaching my senses, the very hairs on the back of my neck standing erect, my whole body stiffening against the side of my wingback. I could not bring myself to turn from the windowpane and confront the creature, lest the creation not be my own but of some other origin.
My gaze held to the glass, reviewing his countenance as he progressed toward me. Did he know I observed him, that I was aware of his endeavor?

I dared not scream, for if it were all my own fabrication the whole household would think me deranged and poorly. I remained rigid as he moved closer to the wingback—his enormous, monstrous frame taking up the entire reflection of all thirty-two panes of rain-splashed glass. He placed his hand on the back of the chair, inches from my neck. His skin was white, tending toward a yellowish pallor. It was dry and flaked, and his nails appeared loose. The stench of charnel house wafted from his rotting flesh as his eyes met and held mine in reflection.

M. Shelley

CHAPTER TWELVE

"*Bonjour*, Francois." Rachel passed from the covered walkway of Château de Chillon out into its first courtyard. The noon sun shone directly into the court, glancing off the heavy stone walls, throwing the indented window casements into dark shadow. A particular aroma pervaded the block work, courts, and corridors that scrambled off in seemingly random directions. Rachel had noticed it the first time she walked across the drawbridge to research in the building's archives, but she'd never been able to define what it was or where it came from. Perhaps it was rotting leaves, or wood, or mildewed stone. Perhaps it was but the slow, natural decay of the history that rose from the eddying waters of Lake Geneva. Sometimes it struck her as pungently sweet, reminding her of meat that had been hung and left to age—bloodless carcasses breaking down into tender and expensive cuts of meat.

"*Bonjour, Mademoiselle* Rachel." The caretaker handed out audio guides to a group of Swedish tourists. He indicated with his hand the direction to the famous dungeon, then rushed over to walk with Rachel through the massive archway into the second court. "But I thought you had finished with our archives, *mademoiselle*."

"As had I, however I've come across a trunk of correspondence that I need to cross-reference." They stopped before the impregnable walls of the keep that dominated the second courtyard. Rachel couldn't suppress an excited smile. "I have access to over thirty letters written by Mary while she was here in Montreux."

"*Madame* Shelley? But that is wonderful. Are they from a personal collection? I have not heard of any such correspondence. I must inform our *directeur* of your find at once."

"Please do. Chillon should have them protected within its archives. Please inform the *directeur* I will gladly join her in approaching the family to secure the documents, if she wishes."

"Yes, yes, oh most *certainement, mademoiselle*."

Rachel pulled a key card from her pocket and raised her eyebrows in question.

"Ah, but of course, I will reactivate your card immediately. You will have full access to the electronic doors of Chillon before you have even climbed the stairs to the Salle de Armoiries." And with that, Francois rushed off to the security room at the rear of the gift boutique.

In no real hurry, Rachel meandered through the third courtyard, the Cour d'Honneur, imagining Mary's thoughts as she had toured this very space. She touched the rough-hewn stonework, admired the awnings over the two chiseled staircases clinging to opposite walls, and peered up at the open blue sky above, rimmed by the battlements and beautiful tiled roofs of the château, knowing Mary would have done the same, as any tourist to this castle must respect the beauty and horror of its history.

Rachel climbed the left-hand stair, through the armory with its display of medieval weaponry and past the petite salon. She squeezed down a corridor of stone barely wide enough even for her, held her key card against an all-but-invisible reader in the side of the solid oak doorframe, and gained access to several rooms directly above the Domus Clericorum.

The walls were filled from floor to ceiling with shelves. Artifacts, ancient tomes, papers, and significant scraps of parchment were wrapped in acid-free archival paper, stored in cardboard sleeves and encased in boxes with handwritten labels across the front. Over one thousand years of history was secured within these rooms, within these boxes. Rachel had spent months scrutinizing the three coffers assigned to 1816, more commonly known as the "year without a summer" or, Rachel recalled with a shudder, "eighteen hundred and froze to death." An unprecedented series of eruptions in Indonesia had led to global cooling, incessant rain, worldwide harvest failures, famine, sickness, disorder, and undreamt-of horror.

"Yes, Mary, you were correct. It was a most ungenial year."

The climate-controlled air conditioning hummed all around her, the air cold and void of any odor or taste. The second room contained more shelves packed with archive boxes, but also an antique, metal-covered workbench—like something in a morgue with a body sprawled on top, the "Y" section crossing its torso sewn closed but still raw and puckering. Rachel shook the image from her mind, placed her satchel on the bench, and spread out a folder containing several of Mary's letters. Behind her was a computer giving access to the archival catalogues. She sat down at it and reread the letters. Mary's concept for her wretch was beginning to materialize from the shadows. It was becoming clearer in her mind and inextricably, yet tangibly, bleeding into her world whether she wanted it to or not.

Rachel worked for several hours with gloved hands, sequencing the letters by date with the documents available in the Chillon archives. The sample of correspondence she'd brought seemed to align to Mary's whereabouts, though it made her wonder whether any of the responses from

Percy or Doctor John Polidori—as most certainly there would have been—still existed. She made a note to e-mail the head librarian at the Université de Genève archives.

Pushing her chair back from the computer, Rachel once again read the most recent letter she'd selected from Mary's trunk, noting the descriptive force of her narrative, of her imagination. *Her imagination*, thought Rachel, folding the letter and peering out the double-glazed beveling in the wall behind the computer screen. At the very top of the defensive slit, Rachel could see the flyover of the Autoroute Du Leman. Her vision was unexpectedly blurred by tears as she thought of Jack. They'd often ridden along the freeway as it tunneled through the mountains and arched over broad valleys and ancient villages up into the Valais. She could still feel the thump of his heart as she held him tight, the fresh smell of leather and alpine air as they sped along.

She wiped at the tears, angry she'd allowed herself to sink back into those memories. She shut the computer down, packed Mary's letters into their protective folder, slid them into her satchel, and left. The sun was low in the west as she walked across the covered, wooden bridge from Chillon back to the mainland. The bus to town was scheduled to arrive in a few minutes, but guessing the sun wouldn't be setting for at least another hour or so, Rachel decided to walk to clear her mind.

She'd avoided the lake edge since that night of the tempest when she'd first seen him, been scared by him. Now, deep in thought about Mary—about Jack really, or was it *him* she thought of, with skin so white and eyes so black?—she missed the turnoff and instead continued following Avenue de Chillon past beautiful villages and walled gardens she didn't even notice as her thoughts shifted back and forth: first Mary, then Jack, then him. *Him.*

A lantern flared above her. It took her several startled moments to realize where she was, when she was. The pavement was cobbled, and buildings rose two and three stories on either side—raw stone work and walls of myriad colors, their shutters secured open to reveal the subdued lighting of apartments filtering through curtains and sheers. Nineteenth-century-style lanterns hung from wrought iron arms jutting out of the buildings, their electricity—not naked flame—giving Rachel a sense of relief she didn't understand. A blue and white street sign proclaimed Rue du Temple. She was in the center of Montreux.

The sky above was still blue but very dark—had she walked so slowly that the sun had almost set? She stood for a moment in the deserted street outside the Caveau St-Vincent. The din of revelers coming from inside was enticing, tempting her to one or more glasses of wine, to conversation and laughter with fleeting acquaintances and perhaps a pot of fondue, half and half, Gruyère and Vacherin, perhaps with wild garlic; no, with cognac and pepper. Hmm, yes.

But the noise reverberating up the lane from Rue du Pont distracted her, and she thought it better to find somewhere simple and get home as fast as possible. She wanted to secure the documents in her satchel and needed a good night's sleep anyway. Too many had been sleepless with excitement, with loss, with wonder. She kept walking.

There was a tiny pizzeria on the bend of Rue du Pont, with a window full of fresh-made dough bases ready for the oven. Rachel watched the chef assemble her pizza then shovel it into the back of the oven amongst the glow of charcoal. The smell of baking crust, artichoke, and mozzarella brought on such happiness that by the time she left with her box of pizza, Rachel was determined to write, to build all her newly acquired details into the current draft of Mary's biography.

Rachel opened the box and continued along Rue de Pont, but it was cumbersome to walk and think about her manuscript and extract each slice of pizza from the box without dropping chunks of artichoke onto the cobblestones. She stopped at a semi-circular platform to enjoy the view of the town, lake, and Alps, as well as her pizza, without the distraction of walking. Thirty thoughtful minutes passed, and with her hunger satisfied and enough pizza remaining for a midnight snack, she brushed the crumbs from her pants and stood.

Only a moment passed before she sat back down onto the wall, facing across the cobbled *rue*, away from the view.

She knew he couldn't see her. She was in darkness, no streetlights nearby.

He was inside a brightly lit store, completely unaware she was observing him.

Light and music blared out into the night from the apartment windows above the store. A young woman was leaning out one window, holding a glass of wine, the hand of an otherwise unseen man resting on her shoulder. The woman laughed and moved back into the room where Rachel could no longer see her.

But he was in the store on the ground floor. The signage above the glassed front blazed: *Think Tattoo*. The walls were covered with designs and photos of ink work. He was staring at a photo, his face very close to the wall, when he turned as if called and stepped further into the parlor. Rachel rose and walked tentatively along Rue de Pont, careful to stay out of the lamplight, until she was directly opposite the parlor and had a full view through the display area into the workshop beyond.

He'd already removed his shirt and sat in the technician's chair facing away from her, a towel hanging over his right shoulder and arm. The tattoo artist stood between Rachel and him, so all she could see was the broadness of his back, the whiteness of his skin under the brilliant fluorescent lights of the workshop. He looked down at his shoulder and arm now and then, talking an unknown conversation with the artist. She moved about him, then placed her face close to the skin of his shoulder and stood back to review her work. Again she placed her hand upon his back to unnecessarily caress it, or at least Rachel deemed it unnecessary. His expression showed no noticeable emotion as the girl touched his neck and stroked his hair before throwing her head back and laughing.

Again Rachel thought of that word: *unbridled.*

She looked again to the upper window from which the music still blared. The lights had been all but extinguished. She could imagine their story . . . their current chapter anyway.

Rachel didn't bother looking back through the windows of *Think Tattoo.* Instead she threw the pizza box into a trashcan and walked home through the darkening night, alone.

The moon had risen and was bright against the flagstones when she crossed the terrace toward her studio. All appeared cold in the pure white light. She reached for her key and urged it into the lock of the terrace door, but then she stopped, distracted. With her hand and cheek pressed against the pane of glass, she peered into the apartment. The room was in utter blackness, except for the trunk and the watercolor painting that hovered above. A shard of moonlight cut through the bathroom, reflecting off an elaborate, gilt-framed mirror to give the trunk and painting of Mont Blanc an extraordinary amity and presence.

The trunk in particular was flushed with verve, and Rachel knew . . .

She needed to touch it, to caress it, to insert and turn its keys, to urge it open within the warmth of her hands, and gaze upon its contents.

She needed to read more of Mary's letters.

CHAPTER THIRTEEN

Almost every evening after kissing Willmouse goodnight and handing him to the nursemaid, Mary sat at her writing desk, quill in hand, and stared thoughtfully through the thirty-two panes of glass that rose before her Maggiolini at the blue lanterns of the *gendarmerie* bobbing back and forth about the hillsides above Montreux. Looking. Searching. Probing. Her window gave her ample view of the far-off proceedings, which she steadfastly wove into her own evolving ghost story.

Her writing was also influenced by a subtle change in the demeanor of the men in summer residence at the villa. Their conversations terminated abruptly whenever she walked into the study or onto the terrace, where they had congregated away from the women. At first it had amused her, thinking she'd disrupted some innocent gossip of subjects men seem eternally dictated to discuss. But their faces, blushed by talk of scandal, were soon replaced by looks of grave concern and worry. After the puffing of cigars and imbuing of port and sherry, this apprehension, imagined or not, distilled into a palatable enthusiasm, invoked by animated whispers and the arching of eyebrows in intimate huddles.

Mary was intrigued—her imagination firing even further as to the possible explanation for this behavior.

She was deep in contemplation, catching the morning rays of sunlight on the villa's terrace and awaiting Mr. Clerval, when her guest walked briskly out from the reception and across the tiles toward her.

"Thank you for meeting with me without a prior appointment, Mrs. Shelley." Henry tipped his hat and pressed her hand momentarily.

"Certainly, Mr. Clerval. But what could bring you to my residence that requires such haste?"

"I regret that I have come to say goodbye."

"Oh, but I was so looking forward to introducing you to Percy and George. You are such good company, and they would have been thrilled to have met your acquaintance."

Henry sat on the elegant wrought iron settee opposite Mary. A waiter stood at the ready as several others attended to the seating, plumping the cushions and readying the tables for morning tea. Beyond the terrace's balustrade, the hotel gardens glistened in morning sunshine and drizzle. Mary straightened the blue pastel fabric of her dress then held up her hand to catch the eye of the waiter, who nodded courteously and went inside to fetch refreshments.

"I am determined to return in a few weeks, but for now I must start my journey before the sun reaches halfway to the meridian. The livery has agreed to deliver my transport to this very residence that I may spend as many minutes saying goodbye as possible."

Mary was about to respond when the waiter approached with the tea set. He placed the silver tray on the sideboard and lifted the silver George III oblong-bellied teapot to fill each of the teacups. He placed the sugar bowl and creamer on the table before offering to get them anything more, but Mary politely shook her head, smiling, wishing he would just go away.

"I will look forward to your speedy return. Do you travel back to Ingolstadt and the University, or follow *Monsieur* Aldini to Bologna?"

Mr. Clerval's countenance darkened. "No, Mrs. Shelley."

Mary said nothing and held his gaze.

"I am afraid I am the bearer of frightful news. A most horrid and unhallowed incident has occurred that makes me weep with even the slightest thought to how it could be possible."

Mary studied the young man before her, now aware of the sadness that imbued his every movement. Tears hung from his lashes, and his fastidious, manicured hands trembled. She moved around the table to take his hands in hers. "Mr. Clerval, would you care to retire to a more private salon? The study, perhaps? I can organize—"

"No, no." Clerval took several deep breaths in quick succession. The waiters had moved to the far end of the terrace as a courtesy, turning their backs that the gentleman might grieve in some kind of privacy. "It should not be my place to show these emotions, as it is my friend Doctor Frankenstein who has been done wrong by. For you see, his dear, innocent younger brother, William—still a child—has been murdered. Strangled."

"Oh my . . ." Mary's thoughts went to her own William, Willmouse, barely five months old, who spent the best part of almost every day sleeping soundly in the nursery with the other guests' children, or at night in the crib Mary kept at her bedside. "The loss of a child . . ." Mary was unable to stop her thoughts sliding back to her first born, a daughter—lying dead in her arms that horrible morning three years previous.

Oh, how she wished she could have brought the young babe back to life, resurrected her through love or . . . by whatever means . . .

"Frankenstein's housekeeper contacted me before sunrise this morning with a message she dare not deliver to her master. I woke Victor from his slumber and, as he came to his senses and the full realization manifest itself, he was of a raw emotion I would never again wish to bear witness to. After all he has been through, that he should now also suffer the loss of one so young and so dear."

"My dear sir! This is indeed unfortunate news, a horror no family deserves." Mary was unsuccessful in her attempts to stop her eyes watering, wishing she could celebrate the life that was with her without forgetting the one that was not. She dabbed at her lashes with a lace kerchief.

"Victor is already in carriage to Geneva. I will follow with a few of his possessions and hopefully some strength to assist him through this trying time."

The *maitre d'hôtel* entered from the main reception, crossed the black and white tiles of the terrace, and stopped short of Mr. Clerval's settee. Mr. Clerval nodded. "Thank you, good sir, I will be at the *porte cochère* momentarily."

He rose from his seat, straightened the shoulders of his frockcoat, refastened an errant button, and placed his hat once more upon his head. "Goodbye, Mrs. Shelley. It has indeed been a pleasure to have made acquaintance with you."

"And you also, my dear Mr. Clerval. I will tell Percy and Lord Byron of your grief when they return to Montreux. We will await your homecoming with the open arms of friendship, as I know sincerely that the carer of those in the path of grief and harm also requires the care and love of friends."

CHAPTER FOURTEEN

Doctor John Polidori
Villa Diodoti, Cologny
Geneva　　　　　　　　　　　　　　　　　　　　　　　　　*July 1816*

Dearest John,
The demon entered my chambers again last night. He sat on the edge of my bed, compressing the feathers of my eiderdown, and told me that someone dear to my own heart had been murdered. "Strangled" was the word he used, though he refused to tell me the name of my acquaintance or where I should go to confirm his utterance.
He sat there, staring at me as I pulled the covers close and moved the pillows between myself and he who invaded my dreams.
And yet I knew I was not dreaming as I observed the smear of dead flesh left upon my sheets and smelt his stench, much stronger than any time I had known previously.
He just stared at me in the candle-lit darkness of my room, and then he smiled—a movement of the lips I am abhorrent to describe . . .

M. Shelley

CHAPTER FIFTEEN

Rachel awoke in fright, her tank top drenched in sweat and clinging, her eyes searching in the morning light to confirm she was alone in her studio. Her comforter had been flung onto the floor, but there was no tell-tale sign of cadaver on her sheets or lingering smell of corpse within the small space.

She pulled off her top as she crawled out of the high bed, flicked on the electric kettle as she passed the kitchenette, and leaned into the compact bathroom to turn on the faucet above the cast-iron tub. The pipes in the walls chugged a few times, followed by the gush of water into the bath and the plume of steam throughout the tiled room.

She sat on the side of the bath, watching as the water rose inch by inch. Her reflection swirled in the eddying movement. She thought about the pizza, wishing she hadn't thrown the last three slices away. The kettle whistled, and within a moment she was perched again on the side of the tub sipping tea—some herbal concoction she'd picked up in the markets. Balancing the cup on the side of the tub, Rachel slipped into the steaming water, fully submerging to look up and out at her world through the rippling water. The bathroom ceiling was a whitewashed wood, and the wall tiles were also white, their enamel cracked from age, the very top row containing an animal motif that was indistinguishable in the steam. With the undulations of the water, it appeared as if the bathroom door was swinging slowly open.

Rachel gulped involuntarily, swallowing a mouthful of water as four enormous, decaying fingers gripped the edge of the door. She rose from the water, catching the reflection of thick black hair and pallid skin in the fogged mirror above the basin. No sooner had she breasted the surface than he was in the room and upon her, a single hand gripping around her neck and pushing her beneath the water once more. His face was without emotion as he stared at her useless struggle, bubbles from her last gasps of breath rising toward the surface until they were no more and the water was motionless.

She stared at him, her mouth and lungs full of water, her body limp and lifeless, her heart no longer beating, and still she could see him on the far side of the water. He was immobile for many minutes, gazing down upon her. He pushed a finger through the surface to trace the outline of her mouth. Ethereal bits of flesh floated loosely about his knuckle and nail. Then, calmly, he pulled her body up out of the tub and into his arms. He placed his lips on hers, now as cold and dead as his own.

* * * *

Rachel awoke in fright, her tank top drenched in sweat and clinging, her eyes searching in the morning light to confirm she was alone in her studio. Her comforter had been flung onto the floor, but there was no tell-tale sign of cadaver on her sheets or lingering smell of corpse within the small space.

She ran around the room, ensuring the front door and windows were locked, slamming the terrace doors closed, and latching them securely. The bathroom was empty, but she couldn't bring herself to enter, instead closing the door and cleaning herself as best she could at the sink in the kitchenette. She pulled on her jeans, shirt, and jacket, and grabbed her wallet, desperate to get out into the sunshine and among the living.

The cafe Rue du Sacre du Printemps was not yet open when Rachel passed by. More to the point, he was not there. She crossed under the railway line and through the village of Clarens until she reached the gardened foreshore of the lake. The full majestic vista opened up before her, the enormity and openness of the lake, Alps, and sky giving her relief from her nightmare. She stood on the park's graveled walkway, watching a young boy running in circles on the grass with a dog. It made her inexplicably happy to watch as they ran and ran in the same tight circle.

She walked over to a bench shaded by an imposing row of plain trees along the lake-walk. Several older ladies walked large old dogs, possibly as ancient as they, all the while talking, smoking, and laughing. A lonesome athlete jogged across the park and disappeared around the bend in the shoreline toward Montreux.

"Any sane person would think I was following you, or you me."

The deep voice at Rachel's back made her jump. She stood as he walked around the bench and took a seat. He was staring at her, his head tilted to the side, a shy but cheeky grin covering his face. "Please sit with me." He patted the bench with his enormous hand. Rachel stared at it. It was as white as she'd recalled, but there were no signs of decay, no signs of rot. The flesh was healthy and strong, the nails slightly bitten but neat. Rachel chewed her lip, embarrassed at being so stupid and rude, and smiled apologetically as she sat beside him.

"Is that your son and dog?"

Rachel shook her head, relieved he didn't know everything about her.

"You don't say much, do you?"

"Oh, I'm sorry. I didn't mean to be rude." Rachel crossed and uncrossed her legs. "It's just that I was, um, I was deep in thought when you approached. I wasn't expecting . . ." He seemed attentive to whatever words came out her mouth. His grin remained, his lips quivering to expose white teeth. Rachel, however, couldn't recall her initial words to him as she attempted to stop herself from scrutinizing every portion of his gigantic frame. *My God, he's big*, was all she could think in such close proximity. Eventually she offered a sensible sentence. "Would you like some café?"

"Thought you'd never ask." He rose to his feet and held out his hand to lead the way, his relaxed, open palm lower than his chest but higher than Rachel's shoulders. "The garden cafe at L'Ermitage should be open by now." He looked up at the sun as if to confirm the time.

They followed the Quai de Clarens around the curve of the shoreline, past multi-storied apartment blocks and two or three large homes that had escaped the plans of developers. The gardens of the hotel restaurant terraced right down to the lake, separated from the shoreline by the Quai de Clarens promenade and the lowest of stone walls.

Rachel climbed the several steps into the garden, noticing how he took them as one, and made her way toward the paved top terrace and an empty table. Some of the hotel guests were already at breakfast in the bright morning sunshine. The cafe manager greeted them with a smile and took their orders: one latte, one double espresso, a small basket of baguettes accompanied by butter, jams, and chocolate spread.

"Look, I'm sorry about the other day," Rachel said. "I didn't mean to be offensive."

"That's cool. Don't worry about it. I had a lot on my mind, too. Still do, I guess."

"Did you finish *Paradise Lost?*"

The question hung as a young waitress of perhaps fifteen delivered the latte and espresso. He watched her movements carefully, as if studying how she placed the cups onto the table. The girl rolled her wrist as she positioned the espresso, elegantly extending her thumb to nudge the handle of his glass toward him. He glanced down to his own hand and mimicked her movement, twice rolling his wrist and flicking his thumb, seemingly in practice.

He appeared thoughtful as the girl walked away, then he returned his gaze to Rachel. "No . . . that one will take me a while yet. More than likely I'll complete several others before I finish that opus. And you, Rachel, are you reading anything interesting?"

"Oh, um, yes I am. Not a novel per se, but I am studying some fascinating papers as part of my research."

"The Shelley biography," he said matter-of-factly.

"Yes, er, you seem to know a lot about me, and I know nothing of you."

He stretched back in his chair. "The people of this village talk. The reason for your being here is interesting to everyone. And you know I read Milton and drink espresso. I would think we know an equal amount of each other." His cheeky grin grew as the waitress delivered their baguettes and spreads.

"Perhaps." Rachel sugared her latte, wanting to choose her words with care, not wanting to repeat her previous error. "Do you work?"

"No."

"Are you still at university?"

"No."

"Are you obscenely rich?" She smiled, not expecting an affirmative answer.

He was quiet for a moment as if looking for something deep within her eyes, then shook his head. "No." Again that smile spread slow and broad across his face. "Not obscenely."

Rachel slumped into her chair, holding her latte close to her lips. She watched as he smeared a thick layer of chocolate across his baguette and munched on it in between sips of his espresso. "Why are you sitting here with me, drinking coffee and eating bread?" she asked.

"Because you are intriguing and beautiful."

Rachel blushed, unsure of how to respond, wondering why she would ask such a question in the first place.

"And why are you here with me, Rachel? Drinking coffee and eating bread?" He suddenly burst into laughter—a genuine, happy laugh that put Rachel at ease and made her chuckle.

Just then, she noticed spots of blood on his button-up shirt. At first it was a few specks below his left shoulder, but then more and more bright red spots plumed through the material on both the left and right of his chest, designating two distinct lines of blood that delineated his arms from his torso.

"Oh my God, are you ok? You're bleeding."

He looked down at his shirt and grunted. "Damn. I'm sorry, I've . . . uh . . . I've gotta go." He pulled several francs from his pocket and placed them under his espresso glass and then indicated toward the blood with a thick finger. "I just had my tats extended. They were already on the arms and I wanted them extended up onto my shoulders to cover . . . They'll look pretty cool when they're finished."

"Do you want me to come with you, to help?"

"It's ok, I have stuff at home from the tattoo place. I should take better care while they're healing. Hey, can I buy you some late supper tonight, maybe a drink or two?"

"Sure." Rachel surprised herself with her own lack of hesitation.

"Harry's at 10?"

"Sure, Harry's at 10."

CHAPTER SIXTEEN

Mary was secreted into a great wingback in the corner of the private library of the residence. All of the other ladies staying at the villa had retired to the main drawing room or their personal parlors, leaving Mary with her diary and pen and a small drop of sherry. Clouds of cigar smoke hung above her, emanating from the gentlemen who congregated about the fire at the far end of the room. She surmised they had forgotten she was in the overstuffed chair, which faced toward the darkened window, for their conversation had moved to topics no lady should ever hear. She placed her pen in its well and listened intently.

"Evidently this atrocity has been ongoing for many months. Graves have been defiled, corpses pulled from their shrouds then thrown back into the ground to be roughly covered again by hallowed soil."

"But to what purpose would any fiend pursue such activity?"

"At first there would seem to be none, but recently there appeared discrepancies that would horrify any of a sane mind."

There was much murmuring and increased clouds of smoke originating from around the fireplace. Mary turned, noting that she could discern the countenance of the men in the reflection of the glass doors of the bookcase beside her. They were all quite young, perhaps two or three years older than herself, about twenty to twenty-two, she guessed. The more elderly gentlemen sat around the card tables, enjoying their own boisterous conversation and haze of cigar smoke. No doubt the younger men were all avid adventurers, much like her dear Percy and friend George, come to conquer the mighty Alps. Astuteness also told Mary, however, that some of the men were likely inclined to partake in a continental enjoyment, a love of each other, that would have seen them socially disgraced or imprisoned back in England, if discovered. She thought of George and the so-called civility of the glorious British Empire. Its prejudice and bigotry sickened her heart. She took a sip of sherry, all her attention directed toward the men's conversation.

"The first they observed was the body of a man, a farmer of extraordinary strength and vitality—his legs known to be massive, but now missing."

"Surgically removed—"

"Then a second, a man of great musculature, recognized for feats of immense strength in his vocation as an axe-man in the forests."

"His thick, muscled arms surgically removed . . ."

"A third man was found, his body discarded in the forest, his heart and lungs no longer with him."

"A fourth . . ."

"A fifth . . ."

They passed around the decanter of port to refill glasses sipped dry. Fresh cigars were cut and lit.

"One young man, known for his vigor and generosity, was found pulled from his grave, draped across the headstone, and surgically deprived of that which had made him known amongst the men of his village."

The group of men gasped as one, downing their port and puffing furiously upon their cigars. Mary held her own hand to her breast, shocked that such could occur. Once more the sight of the body in the ditch resuscitated into clarity, refusing to decay from her thoughts. She wondered for the safety of Percy tramping across Mont Blanc and the Alps. Desperately she wished he would return to Montreux as soon as possible.

The men lapsed into silence.

Mary's own thoughts careened almost out of control.

"Why would you harvest such body parts?" she whispered to her muse, staring at her reflection in the blackened glass of the window. "Arms from one body, legs from another. Heart, spleen, and lungs from several others." She studied her diary and peered for several minutes toward her pen. Ideas formulated within her mind. The horrors of surgical removal, the unthinkable aspects of placing them together, much as a jigsaw puzzle, before shocking them with animal electricity to once more bring life to something God had made inanimate.

But would it be possible? Does the electricity of Galvani bring life to dead flesh, or reverse the death of only those whose spirits have not yet departed fully from this plain? Is the electricity itself life, or is the spirit something different and unique that is somehow intimately connected with the properties of that strange energy?

Mary thought of the sciences she knew intimately and started writing. She thought of the apparent manias and subsisting horrors of recent acquaintances that she knew merely by vicarious conversation. She sipped at her sherry, breathed deeply of the cigar-smoke-laden air, and wrote. She wrote as the card games came to an end. She wrote as the men finished off the last of their cigars and retired to their private suites. She wrote throughout the night, not daring to stop until her mind was exhausted of the thoughts that filled it.

When at last the residence fell into an embracing slumber, a servant entered the library, stoked the fire and approached her.

"*Madame?*"

"Of course. Thank you, I must have dozed after the villa's wonderful supper." Mary collected her diary, quill, and well, smiled at the servant, and retired up the grand stair to her room.

But she wondered whether she would dare sleep, or keep writing that which she had seen.

CHAPTER SEVENTEEN

Rachel always felt a thrill walking along the Grand Rue and into the magnificence of Le Montreux Palace Hotel. Built in the Belle Époque style, it took her breath away with its canary-yellow awnings facing the lake, its grand lobby, and its sweeping staircase within the majestic front entrance. She'd often dreamt of spending a day in its spa on the lakeside and a weekend in one of its opulent suites. *Perhaps when the biography is published*, she thought.

Harry's New York Bar was at the western end of the hotel. With its dark wood paneling, varnished wooden bar, rich burgundy seating and lampshades, and decadent coffered ceiling, it oozed sophistication subdued into a level of cool by the friendly bar staff and smooth, relaxed jazz sessions that ran long into the early hours of the morning.

Rachel had met Jack here. She imagined him standing in the corner, martini in hand, dark blue jacket stretched across his muscled torso and arms, the light of a candelabra glinting off his sleepy blue eyes and wayward blond hair. The thought of him still made her smile; her gorgeous Jack.

She entered the bar at ten past ten. It was hot with the mellow beat of jazz and the voices of a sexy clientele blending into a background buzz. She didn't see him at first, as she urged herself past smiling faces and the welcoming touch and smell of excitement that pervaded the space. *The beautiful people*, she thought to herself, sidling between the silks of Armani and Versace, Chanel and Gaultier, brushing up against the textures of Tom Ford and Yves Saint Laurent, the scents of urbanity and sexually charged pleasure.

He was standing in the corner, whisky swirling in a squat chunky glass, dark blue jacket stretched across his muscled torso and arms, his thick black hair tied at his back with a broad, black ribbon. He raised his glass and smiled before walking over to place his hand against the small of her back and his lips close to her ear—to be heard above the din of alcohol, wealth, and arousal surrounding them. "Would the lady care for a wine or a cocktail this evening?" His breath was hot against her skin, tinted with the rich perfume of Johnny Walker.

"Yes, thank you. A Bitter Sling, please." Rachel took his glass as he moved toward the bar and was devoured mercilessly by the crowd. He was at least two feet taller than anyone else in the room. All the women and, indeed, all the men responded to him with an electricity, a sensuality that made her wonder. None of them seemed intimidated by his sheer size; all seemed more than pleased to be nudged by his massiveness rather than move out of the way. His smile as he made his way back toward her wasn't of embarrassment, but more of unexpected wonder. He swapped glasses with her.

"*Salute*," they mouthed, and he leaned against the wall beside her. He sidled down so she could hear him over the increasing cacophony of saxophone and conversation.

"I tried to get us a table and chairs, but these suits and stilettos . . ."—he motioned toward the crowded room—"are absolute monsters."

Rachel smiled. "That's okay."

"What?"

She tugged at his jacket, pulling him down even closer to her. "I said, that's okay." Her cheek touched his and a tingle reverberated throughout her body. He smiled, watching the people around them, and slid further down the panel, pushing his thick legs out into the crowd until his face was almost beside Rachel's. "This is a great place, hey?"

"Pardon?"

He laughed and rolled his eyes, downed the last of his whiskey and grabbed Rachel's hand to pull her through the boisterous crowd and out onto the *rue*. She still held her cocktail. After taking one last sip, she gave the glass to the doorman.

"We'll come back in a couple of hours when the crowd has thinned and the jazz is nice and soft." He led her across the *rue* between taxis and cars, and down toward the lakeside promenade. He didn't once let go of her hand as they meandered along, pressed against the balustrade to admire the glow of Alps on the far side of the lake, and eventually sat on the grass near the dazzling ambiance of the casino.

"I hope you like French food." He rolled onto his side to face her.

Rachel nodded. "How are your shoulders?"

"Oh, fine, thanks. They've put me together like an ox. Nothing to worry about."

She noted his strange wording and accent and guessed he was fluent in French and German as well as English. Maybe others, too. "That's good, I'm glad."

The lights of Evian, on the French side of the lake, twinkled and rippled across the water. He pointed to a small cluster of illumination a third of the way up the Alps, promising to take her there some sunny weekend. The last of the night ferries crisscrossed the lake, pushing iridescent foam as they made their way to dock. The brightly painted *Chablais* passed close to shore on its way to Bon Port, tourists standing on the deck to admire the view.

"Will your work keep you in Montreux much longer?" He was suddenly tentative.

Rachel thought for a moment before replying. "Perhaps another three months. I may also need to spend a week or so back in Geneva before wrapping up the final draft and returning to Manhattan."

He studied her face, nodding in deep contemplation.

"Come," he said at last, standing and pulling Rachel to her feet. "The finest *grenouilles à la provençale* in all Montreux is awaiting us further along the Quai."

CHAPTER EIGHTEEN

Mary Wollstonecraft Godwin Shelley
Villa Eden Au Lac
Montreux   *July 1816*

Darling Mary (my inquisitive Eve),
Forgive the addressing of this correspondence, but I was uncertain as to the surname under which you had recorded your residence in Montreux. I recognize these Europeans are more acceptable of our lifestyles, but still I am sensible toward your reputation, as you are to mine.
Rumor has, just this morning, reached Geneva of the ghastly occurrences in the surrounds of your village. I will not go into details with this script; however, knowing your penchant for obtaining the most obtuse facts about all affairs, I am certain you are well aware of recent events.
Your stepsister, Miss Claire Clairmont, will journey from Villa Diodoti to Montreux on the midmorning carriage. I must warn you she is still upset to the extreme by Lord Byron's avoidance of her niceties. (Again, I am also aware you know the true subject of George's affection and trust our confidence will continue, for I have grown fond of Miss Claire and do not wish to break her heart.)
I will follow this evening, once I have wrapped up affairs here at the villa and in Geneva.
Please expect me to join you for a late supper. I will be much relieved to see you safe and well.
I hope and trust your host still has a room available for me. If not, do not concern yourself, as I have an uncanny knack of obtaining sanctuary.
Yours sincerely,
Dr. John Polidori

CHAPTER NINETEEN

"You seem pensive," he said. He appeared as little more than a silhouette on the other side of the dining table.

"And you . . ."

He looked at her thoughtfully, a shy curl of the lip delineated by an overhead spotlight. "I didn't realize this place would be so formal. I don't mean to imply anything . . ."

She returned his smile.

The restaurant was very dark—lit by spots and tea-lamps that barely drew the occupants from the shadows. The ceiling was indistinguishable; the walls covered in heavy, gathered, ink-colored silk; the floor a jet marble cloaked in silver and black Persians, scattered with cushions. The furnishings, also, were silver and black—polished, modern takes on pre-revolutionary French styles, upholstered in buttoned black leather that sighed with the slightest movement.

The scent of truffle mixed lucidly with the almost indiscernible musical-resonance emanating from the drapery. The ambient noise seemed to be the gentle, measured breathing of men and women within the tender moments of intimacy. Sporadically, the discreet, sharp intake of breath of one or the other echoed, almost subliminally, throughout the restaurant, followed by a low, satisfying moan—pleasurable, melodic repetition of shared breath and closeness.

None of the tables held more than two parties. Rachel could make out only shadows that may have been male or female, but all were, without doubt, lovers with hands and fingers entwined.

She thought of Jack and the warmth of his embrace.

"Would you like me to order for you?" He rested his forearm on the black tablecloth, the knuckle of his loosely clenched hand almost touching hers.

"Thanks, that would be great." Rachel pulled her hand away to grasp her glass of wine.

He made a slight gesture within the glow of the tea-light and immediately the head waiter was at his side.

"*Deux grenouilles à la provençale, merci.*" Her host ran a finger down the wine list—his own hand almost incandescent in the glow of the flame and more than twice the size of the one serving him. "*Oui, oui. Deux verres Montreux-Lavaux sauvignon blanc, merci.*" For a moment he perused the remainder of the menu, somehow able to see even in this dim space. "Ahh, puis, *magret de canard poêlé à la cannelle infusée.*"

Duck infused with something, Rachel recognized.

The head waiter nodded and collected the wine list before moving off into the darkness.

"The menu here looks good." He lifted his wineglass to his lips.

"Mmmm, it sounds it."

There was silence between the two for several moments, the background noise touching and caressing them in the dark. Rachel felt herself breathing in time with the ambient foreplay, relaxing within its embrace. It was he who restarted the conversation.

"Had you ever been to Harry's Bar before?"

Rachel paused, wondering if she should say. "Yes. Actually, I met Jack there, and we were there the night before he was killed in the accident. But please . . . I don't want to talk about Jack just now. Not yet . . ."

"I understand." His voice was soft, distant. "The trick is to celebrate the life that is with you without forgetting the one that is not."

Rachel was suddenly alert, stiffening in her chair. "Mary wrote that in one of her letters. I read it last night."

"Really? It seems to make sense." He finished off the last of his wine.

"Do you, um, do you have a girlfriend?"

"No." He shook his head, awkward reticence evident in this simple word.

The shadows of two waiters materialized at their side—silver, rectangular platters of *cuisses de Grenouilles* placed before them on the table. The dozen or so sautéed frog legs on each were piled high. The head waiter followed close behind with the saucing dish.

"*Mademoiselle?*" he whispered, his accent charming as in any girl's dreams. He poured the rich, creamy sauce of tomato, parsley, and garlic over the legs, its perfume compulsive and heady. "*Monsieur?*" The waiter's whisper came with just as much sexual intimation as he sauced the second platter.

A smile flicked across Rachel's face as she thought of *Monsieur* Aldini's experiments with frogs over two hundred years ago, but her smile soon subdued as she recalled the ensuing experiments at Newgate Prison. Her thoughtful gaze settled on the massive, pale hand resting on the table.

The waiters placed fresh wine glasses next to the cutlery, and the head waiter uncorked and poured the Montreux-Lavaux Sauvignon Blanc.

"*Bon appétit,*" the head waiter said before dissolving into the dark obscurity of the room.

He held his wine glass across the table, above the tea lamp. Rachel placed

her fingertips around the stem of her own glass and lifted it.
   She touched her glass to his.
   "*Salute.*"

CHAPTER TWENTY

Mary sat within the parlor, separated from the other women who played Commerce, ignoring their squeals of delight and upset with each swapping of the cards. She could understand why the men had removed themselves to the terrace.

Her sister, Claire, was amongst the women, happy with the gossip of her new acquaintances. From her own vantage point, an unread book held in her hands, Mary was positioned to observe the main lobby of the residence, awaiting the arrival of Doctor Polidori. The great old clock that dominated the marble foyer struck ten with chimes that reverberated throughout the house. The last chime had barely completed its final echo when the good doctor strode across the threshold. He handed his hat and cape to the manager, signed into the book of registry, and passed a handful of francs to the head porter who directed his trunks and portmanteaus up the opulent staircase.

Mary left the parlor, closing the doors behind her before she went to welcome her friend and confidant.

"Mrs. Shelley." Doctor Polidori, roguishly handsome at twenty-three, greeted her with a bow.

"Doctor." Mary gave a curtsy before sliding her arm into his and leading him out onto the terrace. "Please do not bother changing for supper, as I cannot wait another minute to interrogate you. Port?"

"Come now. Have you really been in this quaint village far from the bright lights of London and Geneva for so long that you would relegate the needs of your friend?" The doctor chuckled.

Mary smiled impishly and held up a hand to the waiter. "Two glasses of port, please. You may leave the decanter at our table." She selected seating at the very edge of the terrace, far from the groups of men who either read the latest broadsheets just arrived from London or puffed on their cigars while gossiping about the same subjects as their womenfolk indoors.

"Tell me, Doctor Polidori—confirm my guesses on why you have come, for Claire is useless when I question her."

Polidori smiled, his lips already glistening with the glow of fine port. "Should we not discuss the weather first, my dear? Do you not want to know the latest fashions and scandals of Geneva?" he asked with a teasing grin, but she did not succumb to his taunts. "It appears, my Mary, that the dead of the Vaud refuse to remain dead—their bodies exhumed and dissected . . ." Polidori vacillated as he ensured none of the other guests had strayed within earshot.

"Go on . . ."

"Young men of heartiness and verve, not in the ground more than several hours due to natural explainable causes, have been discovered, their graves desecrated, their carcasses incised, their limbs and organs no longer with them."

"Yes, I have heard whispers, but tell me more, tell me all that you know."

"The doctors of Geneva state emphatically that the limbs were removed by a skilled surgeon, the slices precise, maintaining the integrity of sinew, muscle and bone. Clean cuts, without any indication of hesitation." Polidori accepted a loaf of bread from the waiter, who also laid a platter of meats, cheeses, and condiments before them. He ripped a large chunk of the rye with his teeth, then lifted and rolled a slice of pork to push into his mouth. Mary sat patiently until he swallowed and continued. "More than twenty young men over the course of the last few months have been defiled, but in all the cases not once has the same body part been taken."

Mary leaned forward in her chair, recalling the conversation in the library the previous evening, reviewing the words she had written throughout the night and, indeed, over the last few weeks. Was her ghost story even closer to the truth than she had imagined?

"What do you mean?" She hoped her own conjectures had not extended her fictional nightmare into some macabre reality. And although she already knew the discussion and was aware of its components, she needed to hear it again—for surely it could not be true.

"Legs missing from one but no other, hands from a second individual but all others having theirs intact, one missing his heart, another his spleen, another his intestines and stomach, another his forearms." Polidori selected a large piece of ham, some roast pork, and a slice of pheasant, placed them on a lump of well larded bread, slathered it with a thick layer of Dijon, and bit hungrily into his creation.

Mary continued sitting upright in her chair, studying the gentleman, his long dark mutton chops covering a jaw that flexed with each chew. His masculine hands held the bread too tightly, and lard squeezed up onto his fingers, still sullied from his long journey along the northern rim of the lake from Geneva. "The papers surmise"—he paused to take another sip of port—"The papers surmise that the only part of any body left to confiscate would be a head."

A frisson of fear cut unevenly down Mary's spine. Despite herself, she let out a gasp.

The gaggle of gentlemen at the far end of the terrace stopped their conversation and turned toward her and Doctor Polidori. Mary nodded politely toward them, holding up her glass. "*Salute*," she mouthed. The gentlemen raised their glasses, tipping their hats, and then reconvened their own discussion—regarding the same subject, Mary surmised.

She turned back to Polidori. "A head?"

"Yes, it is all the talk of the city. I knew we must come at once to protect you in the absence of Percy and George."

Mary smiled. "But surely it would not be *my* head in danger, as this slight bone structure and wave of curls would not complete the set already obtained."

Polidori returned her smirk, leaning back in his chair and patting his chest to temper a spot of heartburn. "Yes, of course, you have seen through my ruse. I am hoping I may be of assistance to the *gendarmerie* during their investigation of this case. But also, do you not think it exciting that such an adventure should be occurring on our tour? It would make up for all this dreadful weather."

The grand old clock struck twelve.

Mary chided her friend's enthusiasm, reminding him that they were talking of men who deserved to rest in peace, before she rose to take her leave. "I am off to my suite, now. If it is not dismal in the morning, I shall be pleased to accompany you on a walk along the lakeside after we breakfast."

Doctor Polidori rose with her and bowed low to kiss her hand before picking up his port glass and the favorably heavy decanter and striding off toward the smoky haze of gentlemen. He caught the manager's eye, that he may be correctly introduced to his fellow houseguests.

CHAPTER TWENTY-ONE

"It doesn't have a stamp on it." He peered at the first envelope Rachel held up in her gloved hand.

She was silent for a second, considering his statement and working out how best to answer. "I don't think they had stamps in 1816. No, no, they didn't, at least not here in Switzerland."

He took a sip of cola, leaning against the side of his chair to see the envelope more clearly. After walking up through the muddy fields and vineyards to Châtelard, they'd both removed soggy shoes and socks and now reclined in the late afternoon sunshine on Rachel's terrace. Timeworn flagstones were warm beneath their feet, a woody breeze lulled their senses, and amethyst clouds skidded across the sky.

The trunk sat prominently on a table between their chairs. Its keys had been turned, its lid lifted, and the covering tray slid askew so its mouth gaped wide. The treasure it contained lay without obvious confession amongst the rich, red folds and silk froufrou.

The trunk fed off its companions; it drew them closer.

It tightened the sutures of their relationship.

"It's a very beautiful parchment, and remarkably well preserved."

"Mmmm . . . and smell." Rachel lifted the envelope so he could sniff the ancient aroma.

He took a deep breath, holding it within him and stretching back in his chair, bringing up a large foot to rest on his knee. Rachel noticed how pristinely white the naked flesh of the sole was, how beautiful. "Like port and cigars. Wonderful." He grabbed his foot, entwining his thick fingers with even thicker toes. "Now . . . um . . . I'm assuming the mail was couriered by pony or carriage?"

"There would have been services, perhaps a few times per day throughout the region."

He poured more cola into her glass. "How did they know where to deliver it, with no addressee? Apart from the letter from Polidori and a few of the others, much of the correspondence hasn't even a single mark on the front of the envelope. Does that mean she didn't send them?"

"There could be many explanations. These may be copies she kept for her own records, or she may have later reassembled those she had sent and put them in fresh envelopes. But we can't rule out the idea that she just didn't send them to begin with. I'm afraid there are secrets even this trunk will not divulge." She tapped the walnut with her fingertips. "It does, however, seem odd that Polidori apologized for not knowing how to address the correspondence announcing his arrival. That must have been the first letter he sent to her."

"Meaning she most certainly didn't send any of the others you've read so far—because he would have responded to each."

"Yes, you're right. And that may also account for all the letters being together, as they would all have been in Mary's possession here in Montreux, never straying far from this trunk."

They were both quiet for many minutes, sipping their colas, watching the sun reflect off the broad expanse of Lake Geneva. "Why do you think she wouldn't have sent the letters?"

"They may have simply been her thoughts, or even the first version of her manuscript."

"Ah, like a novel told by letters?"

"Yes. It was quite a common device for storytelling at that time."

"So, what she says in the letters may not be true, but rather a part of the initial draft of *Frankenstein*?"

Rachel didn't answer, thinking of the letters she'd read so far, searching each for their own meaning, how they related to the novel and the intrigue surrounding it, or possibly to what really occurred here in Montreux, what really unraveled the wretch from the shroud. "Perhaps she was too afraid to send them . . ." A sudden shudder wracked her body, sending chills out to her fingers and toes.

His massive hand moved over the trunk and onto her forearm in some kind of comforting gesture—the soft flesh of his palm and fingers stretching from her elbow to her wrist. A warm, strange heat emanated from him.

She placed her hand on top of his. Wisps of pale, golden-blond hair crossed the back of his hand, slipped under the wide, leather bracelet at his wrist, and a lighter straw color swept in increasing thickness up his muscled forearm to his elbow, where it receded almost immediately to the smooth freckle-free flesh of his substantial bicep. His T-shirt sleeve no longer concealed the lowest dark lines of his tattoo.

Rachel ran her hand up his arm until her fingertips touched the first mark of ink. All the time, their eyes locked as he held his glass to his lips—not drinking, not moving, just watching as she touched him. She slipped her fingers up under his sleeve, her hand flat against his flesh. He inhaled a short, fast gasp, placed his glass upon the table between them, and placed his hand onto hers to stop its progress.

"Please, I'm not . . ."

Not ready, Rachel thought. She held his gaze and knew she was not ready either. The minutest nod of her head conveyed a subtle understanding to him—and to herself—as she retracted her hand from his upper arm and slipped it back down to grasp his hand.

They lounged on the terrace in easy silence, letting the setting sun engulf their attention and thoughts. They sipped their colas, continuing to hold each other's hand across the open lid of the trunk as the sky kaleidoscoped from dark blue through red, orange, and yellow, with streaks of an irregular green, toward the silky blue-black of a summer evening. The brilliance was tripled as the lake reflected the changes of the sky. The Alps, usually a pristine white, imitated the altering hue of all around them.

The first star dared to shine and pull them from their reverie.

"Rachel, do you really think she was afraid?"

CHAPTER TWENTY-TWO

Polidori placed his foot on the step and hoisted himself into the carriage. His face was pale. "Thank you for coming to collect me, Mrs. Shelley." The blue lantern of the police station shone into the transport's interior, casting a glow across its occupants. Miss Claire gave him a welcoming smile before pressing her nose to the glass to study the townsfolk and tourists on their evening constitutionals.

Mary placed her hand on Polidori's, detected an otherwise unnoticeable tension, and gave him a concerned glance. Tapping the head of her umbrella against the ceiling of the carriage, she braced herself against the first jolting movement as the horses pulled off the curb and through the mud. The talk was small on the several minutes' journey back to the residence, and it stopped altogether as they passed the villa's gatehouse, reminiscent of a Grecian temple, and entered the curving drive. The doorman helped Miss Claire down onto the pavement, but it was Doctor Polidori who assisted Mary's descent down the single step.

Stopping beside one of the columns, Mary held tight to Doctor Polidori's hand. "I had intended to take a constitutional this afternoon but became enamored by an essay in the library. As you can see, I am still in my walking dress without having walked."

"It would be my pleasure to take a turn about the garden and public rooms of the villa with you, Mrs. Shelley. Miss Claire, would you . . ." But Mary's sister had gone, quickly skipping into the foyer to locate her new friends before supper.

Several gravel paths radiated out from where they stood toward candlelit follies and statuary, just detectable in the evening light amongst fiercely clipped hedging. The doctor chose a path that would lead them around to the waterfront, where no other parties were already occupying the rooms and seating of the garden.

"It appears our fiend has become more selective."

"Selective? In what way?" Mary was unable to hide the tremble in her voice.

Polidori looked around to verify no other houseguest was within range of their conversation. "A grave site up toward Château-d'Oex was found disturbed. The soil had been shoveled back and the shroud unwrapped from the young man's head and torso, his lower body and legs still firmly embedded in the ground. We did not wish to desecrate the scene any further, and so I studied the fellow *in situ* as well as I could. The *gendarmerie* of Montreux and Château-d'Oex stood around me as I delivered my verdict."

Their walk brought them to a small rectangular pond, its fountainhead a statue of Diana emerging from the garden, bow and arrow at the ready, hunting dogs at her ankles. Mary took a seat as Polidori remained standing, reviewing the strength chiseled into the marble of the huntress, the savageness into the countenances of the dogs. Light spilled across the space from the brightly lit parlor window above.

Polidori continued moving slowly around the small garden between the pond and masonry of the villa, stopping now and then to pluck a dead leaf from the miniature hedgerow of the knot garden. "My inspection confirmed the use of a scalpel, deftly manipulated to cut and peel back the layers of skin surrounding the cartilage of the nose and ears . . ."

Mary's heart was pounding in her chest as the doctor meandered. He was a gentle man, and she could see the day's excursion had upset him, but she also knew he was wont to hide any feelings that may cause another to doubt his fortitude. She wished George had been here to offer the doctor comfort in the privacy of his suite.

"Come, John." Mary rose from her seat and slipped her arm around his to lead him to the bright lights and gaiety of the front garden overlooking the lake. Groups of guests wandered across the front lawn and along the walkways in quiet *tête-à-tête*, politely nodding and smiling as they passed friends they had not seen since afternoon tea or, indeed, since breakfast. Several guests were already making their way up toward the terrace and into the villa to start readying themselves for supper. "Shall we walk down to the gate?"

Polidori followed her lead until they stood at the wrought iron separating the villa's manicured garden from the public boardwalk skirting the lake's edge. Lanterns had been lit along the boundary, affording light to both the walkway and the garden. The moon announced its appearance above the lofty jagged edge of the far horizon, and Polidori continued the conversation.

"The fragile skin hung loose from the nose and ears, suggesting the possibility it could have been sewn back without much effort, excepting that the cartilage had been removed." Mary looked up at Polidori's own face, the machinations of the scene playing over within his own skull.

"To what end would such acquisitions truly lead? Does this follow from the actions of he who harvested the major limbs and body parts?"

"The *gendarmerie* suspect some sort of voodoo."

"From the Americas?"

"Yes, or from the heart of Africa itself. They feel the sequence in which the parts were obtained by the collector is significant."

"The collector . . ."

"They have sent couriers to the museums and universities of Geneva, London, and Paris, for any who might shed some light on this practice."

"Do you think this 'collector' has kept the . . . the parts, or has he already utilized and discarded them during some ceremony?"

"That I cannot even guess, Mrs. Shelley. If he were to keep them, he would need to store them packed in ice, perhaps in a trunk with blocks cut from a glacier."

"Or remain high in the Alps where the freeze would slow their decay." Mary looked up toward the house; they would need to postpone their conversation for now or neither would be ready in time for supper. "Shall we meet in the lobby within the hour?"

"It would be my pleasure."

They walked toward the terrace, stopping for a moment before climbing the several marble steps. "John?" Mary placed her hand on his forearm ready for the ascent. "Do you think from your study of these events that the parts collected could actually be placed together . . ."

"Perhaps, Mrs. Shelley."

"To be joined in such a manner that they may once again be imbued with life?"

Polidori stared down at Mary's hand on his forearm. His brow wrinkled slightly as he searched for an answer. "It is true that each confiscation would fit into the other corresponding portions of missing flesh. But keep in mind, the absent selection was the most pronounced part of each of the deceased bodies—made massive by their varying vocations as laborers in the forests, pastures, and workshops of the Vaud. On each man, they would have been in proportion, but to place them all together would create a figure over eight feet tall—hardly human."

"Yes . . . hardly human."

"Even then, the creation would still be dead, as life is not found solely in the flesh or by the willing of it to rise."

CHAPTER TWENTY-THREE

It was almost ten—an hour since he'd left her alone with the trunk and her continued research. It had taken several minutes for the awkward goodbye, neither wanting to begin it nor knowing how to accomplish it.

"Tomorrow, you should come to my place—see where I live," he had said before stepping hesitantly off into the darkness with a single wave of his hand and a quiet smile.

". . . *the creation would still be dead* . . ." Rachel highlighted the words on a scanned copy of the letter, even as she still thought about him and his gentle demeanor. She shook him from her thoughts to concentrate on her work. ". . . *the creation would still be dead* . . ." she read again to herself.

The letter had been addressed to Percy Shelley, care of the Hotel de l'Union in Chamonix. The front of the envelope was, however, blank. As with many of the others, it had been sealed by wax embossed with Mary's stamp, with the seal broken at some later, unknown time. The envelope was still crisp and creaseless, perfectly preserved within the silky womb of the document box. Rachel ran the tip of her finger down its edge—almost still sharp enough to cut.

She pulled the next envelope from the trunk, photographed it front and back, and made comments on her spreadsheet, noting a small blue smudge on the bottom left-hand side—possibly a fingerprint of the author herself. She flipped the flap open and extracted the next sheet of parchment with gloved fingers. She'd expected another letter in the flowing script of Mary Shelley that had brought such joy and revelation during the preceding weeks of research. Instead, the unfolding revealed an ink drawing: a young babe with unruly blond hair. His eyes were dark, his nose and mouth petite. The drawing looked to be many weeks of work, many weeks of adoring love to complete in its accuracy.

Rachel studied the illustration, pleased when she detected Mary's initials within the bottom shadows of the work. She knew the subject, but searched 'Willmouse' on her laptop to confirm it. The image of young William Shelley possessed the same eyes, nose, and mouth as the infant in the drawing before her—his ruffled chemise falling from his shoulder, an old-world rose wilting in his grip.

Though little was mentioned in the letters of the trunk so far, Rachel's studies at Chillon and Geneva had proven that Mary doted over young Willmouse, spending the majority of her day playing and singing and reciting stories with her child. Of course, it would have been inappropriate to have him in her company in the dining room or other public rooms of the villa—a child's place was within the nursery or fast asleep in his crib. But without reservation, Mary cuddled and doted over William in the hours he was awake.

Rachel felt suddenly sad, knowing Mary's young boy would be dead not long after her time in Montreux, not long after this portrait was rendered, not long after the first version of *Frankenstein* was released upon the world. How her heart must have broken—yet again.

. . . a life is not found solely in the flesh or by the willing of it to rise . . .

CHAPTER TWENTY-FOUR

His home—or 'wretched hovel' as he often referred to it—was situated on the pastured slopes above Montreux. It was a pleasant walk up the lanes and roadways from the village, through a damp and dark tunnel under the autoroute, and through the beautiful green fields of Sonzier, a valley kissed by uncountable numbers of cattle, embraced by hundred-year-old trees, and cradled by verdant slopes that swept high up into the Alps. At all times, though almost imperceptibly, the gentle roar of La Baye de Montreux could be heard squeezing through the Gorges du Chauderon. The wild river flowed among a thin sliver of virgin, forested landscape that licked along the edge of cultivation—and civilization—to reach almost down into the center of Montreux, where it ejected into the lake.

Rachel didn't know what to expect as the lane abruptly turned from tar to gravel. He stopped at a rough wooden gate that hadn't been opened for a long time. Grass sprouted around it, and defiant saplings had grown askew, making it impossible to swing the gate in either direction. He climbed up and over the entry with ease before lifting Rachel—with one movement of his strong arms—over the wood and down onto the drive beside him.

"Is this the only gate onto the property?"

"Yep."

"So you have no car, or bike, or anything?"

"No. If I want to go up into the mountains, I rent one. Do you prefer car or bike?"

"I don't need a car in Manhattan, and here, well . . . I've been taking the train or walking. I've toured the Valais on the back of a motorbike, though. That was wonderful." A gentle smile came with the recollection of Jack.

The overgrown drive on which they walked, twisted through dense undergrowth before opening up into a large pasture, now wild with flowers and neglect. Birds flitted to and fro, and insects sang from the darker reaches of the forest.

He halted just short of the open space, turned to Rachel with the broadest of smiles, and held out his open hand toward the field. "My wretched hovel." That cheeky smirk crossed his face again.

Rachel looked across the field, past some kind of pigsty. She turned her head and scanned the space before her eyes settled again on the pigsty. She said nothing, instead smiling at him as kindly as she was able and wondering what he was up to.

"What do you think?" he asked, genuine pride in his voice.

"The field and surrounding area are beautiful."

"And my home? What do you think of the place where I spend my lonely hours in solitude?"

Rachel studied his clothes—pristine—and recalled the smell of his body whenever he stood close to her—like a freshly bathed baby, a hint of talcum, a slight medicinal odor. She decided to play along, to see how far he would take this ruse.

"It's beautiful."

They stepped off the drive, which curved around the pasture, and walked through the knee-length grass instead. She studied the sty and its wayward boards of heavily grained wood made gray by years, perhaps many decades of weather and neglect. The walls tilted to one side, as much as a foot, maybe two, as if the building had been blown by a strong wind from the lake. A dozen rusted rabbit traps hung from corroded hooks driven into the planks. Below some was the brown smear of recent blood. A small corral stood to one side, devoid of pigs, the entrance through which they would have passed boarded-up.

Rachel decided that, yes, it was a hovel, but she would reserve the judgment of *wretched* until she saw the inside. He maintained his broad smile, a deep chuckling that made Rachel's suspicions increase. But still she held her course, not wanting to be tricked, not wanting to offend.

She laughed when they came to the front door. An ancient tree had been planted directly in front of it and, over the centuries, its trunk had grown so round it almost blocked the way in.

"It would seem that even the forest is against anyone entering this property . . . er, um . . . home."

He entered the structure, his bulk rubbing against the tree and boards on either side of him as he ducked his head and disappeared inside. His head reappeared at the entrance and, with a laugh, he invited her inside.

She braced herself for what she would find, for a person's home reveals a lot about their nature. She ran a hand against the ancient sun-and-wind-bleached wooden door frame, then pushed against it. Although it was at a slant, it was unmoving and stable.

"Welcome to my wretched hovel. It's what's on the inside that counts."

Rachel stepped down into the hovel, and it was beautiful.

She was amazed she was within the same building. A new structure had been built within the ancient pigsty. Exposed steel girders spanned the ceiling, and whitewashed wood, perfectly vertical, lined the walls. It was a single rectangular room containing all the amenities of a very comfortable home. A sleek kitchen ran along the wall beside her, and oversized chairs were scattered around the living space. One complete wall, at least ten feet high and thirty feet long, contained shelves holding thousands of books—thousands.

"Have you read all these books?"

"A lot of them, yes. Definitely bits and pieces of them all." He jumped up to sit on the kitchen bench.

Rachel walked the full length of the room, looking at the titles—English, German, French, Italian—everything from Keats to Newton, Twain to Sagan, Aristotle to John Smith, the Koran to the Bible.

"You're searching."

"Aren't we all?"

He was right behind her, striding toward the far end of the room. Whereas the entrance and sidewalls had no windows, the fourth wall was all glass. The back of the pigsty was pressed against the edge of the forest, the glass wall opening up to a glen ringed by enormous trees and dense foliage. Rachel wandered out onto the deck, which hung out across a brook. Forest sounds and cool dappled light surrounded her, where the sun could never fully penetrate. She stared up into the canopy and then back toward her host, who watched her in silence.

"Your hovel is beautiful." She smiled. "Wretchedly so."

He returned the smile with a wink. "Would you like café? I don't have any milk, so hope you like espresso."

"Sure."

Rachel sat down at the table just within the edge of the room, looking out at the deck and trees before turning back to watch him make the coffee. He looked more huge than usual in the tiny kitchen, his broad shoulders swaying back and forth as he hovered over the espresso machine.

Between them was a large dining table, a modular lounge suite that faced toward a modern marble fireplace, and then, close to where she sat, his bed —a massive construction that, despite its size, didn't dominate the room. Between the bookcase and the opening to the deck was the doorless entrance to the bathroom—it looked like a conservatory of glass jutting out into the forest.

He returned with the espressos and placed them on the table before reversing a chair and pulling it between his legs. "I have some veal schnitzels and make a good potato salad, if you'd care to stay in for dinner tonight."

"Oh, I should've brought some wine."

"Nonsense. If you'd *really* looked at my bookshelf, you'd have seen it's not all books."

Rachel looked over her shoulder, noting a few dozen bottles of red on the bottom shelf.

"Any white?"

He nodded, blowing on his café before taking a sip.

CHAPTER TWENTY-FIVE

Mary had spent the first hours of the morning in her suite, bathing in the tub of steaming water brought up from the kitchen, selecting her several garments for the day's activities, sewing an errant trimming of lace that refused to stay attached, and casting her eye across the words in her notebook and the last few entries of her diary. The servant who had helped her dress was preparing to leave when Mary saw her stoop at the suite's entrance and pick up an unnoticed envelope.

"*Madame?*"

"*Merci*, Bridgette." Mary accepted the letter and waited for the girl to close the door behind her before she turned the envelope over and broke the seal.

Dear Mrs. Shelley,
Firstly, allow me to apologize profusely for my neglect of your society over the two days just passed. Without doubt I will make amends in due course, but for the time being you must accept my request for forgiveness.

Mary moved over to sit by the window where the ubiquitous morning drizzle afforded a dim light by which to read Polidori's handsome script.

I have just returned to the villa for the first time since last we spoke. The clock in the foyer has recently struck four, and what a miserable time of night this tends to be under the current circumstances. I insist on penning this note so that you may be aware of our progress, or lack thereof, as my current exhaustion has determined I will not be able to share your company until at least supper this evening.
The investigations of the gendarmerie have required my intimate knowledge of surgery and the use of instruments designed for this vocation. I have instructed them in detail of all I know of the various scalpels and other cutting, slicing, and extraction tools. We have visited apothecaries, seeking information regarding whom they might supply to throughout all nearby

villages. We have also sent requests to industrial houses that may have dispatched such to any in this area. But this is only one facet of my assistance . . .

The last two evenings and the entirety of yesterday were the most horrific I have yet endured. I am indeed reticent to share this with you, but I must convey these details so you might understand my current state of mind and also forecast the required protection of your own person and associations.

We were called into the Alps to Château-d'Oex, to the very grave we had inspected previously. We entered the cemetery close to midnight, lanterns held high, and made our way to the site with difficulty over the muddy ground. I would dare say my boots are permanently ruined—the sodden ground having imbued them with an odor I am not wont to describe.

Once more the soil of the young man's grave had been disturbed and the corpse pulled from its repose. The cavity was half-filled with water, and there was naught for me to do but clamber down into the grave, the full weight of my own body pushing the poor deceased further into the mud as I knelt upon his legs and inspected the disturbance about his head and particularly his face. Further incisions had been made along the bones of his cheek and jaw, the skin stripped back and several of the delicate facial muscles removed. I shall not bore you with their Latin terms, but suffice to say they are the elongated tissue emanating from about the oculi (eyes) to cross the cheeks down to the musculature about the mouth and nose. They are key for many facial expressions.

Mary studied her own reflection in the windowpane, imagining the sinew and tissues below the skin of her face.

None of us, however, was prepared for the events that followed. The gendarmerie returned to the chalet that the deceased had shared with his father and four brothers, to make the family aware of the second disturbance and to question them once more for any suspicions they might have. What they found instead was a scene of slaughter the likes of which has never been documented within this region.

The father, a blind and kindly old man of French origin, lay beside his kitchen table, his neck sliced wide open but with no apparent missing organs or tissue. (I am yet to study the body to confirm the gendarmes' observations.) Swathes of blood covered the courtyard, smeared and spread across the cobbles as if due to a struggle amongst many strong men. The bloody wheel tracks of a heavily laden wagon exited the farmyard and traversed the drive to the main laneway and toward the trails leading down to Sonzier and Montreux.

Throughout the night, and the following day and night, the gendarmerie and menfolk of Château-d'Oex searched the lanes and byways of the area, hunting for any clue to the whereabouts of the wagon, to catch the wretch who had committed such an outrageous sin. I joined the men in the search:

inspecting farmhouse and barn, inn and stable, ditch and gorge.

Mary held her fingertips to her lips, wishing it were not so early that she could not afford a sip of sherry. She hurried to her bureau to refresh her powder and perfume and ensure her curls were in order. She had never felt so distressed; indeed, when she looked down at her hand, it was shaking. She closed her eyes and took several deep breaths, thankful Willmouse had already been delivered to the nursery and would not see her in this state. Hastily she grasped the note, folded it, and placed it deep within her décolletage. Within seconds she was in the upper corridor of the villa, her hand on the balustrade.

Several guests were already making their way to the dining room for the breakfast buffet. As she descended the ornate stair, Mary could smell the grease and bacon that so delighted her fellow tourists. She passed the dining room, ran out onto the terrace, across the garden, out the front gate, and along the boardwalk with her umbrella held high. She pressed her hand to her breast, the letter secure against her skin but burning into her mind. She finally reached a small stone bench, shaded by an expansive tree that afforded protection from the rain. Waves from the lake splashed against the wall supporting the boardwalk.

We received word regarding the discarded, blood-soaked wagon in a laneway of Sonzier. By nightfall two score of men were standing before a derelict gateway that had not been opened for many a year. It led to an overgrown drive that twisted through dense undergrowth before opening up into a large pasture, wild with flowers and neglect. Insects sang, and the last of evening birds flitted to and fro. The open space, surrounded by forestation, was lit by the dull, gray light of the moon that made all appear black and white—devoid of color. We tramped across the open pasture toward a relic of a building, our numbers now grown to three score. I surmised it must be a pigsty, for I heard the grunt of one nearby. The building itself was neglected—weathered and decayed, no longer vertical in its construction. "Wretched hovel" was my thought as I held my torch and walked with my associates, dreading what was to be found within this enclosure.

Once more, Mary stopped reading, searching earnestly for the graceful beauty of a swan upon the lake to give some semblance of comfort and sanctity. When none was apparent, she turned to the beauty of the châteaux, the villas, the magnificent Alps, and wondered how something so base, so inhuman, could occur in such an arena. She pressed her handkerchief to her mouth and read on.

The men surrounded the hovel, opening the gate to allow the sows and their offspring to scatter into the night. Some men called for the building to be

torched, no matter someone was inside or not, but the officer in charge kept his head. The pigs' entrance was dark but another entrance with a door offered a way for strategic attack. Several men scrambled through the pig hole, another knocked the entrance door and was followed by a dozen who rushed through to the cramped interior.
There was much screaming, yelling, and sounds of vomiting from within the hovel as the men beheld the scene. I stayed at a distance with the officer in charge, and it was not for many minutes that I was called to inspect the circumstances within the decaying structure.
I am repulsed to place this situation into words. It is a scene of horror, but it is also that which mankind has allowed to evolve and, due to that, my dearest Mary, I feel it is something you also should be aware of, that you may protect yourself, your associates and family, that you be attuned to the world in which you also reside.
The inside of the hovel was but five feet in height—the men had to stoop to move about the mud and stench of animal that filled the rancid space. I entered with my torch and scrambled across the mud to where the dead men lay.
I came to the first and allowed my weight to sink into the mud of the sty, not caring for my own propriety. The four brothers of he whom I had already met in the graveyard lay before me. Side by side—brothers in life and in death. All were massive in structure; all were beautiful, beautiful men. Their bodies appeared intact, their clothing undisturbed, but it was their faces, Mary, that had been desecrated. All had been professionally sliced across the foreheads and down the sides before their ears, the flesh of their faces meticulously peeled down until it hung below their chins and about their necks. Various facial muscles had been selected and removed. All had their lips and related musculature incised—one his tongue, another his eyes, a third his chin.
Bile filled my mouth as I beheld this scene, but the desecration did not stop at their faces. Two of the men had been scalped, the fine muscles and layers of skin from the entirety of the skull removed from each.

Mary stared for some time at the space between the last paragraph and the next. There were very few words left upon the paper. Reluctantly, she looked upon the remaining words, knowing they could not adequately complete the saga that had been burned into her mind.

I must go to bed, for I am exhausted.
I will continue our conversation when next we meet.
Sincerely and with my deepest regret,
Doctor John Polidori

Mary crushed the letter in her grip and wept, not because she was a woman, but because the unknown family had endured so much hostility and degradation, because the people of villages surrounding this idyllic riviera had had their lives irreparably torn, because her dear friend and the *gendarmes* directing him had had to confront scenes of horror that no man, or woman, should ever have to endure.

She wept for reasons she could not even begin to understand.

And possibly she wept for a creature of her own creation, who may or may not be merely in her mind, who may or may not be huddled in the cold dampness of a wood, peering out into the pastures and toward pleasant laneways, searching for innocents who might be beguiled and groomed, to eventually be subjected to his true and horrifying intentions.

CHAPTER TWENTY-SIX

"How's your wine?"

"Fine, thanks." Rachel leaned against the bench, watching him peel and cut the potatoes for the salad. "You're an expert with that knife."

"Trained by the best." He scooped up the chunks and dumped them into a pot of boiling water. "Why don't you check out my music over on the far shelf? Pick out something you like."

Rachel walked across the room and huddled down on the floor in front of his collection. She kicked off her shoes. "It's all jazz and blues."

"But of course it is, *mon chéri*, this is Montreux."

She smiled at him as he jumped around the kitchen, pouring chicken stock into a second pot on the cooker. She flipped *"White Lies for Dark Times"* off the shelf and put it in the player. "Is Ben Harper and the Restless 7 okay?"

"Yeah, great."

She perused the contents of the shelf as the rifts of music bled throughout the apartment. Between tattered volumes of *The Rubáiyát of Omar Khayyam* and *Grey's Anatomy* lay a metal box, about half the size of a shoebox. Peels of red and blue paint curled off of it. Rachel touched one with the tip of her finger, noting how fragile it was, how carefully it must have been protected. It looked like it might be Georgian.

"What's in the box?" she shouted over the music before reaching to turn down the volume.

He looked up from his preparations. "Oh, when they dug this place out, they found some . . . er . . . some pretty interesting stuff. Don't open it, though, I think the box is more valuable and worth preserving than its contents . . ." He stopped his cooking as if to watch her and ensure she didn't open it.

Rachel noted the brightness of its paint—*maybe lead*, she thought—before lying down on the floor, careful not to knock over the glass of wine beside her on the rug.

There was a sudden commotion in the kitchen: the sound of a pot crashing to the floor and the angry slosh of liquid, followed by what could only be the cutlery drawer and its entire contents spilling across the tiles. Rachel turned in alarm to see him pick up the pot and throw it against the wall, liquid flying everywhere. His face was a dark crimson, almost black, twisted.

"Damn." He grunted in obvious pain, pressing the palm of his hand against his temple. He kicked the drawer—scuttling it and its remaining contents over the floor toward the front door.

"What's wrong, did you burn yourself?" Rachel jumped up and ran across the room.

He slammed both his hands onto the granite bench and lowered his head, his hair falling about his face. He breathed heavily, as if counting silently to himself, and let out a final burst of rage, of pain, his hand sweeping across the counter to hurl the carving knife off the surface. The blade flew several feet toward the side wall, the kitchen lights reflecting along its length over and over as it spun through the air before clattering to the floor. He held his hand up toward her and she stopped, tense, watching his slightest movement, searching to see if he had cut or burned himself.

"I'm sorry," he said, his head still low over the bench.

"Are you ok? Did you hurt yourself?"

"No, it was . . . it's a migraine . . . I'm so sorry. Please, why don't you go out onto the deck and enjoy the evening air for a little while?"

"I don't mind helping clean up."

"Please." He motioned with his open hand toward the glass doors. "Go and enjoy your wine. I have things covered here."

Rachel picked up her glass and stepped out to the cool comfort of a deck chair. He had lit a kerosene lantern that hung from an overhanging branch, and it afforded a gentle flickering light across the deck and rippling waters of the brook and up into the foliage surrounding the glen, the nearest leaves glowing yellow.

Through the glass she watched him pick up the pot and place it on the stove once more. He poured more chicken stock into the pot and turned the flame low before checking on the potatoes. They must have been okay because next he stooped to pick up the cutlery drawer off the floor. He inspected it before slipping it back into the side of the bench, then ducked low behind the counter, his head moving back and forth, the cutlery rattling as he rose with a handful of knives, forks, spoons, and spatulas, and placed them into the dishwasher.

He stared at the floor for a few moments, unmoving, then pulled out a mop and ran it across the tiles. Rachel cuddled the bowl of her glass, watching his every move to assure herself he was okay. He hunkered down and picked up the carving knife. Once again, Rachel saw the reflection of the kitchen lights shimmer along the full length of the metal blade. He stayed down on his haunches, staring at the knife, before standing tall and placing it on the top shelf of the bookcase—far above where she or any average person could reach it. Rachel thought his actions curious. She took a sip of wine.

He looked over toward her, squinting as if he was not quite able to see her through the reflective wall of glass. He opened the fridge and then strode out onto the deck.

"I'm sorry about that, Rachel. Really, I am. Sometimes I just lose it—intense migraines . . . It must be something in the way I'm put together." He refreshed her glass with the sauvignon blanc. "All under control now. Dinner will be served in about thirty minutes, okay?" He gave her an embarrassed grin.

"That's fine. Smells wonderful," she said, relieved.

He looked down at his shirt—it was sodden and stained from whatever had occurred in the kitchen, and had been pulled loose from his jeans. The bottom buttons had drawn open, exposing pale flesh and a smattering of dark hair. He brushed down the wet fabric, and Rachel imagined she could see the trail of underlying hair as it twisted in a thin line up his belly toward his chest.

"Excuse me, I'm still a bit of a mess here. I'll be back in a few."

Rachel returned his smile and watched him go back into the main room, grab an athletic shirt and a clean white dress shirt from the wardrobe, and then disappear into the adjoining bathroom. She was content in the darkness of the deck with her glass of wine and the comforting glow of the lantern. The flame jumped and sparked in its glass enclosure, the whiff of kerosene something she hadn't smelled since childhood.

She turned toward the main room and couldn't contain a sneaky smile when she noticed she could see him changing in the reflection of the bathroom mirror. She caught the briefest glimpse of his naked back as he pulled the ribbed cotton over his shoulders and torso, but it was enough to make her feel good. The athletic shirt was white and tight with thin, flat straps across his shoulders, mostly hidden by that hair that now seemed so unruly. The wide armholes accentuated the massiveness of his shoulders and bulge of his biceps and emphasized the patterning of his . . .

Rachel placed her wine glass on the floor of the deck, rose, and took the single step so her nose was almost touching the glass of the sliding door, disbelief clouding her mind. He pushed his dirty shirt into the sink and ran water over it, rubbing the stain from the fabric. His shoulders and biceps flexed with the repetitive motion, making the . . .

Rachel's vision blurred with tears. They came quick, much easier than she would have expected after so many months.

So many months.

She continued watching him without seeing him, as he left the soiled shirt in the sink, as he dried his hands and pulled on the clean dress shirt, as he did up the buttons and tucked the shirt into his jeans, as he pulled his fingers through his hair one single time.

Rachel felt drained. Her vision of him faded through her tears to utter blackness. She knew she was collapsing, fainting, unable and unwanting to breathe, the world toppling about her.

She was unconscious long before her body thudded against the deck.

CHAPTER TWENTY-SEVEN

Mary had been waiting at the base of the stairs for several hours before he appeared on the top step, wearing his favorite evening burgundy frock coat. He looked ashen, tired, and sad. When he saw her, his pace quickened and within a moment he was bowing before her. However, before he could utter even the first requisite pleasantry, she stated, "You must take me to the property, to this hovel. I must confront it with my own eyes or I think I shall go mad with horror."

"But, Mrs. Shelley, Mary—why would you want to be subjected to such?"

"I cannot reconcile with myself that this is not all but a dream, my own imagination, that it is all within my head, that I am so drowned within my own thoughts of horror and fantasy I no longer know what is true and what is not. I must confirm for myself that this occurrence is real, that the hovel is real and not just some occult dream attempting to rip my sanity from me." Her breathing was rapid, her eyes glazed and staring.

Doctor Polidori grasped her hand and guided her toward the stair to the upper landing. "Have you eaten today?"

"No, no, I have been awaiting your company." Her eyes were red-rimmed and teary.

Polidori caught the attention of a chambermaid and indicated for her to open the door of Mrs. Shelley's suite. He escorted her to a settee in her parlor and left her with the maid, running to his own rooms to collect his sturdy black bag. He quickly returned to kneel before her. The maid stood at Mary's side, wringing her hands as the doctor drew a milky-colored opiate into a syringe.

"Now, Mary, I am going to give you something to help you sleep. Do not worry, for I will not leave your side. Is that okay?"

"John? Is what you wrote true? Did this horror truly occur?"

Polidori pushed the opiate into her bloodstream, discarded the syringe into his bag, and placed his hands on both her shoulders to guide her drugged fall along the length of the lounge.

"Locate Miss Claire Clairmont immediately and beg her return to this suite without delay."

The chambermaid looked from Mrs. Shelley to Doctor Polidori and back, uncertain of what to do.

"Good God, my dear woman. I am a doctor. Now leave us and locate Mrs. Shelley's sister in haste." The chambermaid scuttled from the room and down the stairs. "Please forgive me, Mary, for what I have borne upon you. It was, in hindsight, selfish of me to burden you with my horror. I recognize now that I should have availed you of my presence for a full discussion and dissection of the matter, until we were both even minutely soothed."

Polidori remained at her side, stroking her hand, the tremble of his own almost unbearable against her flesh.

CHAPTER TWENTY-EIGHT

"Mary? Mary, are you okay? Are you okay, Ma . . . ry . . . chel . . . rychel . . . Rachel . . . Are you okay?"

Rachel could feel his arms about her, feel and smell his hot savory breath wafting across her face as she regained consciousness. He must have carried her to his bed, for something felt soft and luxurious beneath her body. A cold, wet cloth was run across her forehead and cheeks, and she heard him repeat in a soft, low voice, "Rachel?"

She opened her eyes, comforted to see his just inches from her own.

"You smell like potatoes." Despite the ache in her head, she smiled.

His lips parted in a concerned grin. "And you had me worried." He sat up straight on the edge of the bed, but she placed her hand on his arm to stop him. He appeared puzzled. "What?"

Rachel stared into his eyes, noting how the darkness of one was flecked by blue, the other by brown. "Please . . . please take off your shirt." She bit her lower lip and held her breath, awaiting his response.

"Why?" The word was little more than a breath that caressed his lips.

The music had been turned off and the house was lit only by the kitchen lights at the far end of the room and the kerosene lamp out on the deck. The chicken stock bubbled on the cooktop.

She pressed her hand against his bicep, feeling it flex beneath the cotton of his shirt. Emotions Rachel could not even start to guess at washed over his face and through the darkness of his eyes. He looked at her lips, then her forehead, then down the length of her hair and back to her eyes. He wetted his lips and swallowed.

"Please," she said. "I need to see . . . I need to see your tattoo."

He stared at her for a long moment and then he nodded. She knew he somehow understood, even when she knew he couldn't. He was hesitant, pulling at the buttons of his shirt, his eyes now fixed on the pillow. When the last button was unfastened, he closed his eyes and jerked the hem of the dress shirt from his pants—careful that his athletic top remained tight within the denim. His reluctance was unlike any man she had ever seen disrobe before, as if . . . as if . . . she didn't know what. He sat for many minutes in total silence, with his shirt open. Rachel could not fathom what he might be thinking, as her mind was set upon the tattoo that still lay covered by his shirt sleeve. He turned his side to her, grabbed his collar, and pulled it and the sleeve down the full length of his arm.

The ink swept up and around his arm from the elbow to the top of the shoulder. Dark against the pale skin, tormented roots coiled and twisted around the faces, bodies, and limbs of men, women, and children who, despite their entrapment, seemed content—even joyous. The tree of life. It grew from its foundation, its branches spreading across and around the bulging curves of his bicep and tricep. By some trick of the eye and adept artistry, animals appeared amongst the branches—lions, tigers, monkeys, and elephants, and humans: men and women who looked lost, forgotten, confused, their faces expressing everything from delight to delirium to horror and rapture.

The more she studied the ink, the more she could see, but when she tried to look back at what she'd already encountered, it was impossible to find within the stylized intricacies. The branches gnarled and turned back upon themselves, the subtle flex of muscle and the altering direction of light showing the tree's darker side, populated by satyrs and demons. Prostitutes frolicked. Criminals leered, brandishing knives, bones, and discarded offal. Soldiers lay dead, and stricken mothers begged for mercy.

Rachel looked back toward the roots of the tree, and the once-festive faces now appeared to be rotting flesh and skulls. The branches continued up over the prominence of his deltoid, broad leaves pouring all around the thick, roped muscle and down toward the armpit to intertwine with the luscious sprouting of hair.

He watched her face, her every expression, the most subtle movement of her lips and eyelids, the slightest quiver of her chin. He shivered, running his other hand across the flesh as she continued to study the full length of the arm and the ink that had come with . . . the ink that was a part of . . . the tattoo on his arm . . . *his* arm.

"I once knew a man . . ." She touched the muscled bicep and tattoo with the tips of her fingers. ". . . once loved a man who had this same tattoo. Exactly the same tattoo. It was Jack." She flicked her attention up to his eyes and then back down. "He'd had it done in Chicago—near Logan Square. He said he was sixteen at the time, and that it was an act of defiance."

"An act of defiance?" her host asked before murmuring something unintelligible, staring at the arm and the tattoo. He reached his opposite hand over and stroked the line of ink that curled into the inside of his elbow. "I didn't know."

Rachel looked up into his face. "Didn't know what?"

His face was blank. "I just didn't know."

Rachel spread her fingers across the muscles, her palm pressing against the tattoo and skimming over the skin up onto his shoulder. The ink was fresher here, more crisp, enhancing and extending the original work on the arm up and over an indentation onto his shoulder proper. "Is this what you had done last weekend? You had your original tattoo extended?"

He gave the slightest of nods.

She ran the tip of her finger along the indentation, which appeared to circumnavigate his shoulder under the camouflage of new foliage. It ran down into his armpit, and her fingers brushed past thick golden hair and along a slim black arc that led back to the middle of the tree's canopy and entwined around the fruit at its center. The apple was the only bit of color among the otherwise black masterpiece. It appeared painted, brushed upon the skin in a bright, delicious red.

Rachel rose from her pillow to stare at the apple. As she neared the beauty that reminded her of one but was part of another, she placed her lips upon it and kissed it as hard as she was able.

CHAPTER TWENTY-NINE

The front gate had been shouldered open in the days previous by the *gendarmerie* that the undertaker's carriage might remove the bodies of the four young men. It now remained ajar, the authorities long gone, no indication of what had occurred behind its hewn rails.

Polidori pulled the rented cabriolet off the lane and onto the curb. With his right foot on the carriage apron and the reigns of the petite stallion held firmly in his hands, he turned to Mary.

"I think it best that we walk onto the property, as the track is not sufficient for the wheels of this vehicle." The hood of the carriage had been folded back for the afternoon ride up into Sonzier, but Mary still held a light parasol above her head as she stared in deep thought toward the entrance.

It had been three days since Polidori had helped Mary. Her wellbeing had taken precedence over his involvement in the investigation, of which the authorities were understanding. They had had one full day of sunshine, which afforded them a conversation and constitutional for at least a league past the turrets of Château de Chillon and back. The second day had poured rain, but they had continued their discussions at a table upon the villa's terrace, rarely moving from their positions for the entirety of the day and late into the evening. The host and hostess of the villa had applied every courtesy and service to expedite Mrs. Shelley's recovery—every meal was a personal favorite—and a second girl had been arranged to maintain order in her suite and assist with her daily apparel, possessions, and care of Willmouse.

Mary had recovered admirably from her fears as she dissected the minutest points of the case with her friend. Suspicion had been belied by science, concern and worry by psychology and reasoning, waking nightmares diminished by cold, unmistakable facts.

She looked at the gate now and sensed a minor palpitation ripple across her heart, through her imagination.

The cabriolet's groomsman stepped down from the rear platform and reached up to take the reins from Doctor Polidori. He guided the doctor's foot onto the step, assisted him to the ground, then pulled a small brush from his pocket to remove the dust of travel from the gentleman's full-length frock coat.

Mary turned and gave Polidori a reassuring smile and grasped his hand as she stepped down onto the ground. She pulled her shawl to cover her arms against the minor breeze.

The gate had been left only slightly open by the authorities and would not budge further under Polidori's and the groomsman's strength, but the gap allowed adequate room to access the land without any impropriety. The groomsman remained with his charge, and it took the doctor and Mrs. Shelley just a few minutes to traverse the overgrown and twisting drive, despite the soggy edges and deep, waterlogged grooves left by the undertaker's carriage. They walked along the center ridge, and Mary halted where the drive opened up into the pasture, Polidori at her side. He appeared attuned to his friend and the thoughts running through her mind, for this was also the first he had seen this space in the daylight.

"It's beautiful," Mary said, incredulous. Polidori nodded in agreement. They studied the pasture, its thousands of colorful wildflowers, the magnolias, cypress, fig, bay, mulberry, and other forestation that surrounded the entire space. The steep side of the Sonzier valley rose directly at the property's far edge, and the ever-present, looming, snow-capped Alps climbed further still into the sky above. "One reads of horror, both in novels and in the broadsheets, but it always seems to be in isolated castles, haunted and decaying estates, or in the sordid areas of some vast metropolis, amongst laneways rife with prostitution, vulgarity, and the destitute. But not here . . ."

"No, not here."

They followed the track along the edge of the field against the thick growth of old forest to a meandering brook. By the lay of the land, Mary surmised it must pass behind the building that was their destination, maintaining a fresh supply for the animals the hovel was built to house. "The animals . . ." She stopped several yards from the pigsty under the shade of a tree. "This is near enough, I feel. My observations could not be improved by closer inspection or, indeed, by entering the hovel, as my mind would be muddied by pictures of my own imagination and not by what is really before me."

Doctor Polidori seemed relieved as he leaned against a knotted mulberry tree and reached for his pipe and tobacco. Mary watched as he pushed the cuttings into the head of the pipe and lit it with trembling fingers.

"Thank you, John, for all you have done in these last days. You have been of wonderful company and comfort. Percy and I will be forever in your debt."

He nodded in acknowledgement before pulling his left foot up under his haunches to rest against the tree. He stared at the hovel, his knuckles now bloodless and white against his pipe. Mary felt for her friend but checked herself, consciously taking a step away from him, as her stance was too close and might be deemed improper if viewed by another. She looked to confirm that the groomsman had not entered the pasture.

She wanted to ask the doctor how he fared, to return his favor of fortitude without diminishing his reputation or the social expectations of his gender in any way.

"Have you received any word from the authorities?"

He drew back on his pipe, holding its courage within him for several seconds before allowing the almond-scented smoke to curl out his nostrils and the corner of his mouth. He cleared his throat. "Nothing further has been discovered. The father and his four sons now lie with the one who was already in the ground. Two *gendarmes* stand watch, though hidden, in case the desecrator, the murderer, returns.

"Do they still suspect voodoo?"

"The Université de Genève sent word that this is unlike any ceremony adhered to in that culture. We will await confirming correspondence from Paris and London, but it appears that assumption was incorrect."

"What do you think, John? Are there any assumptions that you believe warrant deeper investigation?"

He tapped the spent tobacco from the head of his pipe and placed it back into the pocket of his coat. "These acts have been performed by a skilled man of science. This person acts without malice or emotion, with precision and a vast understanding of musculature and body structure. He is meticulous and ordered. He has a project and, by definition, that project must have a goal. He is working toward something . . . something grand and yet unthinkable . . . something that has never been done before . . ."

Mary knew exactly what he was alluding to, for she had been consumed by nightmares and waking dreams of this concept for many weeks.

She needed to rekindle her correspondence with *Monsieur* Aldini in Bologna.

CHAPTER THIRTY

It was late by the time they'd enjoyed the schnitzel and potato salad. He was right, it was wonderful. They followed the bottle of white with one of red, which made it all the richer. There wasn't much conversation during the meal, nor did there need to be as they relaxed within each other's company. She helped him clear the table when they were finished, handing him the plates and cutlery across the counter, where he rinsed them and stacked them in the dishwasher. He grabbed the remaining half bottle of red, flicked off the kitchen lights, and led her out onto the deck.

"Would you like some café later?" He seemed to already know her answer.

She shook her head. "The wine is enough, thanks."

"I'm glad you came over tonight, Rachel. I feel comfortable here. I feel comfortable with you."

They sat in silence again, and an insect buzzed out of the foliage to hover around the lantern. They watched as it circled the light, flew toward and away from it, then buzzed down to the brook and to somewhere under the deck.

"It must live down there."

He shrugged his shoulders—a happy, intoxicated shrug, accentuated by the pouting curl of his lips. His eyes were sleepy.

Rachel sipped at her wine, savoring the texture. "You have a tattoo on your other arm as well, don't you? The tree of knowledge, with two bites taken from its fruit."

He nodded almost imperceptably.

"Jack's was never finished."

He rubbed his bicep and left his hand in a loose grip over the muscle as he tossed back the last of his wine. "I don't think it is supposed to be . . ."

"Maybe not."

The kerosene lantern waned and died, throwing them into darkness.

The only visible illumination was the small red light on the espresso machine at the far end of the home.

The boards creaked as he rose from his chair. She stood, too, holding her hand out and brushing her palm against him. His hands sought and gripped her in the dark. They stood motionless, listening to the hum of the dishwasher, the buzz of the insect below the deck. "Don't step backward. You could fall into the brook."

"I won't step back."

With their outstretched hands grasping each other's arms, he pulled her toward him until his embrace encircled her. His body was hot—much hotter than she'd expected. She looked up to where his face must be in the pitch darkness. He must have been looking down into hers as well, as his breath, now heavy with red wine, washed over her. She rose onto her toes, hoping his mouth was seeking hers—knowing his mouth was seeking hers.

Their lips met, an electric charge consuming them both in the darkness.

* * * *

Rachel lay in his bed, still half asleep. His great bulk was pushed firmly into her back, the heavy but comforting weight of his arm resting over her body, his curled hand just below her chin. She wiggled and turned until she was facing him, taking care not to wake him. She slipped an arm over his waist and pressed her cheek against the ribbing of his athletic shirt, content to listen to the beating of his heart as she recalled the previous night.

She felt safe within the warmth of his arms as she lay there, the sheets awry. The slow rhythmic breathing of his slumber was comforting. She wondered that he was again partially clothed now that the sun had risen—his athletic shirt had never left his body in the night; his baggy boxers, at one point discarded in the dark, were once more pulled firmly about his hips and thighs. And, curiously, he once again wore the leather bracelets around his wrists—bracelets that had been flung off into the darkness during a moment she wouldn't soon forget.

She found his shyness quirky and beguiling, a welcome diversion from the distress of her recent past as well as the escalating complexities of her research and writing.

CHAPTER THIRTY-ONE

Rachel turned the two keys clockwise and counterclockwise respectively, swung open the lid of the trunk, lifted out the silk-covered tray, and reached down for the next letter in the collection. She was excited to see she was nearing the first of the two smaller wooden boxes and couldn't even guess at what they contained. The next envelope in the pile was of a coarser paper than the others so far—thicker and darker, with black threads of cotton through the pulp. It was one of the few envelopes that was addressed, written in a serifing script more elaborate than even Mary Shelley's own copperplate. The broken blue-wax seal appeared to be an "A" in a circle.

Rachel photographed the front and back of the envelope, made detailed notes on her spreadsheet, then carefully lifted the back flap and slipped the folded pages out onto her table.

* * * *

Mary was impatient, checking with the owners of the villa several times per day to see if the post had delivered a reply. She once ventured down to the office herself to see if a carriage had arrived carrying anything addressed to her. Finally the host presented it, and she hurried back to the privacy of her suite to break the seal of *Monsieur* Aldini and read his response.

CHAPTER THIRTY-TWO

Madame M. W. Shelley
Villa Eden Au Lac
Montreux
Confederazione Svizzera   *July 1816*

Dear Madame Shelley,
Please accept my esteem and also pass my regards to Mr. Shelley and also Lord Byron if they have returned from their jaunt to Monte Bianco.
I cannot tell you what a pleasure it was to receive your correspondence. I had thought we might never converse again after our short time together on the beautiful Swiss Riviera. I can still recall the glorious escargot we dined upon in the lovely Salon Bernese. What a treat!
I will admit I was surprised, though equally excited, by your line of questioning in the letter. It is indeed a privilege to be quizzed by a student of science such as yourself, as it keeps me searching for answers and also reviewing my previous observations and writings to determine their continued validity and virtue.

    Mary sighed in relief, thankful he had taken her as a serious inquirer and not a bored, gossiping tourist eager for tidbits for around the card table.

I can see you are intrigued by the current circumstances surrounding your village. They are indeed dire, so much so that events have reached the supper clubs and lecture rooms of Bologna. I have come to the same conclusion as your good self, though I do not know how such may be executed, or whether it is possible under any condition. In my thoughts, the purpose of this wretch can only lead to failure—the brutalization and desecration of the dead and the unthoughtful murder of the living to be for naught as his project will not, can not, must not come to fruition.

                            *   *   *   *

"This can't be real," Rachel whispered to herself. Had Mary questioned *Monsieur* Aldini from the viewpoint of an author, or because these horrors were really occurring? She couldn't bring herself to believe Mary's previous letters were of actual events and not a first draft of the manuscript.

* * * *

But, my dear Madame Shelley, I am certain that, as my student, you are not satisfied with such a blunt answer, and so I will attempt to explain my judgment—to back up my own theory.

Mary smiled to herself. "You are indeed astute, *monsieur*."

First, the body parts stolen up until this point—the feet, lower legs, thigh area including knee joint, pelvis, arms, hands, rib cage—have all been obtained from several different individuals of large proportion. Sections of the torso including the heart, lungs, spleen, intestinal tract, various other organs, and two separate spinal cords have been taken from a dozen others. I cannot think why the wretch did not take an entire torso intact other than perhaps each of the items chosen was the largest of each selection and more suitably met his requirements. Recent events have seen the external musculature removed from a number of skulls—all were from the same family, and I must assume these relations possessed physical facial characteristics important or pleasant to the person in question. There are still many key elements of physiognomy not yet collected if our supposition is true. He has yet to obtain an actual skull and its contents. As well, he will have need for large lengths of sinew, vein, artery, plus the finer systems of the body that are not understood. He will require much more skin.

* * * *

Rachel opened her laptop and entered her first note of the day: a reminder to research the archives of Direction de la Sécurité Publique to confirm whether these criminal events really occurred during 1815, 1816, and 1817. She'd need to check all cases as far back as Montreux archival records were kept. She then entered a second note to review the Chillon archives again for any indication of these events.

* * * *

All Mary could think of was there was going to be more desecration or, worse still, murder in its own right to obtain the missing elements.

Second, we must consider decomposition. As you are aware, the body parts have been gathered over a period of many months. Each portion of flesh would be therefore at a different stage of decomposition with the earliest acquisitions probably completely disintegrated by this time. That they were obtained from different bodies presumably brings in to play varying rates of decay depending on the age, overall health, and cause of death of each of the victims. Of course these rates might be slowed or sped up dependent upon such conditions as humidity or temperature. In your letter you mentioned the extreme freeze high in the Alps that might stop this natural process. It would indeed need to be extreme and freeze the flesh solid for there to be a complete stop—anything less and the matter would still break down, even if only gradually. This wretch, if he is planning what we conjecture, would need to freeze his collection as he obtains it, and when all is accounted for, start the process of thawing and assembly.

Mary stared out her window toward the snow-capped Alps on the far side of Lake Geneva.

* * * *

Rachel stared out her terrace doors toward the snow-capped Alps on the far side of Lake Geneva and then back toward the freezer in her studio.

* * * *

The larger elements—bones, muscles—could, of course, be joined and function mechanically, though they would have no feeling and would be cumbersome in their usage for the following reason: It is well beyond our means and current capability to join sinew to sinew, artery to artery, nerve to nerve. It would require a very skilled surgeon, one that neither I nor my colleagues can fathom the existence of, to perform such a task. To discuss connection of the sensitive tissues and organs within the chest, to say nothing of the intricacies of the spinal cord and brain, we step outside science and move firmly into the realm of fiction.

* * * *

Rachel thought of the Frenchman who lost his arm in a farming accident and had it surgically replaced with another; of the woman, her face destroyed by cancer, given a new face from a cadaver, every artery and vein and nerve surgically joined to her own. She set down *Monsieur* Aldini's letter for a moment and wondered. Would Frankenstein be able to create his "monster" in this day and age?

* * * *

Mary thought about the impossibility of her basic dread, hoping it was indeed impossible, for it could cause only horror. But two words caught her attention and stayed with her as a contrasting juxtaposition, an oxymoron that excited her. Science. Fiction.

Now, Madame Shelley, our supposed creator's dilemma does not stop here, for if he were able to perform the miracle of assembly—even at the most corrupt and perfunctory level of construction—his next hurdle would be animation. One may imagine bellows pushing air into the lungs and perhaps some sort of distillery to alternatively drain the blood or some similar fluid from the body, purify it by evaporation or other means, and then, by gravitation or pump, allow it to flow back into the creature's system.
I am afraid, however, that such devices would still be a sham, an illusion and hoax, for the flesh would still be dead. It would still be decomposing at a rapid rate. Our creator would require his creature to be imbued with the "spark of life," with "animal electricity," for it to be self-sufficient, regenerative, and not require external means to keep it alive.

* * * *

Rachel read the paragraph several times, attempting to relate it not only to the thinking of the nineteenth century but also to her own time.

* * * *

Mary read the paragraph several times, attempting to relate it not only to the current events in and around Montreux but also to some inexplicable future where, perhaps, it would not be classified as horror but as an everyday incident to assist in the extension of life beyond its current barriers.

You are well versed in my theories of electricity and how it might be utilized to manipulate the dead, to make muscles twitch and react in a lifelike manner. My experiments at Newgate Prison are testament that a charge may make inanimate objects jump, quiver, and jerk, but I have concluded that this indication of vibrancy is not life itself. Perhaps it is the means by which "life" makes a body move. I would conjecture that an apparatus might be designed utilizing electricity to "bring someone back to life" but, by virtue of each individual circumstance, I doubt victims could be "absent" for more than a few seconds—perhaps as long as a minute— without irreparable damage to their brain and vital organs. A being whose heart has stopped may require the shock of electricity to restart its rhythm, but I fear once a being has actually left their corporeal representation, there is naught this energy can do for the cadaver left behind.
Of course, one does hear of romance novels and perhaps a handful of

incidents in the broadsheets where a loved one has appeared dead for many minutes or even hours until a distraught wife or husband or mother has cried over the corpse and called its name, only to see the unexpected flicker of an eyelid or feel their hand grasped by the one they thought they had lost.

Mary pondered whether it was a question of science, theology, or romance, and whether anyone's research had delved into success beyond the thoughts of *Monsieur* Aldini and his works. Could love bring someone back to life, or is this realm relegated only to God and His wisdom?

* * * *

Rachel left the letter on her table and walked out onto the terrace, her thoughts with Jack and their wonderful times on the Harley, riding through the Valais and up to Château-d'Oex to see the balloon festival. She thought of their nights together, their passion which seemed perhaps addictive and extreme. She thought of his cheeky smile, the glint in his eye, his muscled body and arms, and his tattoos. The tree of life and the tree of knowledge were burned into her mind, were part of her psyche thanks to nights and mornings and afternoons that would always be with her.

* * * *

And finally, I come to my conclusion: No architect, no matter how skilled and educated he might be, could create a new life from death as gallant or as complicated as mankind is—save for He Himself.
We might try, and we could perhaps craft a sorry representation that would be cumbersome in its movements, simple in its thoughts, and devoid of any sensible human emotion. Its complexion would be pale, the underlying circulatory systems disrupted in their smooth functioning, decay imminent. The wonders of the human mind and brain would be damaged—caused by the death of its original proprietor—the dislocated and corrupted electrical currents of this mysterious organ making the creature prone to headaches, inexplicable fits of rage, and outbursts of violence. It would be incapable of love, except perhaps for the more animalistic actions and perfunctory motions of the body itself. It would not know mercy, if ever it were placed in a situation where mercy was required.
These last few words are merely my own personal conjecture, but it is conjecture based on an intimate knowledge and close observation of both death and life during my many experiments with the human body and condition over the past decades.
The answer to your question is possibly more within the realms of a priest who truly knows Him, or someone who has loved another without question, without judgment, rather than a man of science such as myself.

I look forward to your response.
Yours sincerely,
Giovanni Aldini
Villa Forli
Via di San Luca
Bologna, Italia

Mary folded the letter, slid it into its envelope, and placed it into her document trunk. She pulled a fresh sheet of paper from her drawer, dipped her quill into the inkwell, and started to write.

* * * *

Rachel sat out on the terrace looking off into the distance and, although she was not certain why, her thoughts were completely of him.

CHAPTER THIRTY-THREE

"You can trust me, you know." Rachel snuggled into the crook of his arm as they lay before the open fire in his hovel.

He leaned against the bottom of the couch, one arm around Rachel, the other extended along the lounge—comfortable in only his boxers, athletic shirt, and thick white socks. His legs splayed across the floor toward the fireplace.

"I know."

She fell asleep within his comforting embrace, at least for a couple of hours, for when next she opened her eyes it was dark both outside and in—except for the fireplace, which cracked and popped and sent shape-shifting specters of light around the room and across the ceiling. He was still beside her, awake but with eyes closed, his chest rising and falling in an easy, relaxed rhythm. The neckline of his athletic shirt exposed the very top of his hairless chest. She ran her hand over the bare skin, up across his neck—feeling more than seeing the crease of a faded scar below his Adam's apple —and then along the smooth, taut skin of his jaw. He smiled and murmured in delight.

The light from the fire gave him a glow, a color that seemed healthy but unnecessary. It made him look unusually beautiful, untouched. Her hand fell back to rest just over the collarbone, the tissue of the indentation above it thicker and less elastic than that surrounding it. He opened his eyes and stared at the metal girder in the ceiling overhead, his brow furrowing and his eyes squinting in deep thought. His tongue flicked out to wet his lips and then he turned his attention toward her.

"I do trust you," he whispered, continuing their conversation from before the sun had set.

Rachel expected no more than that, but he started to sit up properly. She rose beside him so he could get comfortable, but he scooted toward the fire and turned to face her. He licked his lips again, a habit Rachel surmised was linked with worry, maybe even fear. She said nothing, just watched him, the glow of the fire at his back, playing against his silhouette.

Outside, the wind whistled through the trees, and many pairs of glowing eyes clustered in the branches. Inside, the fire cracked and spat, amber reflections of Dante swelling into every nook and cranny.

His gaze held hers for a long time as he sat cross-legged before her in his underwear. He mouthed, "I trust you," and reached down to unclasp the broad leather bracelet from his left wrist, then his right, before placing them at the side of the hearth. The shifting movement of firelight showed the scarring at his wrists. At first Rachel thought he might have once attempted to harm himself but then noticed how the pink blemishes went the full perimeter of each wrist in a single precise sweep.

His hands clenched upon his knees and his breathing became heavier. But still he gazed at her intently, as if studying her every emotion, attempting to read her thoughts. She once had a friend who'd broken her wrist in hockey. The reconstruction had taken years and left wide crimson welts around her hand and wrist where the bone had broken through. His scars were different, inflicted by an expert surgeon using accurate incisions and minute sutures. They were well healed. The lines would fade in time, becoming one with the natural wrinkles of his wrist.

He pulled off his large, white cotton socks, scrunched them, and threw them toward his bracelets. In keeping with every other part of his body, his feet were massive, their pristine whiteness unblemished. He stretched his long, thick toes in the heat of the fire, and Rachel saw that here also were faint, well-healed wounds around his ankles. Fine scar lines, dozens of them, crisscrossed the ankle around the Achilles tendon and heel. The almost invisible web orbited the flesh of the joint between his lower legs and feet—as if they'd been smashed in an accident, as if both had been substantially damaged, maybe severed, and undergone major surgery to rectify bone, muscle, tendon, and skin.

Rachel's attention flicked from scar to scar, ankle to ankle, wrist to wrist, shoulder to shoulder, to neck. And then into his eyes, which showed the depth of pain he must have endured, must still be enduring, that these physical scars only hinted at.

He placed his hands on the floor and pushed himself up to stand between her and the fire. A shimmer of fear passed across his eyes, but he squeezed them shut and rubbed his face brusquely with his hand. Then he returned his attention to her . . . completely to her.

He took a deep breath and let it out slowly, his tongue again wetting his upper and lower lips, and then pinched the bottom of his athletic shirt and pulled the cotton ribbing up over his stomach, his chest, his head and arms. He threw it onto the floor then grasped his boxers and pushed them off his hips, past his thighs and lower legs, until they were also on the floor. He kicked them to the side.

He was exposed, showing her flesh she'd touched in the blindness of night but never seen, that perhaps no one had ever seen. She felt humbled at his willingness to bare his soul, to reveal to her something he had obviously kept hidden, something that had affected him and his life. The skin barely covered the muscle, sinew, and vascularity that swelled prominently beneath. The fire flickered, seeming to pull him from the darkness as it caressed the curve of masculine tissue and licked the lengths of unblemished flesh.

Like his ankles, his pelvis and upper thighs were a web of fine scarification radiating out from his groin, mostly camouflaged beneath a layering of scattered hair. They, too, must have been the aftermath of a score—or more—of surgeries.

Rachel's silent study of his body moved up over his muscled torso. A puckering pink scar that would still take many more months to heal, even with corrective surgery, extended from just above his groin, between the swell of abdominal muscles, to his sternum. Here the pucker split, one branch crossing his chest toward his right shoulder, the other toward his left.

Rachel didn't know much about surgery, other than what she'd viewed on documentaries and television dramas. She attempted to recall a program she'd seen about heart and lung transplants and the suture wounds they left on the chest, but the more she stared, the more she thought of the autopsy scenes in crime shows rather than the operating tables that saved lives.

She raised her eyes to his face, the glint in his eyes confirming his trust in her.

"I was told I was in an accident recently," he said, his voice somewhat hoarse. "A motorbike accident. But I don't remember. I don't remember that or anything of my life before that. All I know is what I was told."

Rachel's heart wrenched, both with pain and an ever-growing affection.

Feeling as though time no longer passed within his wretched hovel, she rose from the floor until she was standing before him. She undid the buttons of her blouse and the clips of her bra and let them fall to the rug. She undid the button and zip of her jeans and pushed them down.

She held out her hand.

CHAPTER THIRTY-FOUR

She held out her hand to Polidori, requesting he stay with her awhile before joining the company of the other men in the study. The three young gentlemen who hovered at his side tipped their hats in respect before retiring toward the aroma of port and cigars.

"It appears you have acquired a group of avid admirers, Doctor Polidori."

"I am afraid, my dear, they are men more of means than of substance. Whereas you pry me for intellect and facts, they only wish for the tawdry snippets and scintillating gossip."

Mary laughed. "I have no doubt you are more than amply giving them what they desire."

Polidori's eyes gleamed, his subtle smile broadening between perfectly clipped mutton chops. "Do you mind if I smoke?" He lifted the port decanter and filled their glasses.

"Please, be my guest." She accepted the glass and took a small sip as Polidori called for a cigar. The waiter was at his side momentarily with the box and assisted him with selection, cutting, and lighting. Polidori puffed as he relaxed into his regular overstuffed chair on the villa's lakeside terrace, his jaw and cheeks working as he swirled the smoke around his mouth then allowed it to escape his lips. The smoke was sweet and earthy.

"You seem distant, Mrs. Shelley."

Mary pulled her attention from the dark, moonless night beyond the lights of the garden.

"Do I? Yes, perhaps. I was thinking about my creation."

"Your ghost story?"

"Yes. The horrible occurrences you are investigating in Montreux have steadfastly woven themselves into my manuscript. But it seems to me that my imagination has, at times, pre-empted several of the occurrences—as fantastical as that may sound."

Polidori did not respond, though Mary could see he was deep in thought. He placed the cigar to his lips, drawing back heavily then resting his head against the cushions, closing his eyes. Two languorous curls of smoke eddied from his nostrils and about his face. His face spread suddenly into a smile. "That would mean, Mrs. Shelley, that you should be able to tell us who this demon is."

Mary chuckled. "I am afraid my reasoning and solution for these events is explicitly in the realm of fiction and not fact."

"But have we not seen that fiction does quite often predate fact and, I dare say, may be the catalyst for such to occur?"

"Perhaps." Mary took another sip of her port as she attempted to discern the lights of villages on the far side of the lake. "It must be raining over in Evian. I cannot see even one light on the hillside. So very dark."

Polidori looked over his shoulder to appreciate the view, then fell back into his cushions and closed his eyes again. Mary stood and walked over to the balustrade, ignoring the lanterns in the garden and concentrating solely on the darkness beyond. "Tonight, when I return to my writing desk, I shall breathe life into my creature, something that was and probably still should be dead. But I wonder if I have the right to animate this demon—even as only part of a ghost story. And what of he himself? What sensations and thoughts would he have upon awakening for the first time? Would he know his history, or would his mind be wiped clean by the deaths of those lives that came and ended before his? Would he be the sum of his parts, or less than any single part of his own puzzle?"

Polidori was now at her side, leaning against the balustrade. "One could not assume he would be as innocent as a newborn babe. By the very nature of his creation, I would think he'd maintain some memories—even if only those that assist us to walk, to feel our way through the world." He puffed on his cigar. "Also, as we know very little about the operation of the brain and how memories are stored—whether in the convoluted gray matter in our heads or in the cells throughout our bodies—he might indeed recall everything that one or all persons involved knew. Or, if not, he might be inexplicably drawn to the families, acquaintances, and environments his predecessors inhabited."

"And yet he would be innocent—innocent of the desecration and murder necessary to create him."

"Would he?" Polidori asked, not really knowing the answer. "If any semblance of memory has been retained, then he might know what death is —several times over. He might also know the pain and shock of being murdered. Whether he knows these events completely, or as nightmares, or as severe migraines and confusion, or as only a current of underlying thought, they would without a doubt affect his very nature, his every venture. It would be my assumption that he would, sooner or later, with the realization of who and what he is, go mad—with two possible routes to take: a self-inflicted fatality, or further desecration and murder by his own hand."

Mary continued peering off into the night to discern any possible light, but there was none.

"Yes. I believe you are right."

CHAPTER THIRTY-FIVE

The police archive was in a room at the rear of a long, low, concrete building on the corner of Rue du Lac and Chemin du Pierrier in Clarens. A sign by the bus stop outside proclaimed *Police Riviera*. It was an easy walk down the hill from Rachel's studio in Le Château du Châtelard, where she'd returned that morning from his hovel to collect her notebook and papers. The walk should have taken less than twenty minutes but it actually took Rachel three hours as she thought of him, looked in the windows of shops, thought of him and the pain he had endured, lost an hour in an ancient bookshop and thought of him, sipped an espresso and thought of him. She could, in fact, think of nothing but him, but the deadline for her book was getting ever closer and the letters from the trunk had exposed major gaps in its timeline.

She stopped at a cafe within view of the police building, holding her fourth espresso to her lips. And she thought of him.

The scarring on his wrists and ankles, shoulders and pelvis was almost negligible, explained by the motorbike accident and the need to rebuild and reconstruct damaged bone and joints. The imagined horror of the accident played over and over in her head—his body thrown from the machine at an unknown but terrible speed to tumble and break and rip across the roadway. She thought of him. She thought of Jack. They both had experienced similar horrific events, but only one had survived.

She peered into her espresso cup and swirled the black liquid around before taking another sip.

The scarring up through the center of his belly and across his chest toward his shoulders she could not grasp. She imagined massive internal bleeding, the need to cut the body open to contain any damage and stop him losing his life. It frightened her to think someone was just a piece of animated meat to be ripped and cut and stapled or sewn back together. It frightened her more than she could think.

They'd made love again that night, last night, after he'd dared to show her the truth of his body, had dared to reveal something no one should ever have to endure. And when they were done, when the light of the new day intruded into his hovel and exposed the naked passion of their night together, a grief had cascaded throughout his entire body and erupted in a wrenching guttural sob that pulled Rachel down with it. She'd held his face and kissed him as he cried, comforted him with her words, caressed him with her lips. And when at last his body stopped shuddering and he lay at peace within her embrace, his mouth found hers and again they let their passion consume them.

Rachel held the espresso cup high, tapping the end to make the last drop slide down into her mouth. It was already mid-afternoon, and she needed to at least start work on the police archives, to become familiar with their layout and cataloging. She took out her laptop and scanned through several pages of bullet points detailing the crimes mentioned in Mary's and Polidori's letters. If she could confirm whether they were fact or fiction, that would be a start. If they *had* occurred, then knowing their full details, sequence, and the results of any investigation might fill in gaps not covered by the documents in the trunk.

She made her way down the *rue*, entered the police building, and asked the *gendarme* at reception for the archivist she'd already spoken to on the phone. He chuckled as he talked into his phone in Swiss-French—much too fast for Rachel to understand many of his words. She guessed the reason for his amusement when the "archivist" entered from a side door—a very young man, not yet sixteen, in a suit three sizes too big, his eyes still bright from having escaped school for some work experience. Rachel followed him through the door, down a flight of stairs, and along a basement corridor to the farthest corner of the building. He ushered her into a room no bigger than a windowless broom closet, the walls overcrowded with shelves holding tens of thousands of microfiche files. The door had to be left open if there was to be space to sit at the chair in front of the reader, which took up most of the room. The chair looked uncomfortable and Rachel soon found that it was.

There was no master catalog for the files, but the untitled containers seemed to be in chronological order. She checked a few dozen, flicking at least forty micro files from each before placing them on the reader to confirm dates and sequences. Yes, the files appeared to be in date order. But she wanted to be certain, and that meant sampling every box for confirmation. By the time the archive was closing for the day, she had made it back to the 1960s. One hundred and fifty years to go.

The sun was low when she walked out onto the *rue*.

He was there, sitting at the bus stop, waiting for her.

He was wearing his blue jeans and a short-sleeved, light-colored Polo shirt that somehow managed to stretch around his muscles, the naked bulge of his tattooed biceps. His long hair was gone, reduced to a handsome buzz cut that made him look like a marine. Also gone were the wide leather bracelets. One wrist was bare, the gold hair of his forearm glinting in the

sun, the other was adorned by a Patek Philippe watch.
  Rachel smiled.
  "Hey." He rose from the bench to approach her. "Would you like an espresso or should we go straight to Harry's?"

CHAPTER THIRTY-SIX

By the time Mary had set her writing paper, filled her inkwell, and arranged her quills, the moon shone through the thirty-two panes of her window onto the Maggiolini desk. She could already hear the rasp of his breathing in her ear, could feel his pulse beneath her fingertips, knew he was waiting for her to put her pen to the paper and awaken him from the subtle insinuations and scattered thoughts of her imagination.

CHAPTER THIRTY-SEVEN

Rachel had crawled into the stuffy confines of the police archive for three days in a row. She had progressed back to the early 1800s and isolated the single container of microfiche that held the first and second decades. The film in this one was not as tightly packed as the more recent ones, and she hoped she'd be able to scan through the documents on every sheet within another day or so, to determine the relevant frames. But for now, her eyes ached, her head ached, and even her stomach ached from the dizziness brought on by the rapid back-and-forth swing of frame after blue-and-white-negative frame in front of her eyes. It was time to go home and relax.

    She had intended to walk up the hill to Châtelard, but when she turned the corner outside the police station the autobus to Sonzier was pulling in. Impulsively, she jumped onboard and within fifteen minutes she was meandering along the lane that led to the front gate of his property. The sun was just starting to set. Long, deep shadows were cast across his pasture, but the hovel sparkled in the last yellow rays reaching down into the valley. Rachel stood awhile, halfway across the clearing, knee-deep in grasses and wild flowers, admiring the change of light from yellow through orange to magenta and blue-black. She knew why he loved living here—so close to the town, yet so completely isolated.

    "*Bonjour* . . . hello?" Rachel nudged open the front door of the hovel. It was dark inside, but she didn't want to flick on the lights in case he was sleeping. After pushing the door closed behind her, she stood in the entry until her eyes adjusted. The room was empty. Her watch said six pm. She turned the kitchen lights on, grabbed a cola from the fridge, and went out to the deck to wait for him. The kerosene lantern refused to work, so she sat in the subdued darkness listening to the crickets and the gurgling of the brook flowing under the boards.

    The last of the light shimmered through the canopy of trees. When the daylight and the cola were finished, she went inside, turned on one of his side-table lamps, and sat on the lounge. She thought she might start preparing dinner but decided against it when she couldn't find anything that inspired her in the fridge or freezer. She didn't mind a night of wine and making love. Who needed food?

Her attention settled on the bookcase, and she ran her fingers across the books, across the titles on shelf after shelf. She was about to select a Hemingway—*For Whom The Bell Tolls*—when she spied the large volume of Milton on the floor by his bed.

She fell onto the quilted comforter and pulled the book up onto her stomach. Heavy and cumbersome to hold, it tipped back and forth in her grip.

Several photographs fell from the back of the book—a few Polaroids, a number of paper clippings, a couple of regular photo prints. All were of men about the same age as him. They looked like members of a football team, due to their size. One of the photos made her smile—the young man's scruff of hair sticking up at an odd angle; he was handsome, though. Another man in a striped rugby shirt reminded her of him—he had the same thick facial features, but gray eyes. A brother, perhaps?

Several more photos peeked out the fold of the back cover, so she slipped the ones that had fallen out back behind the jacket flap where they belonged.

As she flipped to the beginning of the book, she noticed the last pages were not part of the book at all. They were separate sheets of paper of comparable dimension, each covered from edge to edge, top to bottom, front and back, by a large, awkward and uneven handwriting.

In the beginning there was nothing.
Nothing.
Sudden cataclysm. Bright light and intense pain, unknown pictures—shifting, imploding, splintering, shattering, evaporating.
And then once more there was nothing.
Almost nothing.
Surging current, severe agony, an offense that made thoughts shimmer, memories flash beneath detection, and perhaps the sense of knowledge—of something that was able to be known.
And then a sound came from somewhere within, within the world I was able to sense. A rasp, a rattle, a vibration. I recognized, I do not know how, that it maintained a rhythm, a regular timing, a repetition that stirred emotions I could not begin to understand. It was as if I could feel the movement of the rhythm—moving within me, expanding and contracting my world as it continued. I monitored the recurrence—it intrigued me. I could not reason why, but I concluded that I might be able to play with this phenomenon. I willed it to stop, and it did. I willed it to start, and it did. Again I willed it to stop, to see if it would start again on its own account. The nothing, the blackness seemed to tend toward more nothing, toward more blackness, and I was again no longer aware of anything . . .
A violent shudder went through my world, a strange delirium I somehow

knew was caused by stopping the rhythm. And then once more the rasp, the rattle, the vibration settled into its easy resonance.

I stopped the rhythm a second time, and a second time all sensation faded and ceased before an urgent shudder threw me back into my bare awareness and allowed the pleasant rhythm to resume. I thought perhaps I might trick it, force it to go faster, but the action made me feel so euphoric I could not maintain it, and so allowed my companion to resume its regular pattern.

I listened to and felt this world for many a rasp, rejoicing in the wonderment of it all, when I sensed there was more. There was more to be known. From somewhere within my planet came a second cadence. I listened to isolate it from the first. The more I concentrated on it, the more dominant it became. The beat, beat, beat was slightly faster than the initial rhythm. The harder I focused, the more I could feel the beat, beat, beat, as if it caused a coursing through my very existence. It seemed to affect a surge, a pulse that gave depth and a feeling of . . . a feeling of . . . more. Although it seemed centered close by, the pulsations went further than I was previously aware, moving out to extreme limits that increased my wonderment. The pounding I envisaged as traveling to the very end of my universe caused a tingle . . . a tingle in a thickness of something that was not nothing. I imagined I was making this something move, animating it, making it shake and shiver, and yet I knew not what it was, whether truth or imagination.

By stealth I followed the pulsation wherever it would allow me, sensing more of the something that was not nothing, as if it encased my . . . me . . . I became more and more aware of edge . . . yes edge . . . the edge of "me." I could feel the tension that kept the something, that kept me together, could feel the thickness that allowed the pulsations to travel throughout this interior. My awareness traveled to a thickness at the edge of me that seemed connected to the original rasp, rattle, and vibration from deep within me. Directly above this—beside this?—above this, the edge seemed thinner, more translucent, as if it were a portal to what lay beyond. A possible doorway to something that was not me.

No sooner had I recognized it than the portal was flung open and I was assaulted by an external brilliance. I felt frightened and my world shuddered. A horrific utterance resounded . . . was that me? I did not know but it resembled the feelings within me . . .

There was movement external to me, around me, noise and emotion, the feeling of pressure against my edge . . . first here, then there, reconfirming my sense of extremes.

The noise was fast and urgent, of tones high and low. I imagined many somethings, each separate and unto themselves, moving freely, emanating noises of their own, causing pressure on my edges as theirs pushed against mine.

The intensity piercing my portals became unbearable. Without knowing

what was occurring, I could feel a pendulous part of my edge move up and away from the rest of me. It slammed into the edge of another, causing it to fly out of view with a noise that was loud and made me ache. Once more a thunderous utterance filled me, was created by me, and caused sound in the space external to me. The somethings appeared to fall back but then one rushed toward me, causing a sharp prick of pain in the thickening edge of my being.
All went dark, and nothingness once more swallowed my awareness.

Rachel lay in silence on his bed. Her mind was blank as she thought to decipher the meaning of the passages. She had to continue.

I became aware again and could hear them around me, moving and making noise. I felt I was in control of the portals . . . of the portals . . . of the eyes that would allow me to view their movements, but I chose, yes, I chose to keep them from my sight. I studied my feelings and thoughts, as they were very interesting to me. I know not where they came from or why they were, and yet I felt these feelings and thoughts could serve me, could be of use. The noise subsided and I decided to open my eyes. I cannot describe the delight I felt when they did my exact bidding. I willed them to close again, and they did. I willed them to open, and they did. There was no movement around me and the brilliance of before was no more. I suspected the others were not aware of my awareness.
I kept my eyes open that I might review the universe around my planet. It appeared I was within something larger than myself, something contained by its own nondescript edge. By subtle movements within my own sphere, and by applying tension to the edge of myself, I was able to alter my view. I don't know whether it was by some inner knowledge of orientation or direction, but I sensed I could view the external surface of my own edge. It was the same paleness as all other surfaces within my sight, but it appeared more complex—a symmetrical slab with appendages that in turn had smaller appendages. I tested my knowledge of the pulsations throughout my inner self, attempting to follow one to the farthest extremity I determined was still me and not the outer world.
It moved.
A moan reverberated in the space around me. I knew instinctively that it was me. I forced several of the far appendages to wiggle, and then a thoughtful sigh escaped from within me to the outside world. I am unable to communicate the sheer joy these actions brought me. I turned my attention to the appendages closer to my point of view. I willed the smaller ones to wiggle and curl, but the larger one to which they were attached was stuck to the outer world. I attempted to pull myself free, sensing the connection could be severed. I jerked and pulled at the appendage, flexing the, the, the fingers, clenching the fist, and yanking as hard as I could. I saw how the appendage, the . . . arm . . . flexed and throbbed with the exertion. But I

could also see that the connection to the world was breaking. So, too, was the one that held my other arm.
Frustration grew within me, a deep pressure and anger that pulsated throughout my very being, throughout my own—MY OWN BODY. The emotion of my fight manifested into a roar that frightened even me, but that gave me more strength to pull against the bonds. They snapped, and I was free—complete within myself and no longer attached to the whiteness that surrounded me. I swung the larger appendages . . . my . . . my legs to the lower surface of the world, stumbling onto them and allowing them to support the rest of me. I will admit it was as if they knew what to do as they held me up off . . . off the floor. The noise that emanated from within me had continued unabated, forming garbled sounds and tones that meant nothing, but that meant everything to me.

Rachel's vision blurred with tears of unexpected emotion. Was this fiction? Could it be his writing? Could writing this down be part of his rehab after the motorbike accident? Is this how he saw the world upon first awakening?

Suddenly the others were there again, entering the universe by some unknown way I had not yet recognized. I stood looking down at them, attempting to communicate, but they seemed frightened and concerned. I held out my arms, allowing my emotions to control the emanations, the sounds emitted from me toward them. They moved back toward the outer limits.
Another came into the universe . . . into the room. He, like them, was dressed the same color as the room. He was taller than the others, but still I looked down upon him. He made noises of kindness, his hand reaching out and stroking my arm and my side. I stared at him, feeling the softness and warmth of his touch against my skin. His eyes were thoughtful and worthy of worship.
I attempted to speak to him, to ask him whether he was my creator, but my words were ragged and unintelligible. And so I became silent.
I looked down at myself as I stood before him.
I looked down and I saw I was naked.
I looked down and I was ashamed.

Rachel closed the book and placed it on the floor by the bed where she'd found it. She pulled his comforter around her as she lay on his bed.

She thought for a long, long time, until finally she succumbed to a temporal slumber that fled across the shallow graves of buried nightmares.

CHAPTER THIRTY-EIGHT

Mary lounged into the deep comfort of the wingback chair. She gazed at the papers upon her desk, recalling what she had dared to write upon them. The horror of her waking nightmare had finally been exhumed into her own world, been given a face, been given a voice. He had been brought out of the shadows. He was now real, and she knew she was responsible—completely and utterly responsible for the horror and pain he was about to inflict on those around him before her story was done.

CHAPTER THIRTY-NINE

Rachel was roused from her slumber by the sound of running water. The lamp had been turned off and the main room of his home was in darkness except for the light emanating from the bathroom. She swung her feet onto the floor, pulled her clothes off, and went to join him in the shower.

She was not prepared.

He was hunkered down naked, holding his hands to his head in obvious agony as the steaming water fell over him. His hands, forearms, and legs were swathed in blood. His clothes were scrunched into a pile under the running water, blood oozing from them to wash down the drain between his bare feet. Rachel stood, horrified. He turned, saw her, and stood.

"It's okay, it's okay. I'm all right—just another damn migraine."

"But . . . the blood?"

He looked down at his body, at the water splashing the blood from his skin, thick red rivulets spilling from his hands. He let out a low choking sound before grabbing the bar of soap from the rack and scrubbing his torso and arms and hands. He ran his lathered hands up and down and around his thighs and groin, his feet and toes. He was mumbling, but Rachel couldn't understand the words.

"I'm okay, I'm okay," he said, a little louder, as the blood washed down the drain and left his skin as pristine and white as before. He stomped on his clothes to push the last remnants of red liquid from them. He picked them up and wrung them under the showerhead before throwing them into the laundry basket. Once more, he grabbed the soap and lathered his body from top to bottom, squeezing and rubbing the flesh until he appeared certain he was clean. Without looking at Rachel, he leaned out of the shower and opened the cupboard under the sink. He pulled a bottle of bleach from the lower shelf, yanked off the top, and squirted the thick blue liquid over the tiles and glass.

Rachel watched, numb, as he scrubbed the tiles and glass and squirted more bleach onto the surfaces and down the drain. He sniffed at his hands and lathered himself up a third time.

"Rachel, it's okay. It's all gone now. It's okay." He was out of the shower with his arms around her, his hands on the small of her back, holding her to his dripping wet body.

"But . . ."

"It was a rabbit, Rachel. I had set the traps earlier today and when I went out to check . . . well, suffice to say that one of them was a real bleeder. I'm sorry I frightened you."

"A rabbit?"

"Yeah, as in stew."

"But there was so much blood." She looked up at him.

A grin spread across his face. "It was a big rabbit."

Rachel punched her fist against his pectoral, knowing he would hardly feel it but that it would give her some satisfaction. "You scared me." Then she let out a sigh of relief and rested her cheek against his chest. She studied the edge of his tattoo, where it curled around his bicep—a demon peered over the shoulder of an angel and stared at her. "How's your migraine?"

"It's bearable now. They seem to be coming less often."

"Do you feel like another shower?" She was hesitant, letting her hands fall down to rest on the curve of his butt. "Would that help?"

"With you, my darling Rachel, yes."

CHAPTER FORTY

Although the heavens continued their assault with a rain that rarely abated, Mary was happy to leave the creature to his own devices while she joined Claire and Doctor Polidori on a tourist boat excursion. They crowded into the windowed viewing cabin with two other couples from their villa and took a seat on slippery wooden benches. Faded cushions gave a modicum of comfort and reminded Mary of the patterning on her own hallway chairs back in England. White paint peeled off red paint, which in turn peeled off yellow paint from the cabin ceiling and the wood surrounding the windows.

"There is some history in this old vessel," Mary said with appreciation, considering that the rustic feel added to the adventure.

The boat pulled out from the shelter of the dock into the current of the lake as the captain unfurled the main sail and let the wind take her. They sped out into deeper water before heading back in toward land in a gentle curve. Rain fell against the windows, making the vistas hazy and sublime. Even though it was mid-afternoon, the lights of Montreux quickly faded into the gloom as they slid past a shoreline where villa after villa leapt out at them like apparitions—intimidating white walls, public lanterns casting shadow and light through damp uninhabited gardens and across deserted walkways. Wood creaked, canvas fluttered, and ropes whistled and sang. Rain splattered upon the roof. Waves thudded into the well-worn planks, both outside and in, as Mary could sense the slosh of the bilge below.

Notwithstanding the rain, the waters of Lake Geneva were calm and afforded a smooth journey along the lake's edge. The captain advised they would see naught if he ventured to the center of the lake. Much better to skim in the shallows where they might see the buildings, flora, and fauna that meandered down to the water's edge.

"Positively Gothic," Claire muttered at her side. "No wonder you wish to reside here, my sister, while you write your ghost story." It was as if all color had seeped from the Swiss Riviera. All tended toward the many tones of gray—from specter white through funereal tones that shoveled toward clump-of-dirt-on-your-coffin black.

The vessel lurched around the broad curve of the bay, bringing the tourists in close to see soggy pastures and waterlogged cattle huddling under bucolic stone and timber shelters.

"I am glad you are taking a rest from the case, Doctor Polidori." Mary wiped the condensation from the window.

"I am afraid it was not by my own choice."

"What do you mean? Do they no longer require your services?" Mary was quite shocked that the *gendarmerie* would not need the assistance of her esteemed friend.

Polidori shifted in discomfort. He rose to plump his cushion before once more taking his seat and staring out the window. "The head of the *gendarmerie* feels I am too close to the investigation, that my being a doctor in the vicinity might be a compromise."

"Oh my . . ." Mary placed her hand on John's forearm, then quickly removed it. "You cannot mean they suspect you."

He raised an eyebrow, pressing his index finger to his lips as the captain's daughter approached with cups of tea and a plate of cut sandwiches.

"Well, so be it. I shall be your companion and your alibi for the days to come. You will see, they will come beckoning you to rejoin their ranks when the next murder occurs."

Polidori stared into his teacup. "Yes, I agree. It is a matter of time, and I fear a very short time, before another takes place."

There was excited commotion from the front of the boat as they approached Château de Chillon. Mary placed her tea on the table next to her uneaten sandwich and rubbed the window once more for a better view. The edifice loomed, appearing larger and more foreboding than it had on her infrequent but pleasant afternoon constitutionals along the lake walk. The vessel tipped to and fro, causing screams of excitement from all within the cabin. Both Mary and Claire slipped their arms through Polidori's, that he might offer support. The captain pulled his vessel to, so everyone had a view into the barred sea entrance of the dungeon. Claire said she imagined she saw a decayed phantasm peering out from the darkness and clamped both hands around Polidori's upper arm. He bellowed and chuckled, catching Mary's eye in shared enthusiasm.

"I think I shall set the climax of my story in this wonderful fortress."

Polidori peered out the window, his face close to both Mary's and Claire's as the three of them looked into the dungeon and up at the massive fortress in awe. "I thought you had decided upon Mont Blanc as the background for your key scenes, followed by the ice-covered desolation of the Arctic wastelands?"

"We shall see." Mary considered the mollusc-covered stone before her. "My story is tending to have a mind of its own, to take me where I had never expected it to. Last night I dreamed of my tale and, without prior knowledge, another character crept from my quill. I do not yet know whether she is heroine or victim . . ."

CHAPTER FORTY-ONE

"What happened to the rabbit you trapped the other day?" Rachel cuddled into her pillow. "I was looking forward to your promise of stew, or is it more appropriate to say *Lapin a La Cocotte*?" She smirked at her attempt at French.

He looked at her, his face blank, his eyes glazing over before a spark of anger—no, recognition—rippled across them. He rolled over on the bed so his lips touched her ear and whispered his answer.

And before she could respond, he placed his mouth over hers, the moisture of his tongue dissolving her thoughts, stifling any words she might have been able to form.

CHAPTER FORTY-TWO

Both the doorman and the valet held umbrellas high against the wind and rain that forced itself under the *porte cochère*. Claire was the first to alight from the carriage, with Mary and Polidori at her heels. They jumped across the gravel and up the stairs into the main reception of their villa as fast as they were able—all dripping wet from their prior dash between the tourist boat and the awaiting carriages. They looked a sorry mess—so much so that Mary was unable to suppress her laughter upon viewing her sister and friend in the ornate surroundings. The other couples rushed into the reception from their own carriage. "What an adventure," one of them said, and everyone laughed and agreed.

"Best we collect ourselves and change before we catch pneumonia." Doctor Polidori motioned toward the staircase.

"Always the doctor. Tea in an hour on the terrace?"

Polidori nodded and offered his arms to escort both ladies up the staircase.

"Mrs. Shelley, excuse me, *madame*." The manager scurried across the oriental carpet that stretched over the marble floor of the lobby. He gave a slight bow to each of them before holding out a platter conveying a letter addressed to Mary in the recognizable script of *Monsieur* Aldini. She accepted it, and Polidori delivered Mary and Claire to their suite before retiring to his own.

The unopened envelope sat for many minutes on her dresser. She scrutinized it from afar as the maids assisted her and her sister from their sodden afternoon apparel. Finally, Claire was deposited into a steaming bath in the corner of the bedchamber, and Mary wrapped her robe about her and took a seat in the parlor to await her turn and read the letter. She sliced the blade of her letter opener under the envelope flap and through the wax seal before extracting the single sheet of paper and holding it up to the light.

Madame M. W. Shelley
Villa Eden Au Lac
Montreux
Confederazione Svizzera *July 1816*

Dear Madame Shelley,
Dovete perdonare il temperamento di questa lettera . . .
Ah, please forgive me, as I am tired and upset and must finish this letter while I am able. I have some very sad news to convey regarding our mutual acquaintance, Mr. Clerval.
Our dear Henry.
My heart is heavy to tell he has passed away.

Mary pushed the document down into her lap and pressed the back of her hand to her mouth. Tears ran down her cheeks as she thought of the handsome young man, so full of knowledge and promise, who had escorted and conversed with her for many days in such a trying time for both him and *Monsieur* Aldini during Doctor Frankenstein's illness. For several minutes she could not bring herself to read on, but eventually she regained her composure, lifted the letter, and continued.

As you know, our friend followed Doctor Frankenstein to Geneva to support him in his hour of need. Already that household had been plunged into the depths of sorrow by the murder of the doctor's young sibling—a boy barely ten years old. The story that follows is intricate indeed and well beyond the means of my communication to you today. I will not bother you with the distress and grief that surrounds it.

Mary thought on what could be more concerning than the murder of a child. Her imagination flared, and she knew instinctively that many things could indeed compound even that most heinous of crimes.

Suffice to say that Henry has now suffered the same fate: strangulation.

Her attention could not pass that terrible word. Her own throat constricted as disbelief attempted to consume her, until it was replaced by an anger she had never before felt.

My immediate thought was that both murders were the work of the same culprit, until I was informed that the monster responsible for the first had already been sentenced and executed. It does not seem probable that such misfortune could strike in the same vicinity with such cruelty—but indeed it has.
Henry was a valiant and strong man, proficient in the art of fist-fighting. I once saw him practicing in the gymnasium against the punching bag, and

he went a number of rounds in the ring with men of great stature. *If it was truly a lone murderer, and not some gang of ruffians, the perpetrator must have been of immense and muscular build to have overpowered our Mr. Clerval.*
I cannot bear the thought that I will never converse with my friend again.
Yours sincerely,
Giovanni Aldini
Villa Forli,
Via di San Luca
Bologna, Italia

"The stuff of nightmares is not only relegated to unconscious thoughts upon a pillow, safely beneath an eiderdown," Mary whispered to herself, her lower lip trembling.

She leaned against her desk, strumming her fingers upon the inlaid wood, staring at the drizzle of rain as it coursed down the windowpane, dappling the light in the parlor. Less than an inch from her hand lay the document trunk that held her letters and incomplete manuscript. She ran her fingers over its polished walnut. The monster within, the one *she* had created, was no more cruel or vulgar than the ones that already populated the society. Indeed, though the scratching marks of her quill were intended as fiction, they were in fact a mirror to a harsh reality—both current and future. Her words were closer to the truth than she would ever have wished. For hers was not the box of Pandora—it was merely an encapsulation of an evil that had long been walking this earth, and that would continue its quest long after her ghost story was complete, long after the summer of 1816 was over, long after her own flesh had been devoured by worms and her bones disintegrated to dust.

Mary lifted the lid of the trunk so she might set her eyes upon the parchment, upon the innocence, naïveté, cruelty, and murder, upon him—to determine for herself who he truly was.

CHAPTER FORTY-THREE

He walked with her from his pasture down through Montreux to Clarens, where they enjoyed breakfast in the lakeside garden of L'Ermitage.

"You become more beautiful every day, Rachel," he said as he slid a fork through his soufflé.

"Thank you. You're not too bad yourself."

He smiled and reached across the white tablecloth to hold her hand in his as they both continued to eat.

"I hope to finish the research in the archives today. There are only a few microfiche left to study, but I may have to stay there till about seven so I can wrap it all up."

He nodded, rubbing the pad of his thumb back and forth across the side of her hand. "I can book a table and meet you here if you like."

"Sounds good."

He turned his face toward the sky. "It should be a nice evening for dining out, and then I can walk you home to Châtelard—keep you safe through the vineyards and Cimetiere de Clarens." He punctuated his words with a wink. Then, without warning, he extended his arms over the dining table, the fingers of both hands clawing the air, the muscles of his face slackening, his eyes deadening as he swayed his enormous bulk from side to side and let out a pathetic Boris Karloff moan.

Rachel looked around at the other guests eating their croissants and sipping their café before throwing her napkin at him. "Idiot," she whispered affectionately. "No more reading my notes for Mary's bio."

He chuckled and took a slurp from his espresso before lifting a quivering chunk of soufflé into his mouth.

Rachel could see he was much better than "not too bad." He had blossomed during the short time she'd known him. His shyness and reticence had dissipated. He was a handsome, sexual, gregarious, and confident young man.

A beautiful creation.

She noted how his lips moved as he savored his breakfast, and she knew that, for a second time in the picturesque setting of Montreux, she was falling in love.

It was almost nine by the time she left him to go to the police archive building. He leaned against the metal balustrade on the lake walk, kissed her, and waved her off. Several times along her walk, she turned to see if he was still there. He was, and each time he lifted his hand in salutation. Before she rounded a corner, she stopped beneath a thick copse of trees to take one last look. She knew he couldn't see her, as she was camouflaged by dense foliage, but still he gazed in her direction for many minutes before turning and walking back toward Montreux, running his hand along the top of the balustrade.

She wondered what thoughts filled his mind.

Rachel made her way down the *rue*, entered the archive building and asked the *gendarme* at reception for the student who'd been assisting her. The young man—boy—still wearing his three-sizes-too-big suit escorted her through the door, down the flight of stairs, and along the basement corridor into the small, windowless, broom-closet-sized archive. Rachel reached for the microfiche box she'd isolated as relevant and took her seat on the uncomfortable chair before flipping open the lid and switching on the archaic reader. The machine clunked and buzzed, and the screen filled the room with a bright blue light that seemed to drain life from everything it illuminated.

There was about an inch of negatives that would confirm the truth about Mary Shelley's letters—confirm whether they represented actual criminal occurrences or the imaginary basis for *Frankenstein*. She placed the first negative into the cradle and moved the control from left to right, down, right to left, down, and so on, looking for key French, English, or German words that might indicate a murder investigation. She scanned through negative after negative: 1816-2-1, 1816-2-2, -3, -4, -5, through the months and days of the "Year without a Summer."

A few cases referenced *"la morte,"* but these deaths occurred due to farming or carriage accidents rather than murder. By noon Rachel had discovered one event that mentioned *"meurtre,"* but even this was of no relevance, as it involved two neighboring vintners in a long-standing feud that ended in both of their deaths—explainable and quickly solved by the *gendarmerie*. No missing body parts.

The negatives were muddled in their sequencing, but Rachel handled that with a tick sheet of weeks and months on a page in her notepad: February, September, May, August, January, etc. The hours wore on, and month after month of 1816 was ticked off.

By 6:00 p.m., Rachel had one last negative to peruse. She guessed it was unlikely she'd find any clue to the murders indicated by the Shelley papers, and was resigned to the assumption that they were fiction—a part of Mary's process of creating and evolving her iconic novel. Rachel reviewed frame after frame documenting the last days of June 1816: a stolen bull, a

Fire on the Water

pickpocket, indications of prostitution in a villa on the Grand Rue, a petition signed by several guilds on why the investigation should be discontinued. The microfiche flicked back and forth until Rachel reached the final line of frames.

She turned her wrist to see her watch: twenty to seven. She could wrap this up and meet him for dinner. She could already taste his lips on hers.

Rachel clicked to the third-to-last frame: *"fraude et déception."*

The second-to-last frame: *"cambriolage."* Burglary.

The last frame: *"désécration in Cimetiere de Clarens."*

Rachel's heart pounded. Yes, it was the last frame of the negative. She pressed the print button and, after two minutes of clunking and buzzing, the old machine spat out a black and white printout of the negative. She tested every bit of her skills in reading French to decipher as much of the text as she could.

Case XXIIa
Report: Gendarme Zuelle
Location: Cimetiere de Clarens
Date: 30 June 1816
Gendarmerie notified by Vintner Christen of a disruption discovered in the Clarens cemetery at sunrise on this day. Gendarmes Zuelle and Cheda dispatched and discovered desecrated grave. One Thomas Albbrecht, buried the previous evening, was found several yards from his tombstone, partially stripped of his shroud. Both feet were missing. Undetermined at this point whether feet were with corpse at time of burial. Graveyard attendant ordered to return Thomas Albbrecht to his grave. Further enquiry recommended.

Rachel pulled her laptop from its satchel and transcribed the document word for word. Could this be the one instance that sparked Mary Shelley's imagination into a whole slew of cases relevant to her storyline?

Case XXIIa
Report: Gendarme Cheda
Location: Cimetiere de Clarens
Date: 30 June 1816, 9:35 post meridian.
Christophe Christen, tenant vintner of Châtelard lower vineyard, alerted the gendarmerie at 6:50 on the morning of this day to an offense discovered in Cimetiere de Clarens. Christen escorted Gendarmes Zuelle and Cheda to the cemetery where he led us to a shrouded body under a tree. The deceased was a man of impressive structure. We determined this was not a scene of murder but that the body had already been resident in the cemetery —interred on 29 June 1816. Gendarme Zuelle discovered the grave of a Thomas Albbrecht that had been disturbed. He discerned that the body was Albbrecht's—pulled from the ground and dragged to its current position.

There was evidence of ripped shroud between the grave and the body, and review of Monsieur Albbrecht determined that his shroud had been unwrapped from his head, then loosely and unprofessionally rewound. All material had been ripped and cut from about his lower legs, and it was there the true desecration was apparent. His feet had been removed just above the ankles—a clean incision through the flesh. The bones also appeared to be . . .

"What?" Rachel stared at the end of the printout and compared it to the original microfiche on the screen. Both ended there. "But that can't be all . . ." Her voice echoed off the walls overcrowded with hundreds of microfiche containers. "The bones also appeared to be *what*?"

There were no more negatives to review. That was the end. And yet there must have been more negatives, as the report was clearly incomplete and the first *gendarme* had recommended further investigation. Rachel studied her notepad where she'd ticked off the weeks and months of 1816: February, September, May, August, January, March, April, October, November, December, June.

There was no July.

July 1816 was when Shelley took up residence in Montreux.

Rachel looked around the walls of the archive. Could she have missed it? She looked down at the white plastic microfiche box on the desk in front of her. The fiche were loose—not as tightly packed as in every other box she'd scoured through. She drummed her fingers against the desk and reread the 30 June report on the reader and then again from the printout. The investigation may or may not have continued—but if it had, it would have been in July 1816.

Rachel pressed the button next to the archive door. She waited for several minutes until the boy came down the corridor and into the small room.

"*Bonjour, mademoiselle.*" The boy's voice hadn't broken yet, despite his age.

"*Bonjour*, Alain, *pourriez-vous m'aider*, umm . . . could you help me?" She tapped the box on her desk.

"*Certainement, mademoiselle.*"

"*Dossiers absents* . . . er . . . um . . . *Juillet* 1816—umm . . . *dix-huit seize.*"

"*Oui, un moment.*" He rushed off down the corridor. Rachel heard his cumbersome feet stomping up the steel staircase to the next level.

Several more minutes passed. It was now seven-thirty. She imagined him sitting alone at a table on the L'Ermitage terrace. She knew he'd understand. She hoped he'd understand.

The stair at the end of the corridor clanked with sure-footed steps, followed by those of a second and third person. Rachel leaned back in her chair to peer down the hall—three *gendarmes*, their uniforms sculpted around toned physiques, walked briskly toward her. They stopped at the door and peered in.

"*Mademoiselle* Rachel Walton, *promenade avec moi*." One *gendarme* held out a stiff hand, indicating for her to walk before him.

"*Qu'est-ce que c'est?*" Rachel asked, her brow furrowed.

"Please, *mademoiselle*," the *gendarme* requested in English. "Please come this way."

Rachel walked along the corridor, for the first time noticing how it echoed her every footstep, how reflectively white it was—as if it had been painted minutes before and was still wet. She climbed the metal stair to the first floor but, instead of going through into reception, the *gendarme* motioned down another corridor that led deep into the police station. One *gendarme* moved past them to hold a door open near the end of their path. His eyes were blue, and they pierced right through Rachel. She stared hesitantly into the room at a single table and two chairs—one on either side.

She looked toward the *gendarme* who'd originally spoken to her, but he just held out his hand toward the open door and repeated, "Please, *mademoiselle*."

Rachel stepped into the room.

The door closed behind her, making the grating and thudding slam only a metal door in a police station—or prison—could make.

She was alone.

The room was white. The table was bolted to the floor. The two chairs were plastic. She wondered why there wasn't a mirror on one wall, like in all the television shows. There were, however, two cameras on the ceiling behind protective white bubbles.

She took a seat on one of the chairs, wondering what she was doing there. She was considering trying the door handle when a man dressed in a finely tailored, dark Brioni suit entered and took the seat opposite her. He placed a thick manila folder on the table and pressed his hands, his fingers spread wide, against the metal tabletop. His face was plain, forgettable, his nose blunt, but the intensity of his gaze unnerved her.

"*Ce qui* . . ." Rachel swallowed, fear creeping over her initial confusion.

"*Mademoiselle* Walton, I will ask the questions. May I call you Rachel?"

Rachel nodded.

"I am Detective Baertschi with the Geneva *Gendarmerie*, seconded here to Montreux for several specific investigations. Do you know what I might be investigating?"

Rachel felt numb—her confusion dissipating into nothing. "No. Why—"

He held up his hand. "May I ask what you were researching in the archives downstairs?"

"Um . . . yes."

He stared at her, waiting.

"I'm . . . completing my . . . um . . . research for a biography of Mary Shelley. Mary resided in Montreux for several weeks in the . . . in the summer of 1816."

The detective nodded, studying her face. "What does *Madame* Shelley have to do with police files from two hundred years ago?" He flipped open the top of the manila folder and pushed a smaller envelope from it out onto the desk. Rachel could see a score or more of blue microfiche sticking out of the envelope.

She glanced up at the blunt nose of the detective, then back to the microfiche.

"My study has indicated that she may have been influenced by . . . by several occurrences in this area."

"Police investigations?"

"Yes, desecrations of bodies plus a number of murders."

The detective straightened in his chair and pulled the manila folder an inch closer to his side of the table. "And what made you conclude that *Madame* Shelley was involved with these . . . occurrences?"

Rachel blinked, pondering what the microfiche in the envelope contained. "Are those the files from July 1816?"

"What made you conclude that *Madame* Shelley was involved?"

Rachel glanced sideways at her watch. 8:30 p.m.

She thought of the trunk full of correspondence. There were still several letters and the two smaller document boxes she hadn't yet opened.

With her attention still on the microfiche, she pulled a single letter from her satchel and placed it on the table. The envelope was laden with the script of *Monsieur* Aldini.

Detective Baertschi pulled the envelope toward him, urged the top flap open, and pulled out the letter. He read the yellowed parchment front to back and his eyes narrowed. "Is this the only letter you possess?"

Rachel was silent.

"Is this the only letter you possess?"

"Yes." She couldn't believe she'd just lied. "Yes," she said again.

The detective folded the letter and inserted it back into its envelope. Rachel's heart sank as he placed it on top of the manila folder between them.

"That's my letter."

"Is it? Now it is part of my investigation."

"And the microfiche?" Rachel nodded toward the envelope of film.

"I am afraid, *Mademoiselle* Walton, that even with the policies on freedom of information these items are related to a current inquiry. As such they will not be available for public review for at least several years after my investigation is completed."

"Then there are more cases in 1816? The microfiche contain details of those events?" The pace of Rachel's breathing picked up. "They happened?"

The detective stood and nudged his chair behind him with his foot. He collected the letter from *Monsieur* Aldini, the manila folder, and the envelope of microfiche and walked out of the room without another word.

It was 9:00 p.m. the next time Rachel checked her watch.

And then it was 10.

She waited in silent contemplation. Her mind went over the questions she'd been asked, the answers she'd given, the lie she'd told.

She bit her lip. Were Mary's letters true? They must be.

11:00 p.m.

The door opened. Detective Baertschi entered and sat on the chair opposite Rachel. Once more, he placed the manila folder on the table and opened to about halfway through the thick wad of documents it held. He extracted an envelope and opened it so that only he could see its contents.

Rachel didn't dare speak. She could feel the blood thumping through her heart, coursing through her veins. She jumped when the detective flicked an object from the envelope into the center of the table.

A photo of a young man with red hair. Rachel stared at it without recognition.

A second photo—a polaroid—of another young man. The detective seemed to sense her confusion, but still he flicked a third photo, a fourth, a fifth.

A sixth photo—a young man with a scruff of hair sticking up at an odd angle. *Handsome*, Rachel thought for a second time.

"You know this boy?" the detective barked. He reached over and tapped the photo with his fingertip.

Rachel shook her head.

11:30 p.m.

A seventh photo.

It reminded her of him—again—the same thick facial features, but gray eyes. A brother?

The detective pushed the photo to the side along with the one of the young man with the scruff of hair. He tapped one and then the other with his index finger.

Rachel stared—not daring to lift her gaze to his.

"Rachel?"

"Yes?"

"Do you know either of these men?"

"No." Her voice quavered, almost inaudible.

He was silent for several minutes. She listened to his breathing—it seemed to mirror her own heartbeat which had now slowed to a sluggish cadence but still managed to make her entire ribcage rattle and vibrate when it did have the courage to beat.

"You were in New York when most of these men died. You were in Geneva when these last two were—" He stopped tapping the photos. "You were in Geneva." He sat very still, waiting for something. Rachel finally looked up at him. "You definitely know this next gentleman."

He pulled a photo from the envelope and placed it face down in front of her. He withdrew his hand and left Rachel staring at the back of the print.

11:50 p.m.

Rachel slipped a nail under a corner and started to peel the photo off the tabletop. The detective studied her every move, every mannerism, every bead of nervous sweat.

She flipped the photo over.

Jack.

Jack.

She stared up at the detective and then back to . . .

Jack.

"Why is this photo here?" she mouthed, without a wisp of breath.

The detective was silent.

She found her voice with an anger that welled up from . . . from where? "Why is this photo here?"

"You do not know, do you?" He seemed apologetic.

"Know what?"

He collected the photos from the table and placed them back into the envelope.

"Know what?" Rachel repeated, exasperated.

He put the envelope into the manila folder and closed it before pulling the entire package under his arm and rising from his chair. He strode to the door, tapped twice, and a uniformed *gendarme* opened it from the outside.

"*Elle est libre pour aller*," Detective Baertschi said to the *gendarme*. He turned, placed his hand on the doorframe, and leaned back into the room. "Be careful, *Mademoiselle* Walton," he said and nodded before walking off down the corridor.

12:01 a.m.

CHAPTER FORTY-FOUR

The clock in the lobby downstairs gave the single chime of a quarter past.

"Just after the witching hour," Mary said. She looked down at her ink-stained fingers. There was no moon or starlight outside her window, and the street lanterns had long been extinguished and brought inside. Not even a drizzle of rain kept her company in the midst of the evil that lurked upon her pages.

She could smell him on her fingers.

Claire stirred in the bedchamber. Mary rose from her desk to cross the parlor, peer into the darkness of the second room toward Willmouse's crib and, satisfied both her babe and her sister were sleeping soundly, closed the connecting doors. She leaned against them, rubbing at the ink on her hand, thinking of the girl she'd just written about, wondering whether she should kill her or not, whether her characters deserved some happiness. But then she thought of the delight she would feel to make her friends shiver and creep with fear. She thought of her Percy begging her not to expose the horror that was approaching.

Mary smiled in the dimly lit parlor, with perhaps a touch of sadness holding a scalpel against the side of her heart.

She stepped to the window and pressed her nose against the cool glass to search for stars, but she could not even discern the clouds she knew must be up there, stopping the light. A sudden glow distracted her, and she turned her attention to the terrace below. It flared again. A cigar. The glow waved in the darkness and she knew instinctively.

"John."

She drew the empire shawl about her, checked again that Willmouse and Claire were still fast asleep, and then left the suite.

The lobby was empty as she tiptoed down the grand stair in the shadows, not wanting to wake the other residents of the villa. The blackmoors at each turn held their unlit candles high and stared at her through chiseled, painted eyes. One grabbed at her shawl, attempting to pull it from her shoulders. Another smiled a toothy grin with the same subtle glow as the dying embers huddled in the depths of the ornate fireplace.

The first door to the terrace was locked, the second kept ajar by the upturned corner of a rug. She gave the door a nudge, careful to make no sound in case her friend was entertaining another. When she discerned he was alone, she sped up, not minding that the wooden heels of her slippers gave her away.

He smiled in the darkness, his teeth and mouth lit by his cigar.

"Ah, Mrs. Shelley. I noticed the light in your window."

"Doctor." Mary took a seat beside where he stood.

"How does your story progress?" He puffed on his cigar, and it flared once more in the otherwise pitch darkness.

"It progresses well."

"Good. I don't suppose you managed to secret a decanter of sherry out with you?"

Mary shook her head but then realized he could not see her and said, "No." She watched the glowing end of his cigar move to his mouth and away, down to his waist, then back to his mouth. "Did anything happen in the study this evening while I was with my creatures?"

"The card games fizzled. The gossip was rhetoric."

"Was there no new word of the occurrences?"

"Well . . . yes. Two *gendarmes* visited late this evening, requesting that I attend their muster in the morning. Once again they require my expertise. I must admit I am quite apprehensive, but I do wish to help them in any way I am able."

Mary stared out into the darkness, waiting for him to continue, to comment on why he had been recalled, but he did not. "I am glad. I know without doubt your assistance will be invaluable. Has another body been desecrated?" She strained to see his face in the black.

Polidori sat beside her on the lounge. His thigh brushed against her skirts but he did not bother moving an acceptable distance from her person. "Another murder. This one just as gruesome, more so, but apparently without souvenirs removed."

"Another man has been killed? Killed and disfigured for no purpose, without the confiscation of any part of his corpse?" Mary fell again into a sad, troubled reverie, thinking more of Mr. Henry Clerval's recent demise than that of an unknown, but just as unfortunate, stranger. The cigar glow moved in front of her and was dashed out in the sand tray beside the lounge.

Polidori placed his hand on the bench by Mary's knee. She felt it shake in nervous apprehension.

"No, Mary. It was a woman. This monster has murdered and mutilated a woman."

Mary could think or see absolutely nothing. She was blind to everything, though she could hear Polidori's breathing and was aware of the heat emanating from his hand by her knee. She could not discern whether the look on his face was of grief or anger, frustration or uselessness, fear or numbness. In the distance, waves broke on the shoreline, wind rustled through shrubbery, a shrill sound came from very far away, but she would never know what it was.

Heavy footsteps sounded in the background upon carpet and marble. Several yards down the terrace, the French door creaked open from the villa's reception.

Polidori stood. "I must take my leave of you, *madame*. I became acquainted with a like mind at this evening's port and cigars whose wishes coincide with my own. This night is surely something I will need—that I might endure the horror of the coming days."

"I understand." She held her hand out until it touched his waistcoat. His fingers encircled hers and lips brushed her hand.

"Take care, Mrs. Shelley."

"And you also, my friend."

CHAPTER FORTY-FIVE

1:00 a.m.

Rachel stood on the front steps of the police station. The late night sky had become overcast—clouds yellow with the reflected street lighting of Clarens and Montreux. A drizzle made the air cold and the streets shine. Water slipped down the gutters. She stood for almost thirty minutes waiting for a taxi, but the *rue* was deserted. She could hear the distant echo and shout of revelers around the bay in Montreux, but she saw no signs of life from where she stood. She looked back toward the glow of the *gendarmerie* reception and then strode off into the desolate streets of Clarens toward Châtelard.

Instead of following the main roadway, she chose to walk directly north on Du Pierrier. A large, deserted school building loomed on her left. On her right, a stone wall separated her from the gurgle of a stream, dense concealing foliage, and large trees that clung to the otherwise invisible watercourse. As she approached the railway line, her walkway was sidetracked into a narrow black tunnel without any apparent light at the other end. She didn't care. She just wanted to get home to Châtelard on the other side.

A gauntlet of shrubbery pressed in on either side of the path as she approached the tunnel. Above her, chalets perched on the natural ramparts, but they too were dark and lifeless. She plunged into the concrete passageway, her every breath reverberating off the walls, ceiling, and floor to hit back at her. She didn't stop to listen to them, thoughts in the back of her mind telling her she shouldn't be in this place at this time, that she'd made a terrible mistake and must keep going without even glancing back. Her heavy footfalls echoed as she gained speed, and the drizzle from the open sky was upon her again.

She turned in a circle to get her bearings. Her path appeared to follow the brook then veer off into pastures away from her destination. To her right, however, a footbridge led to the other side of the waterway and up into what looked like a factory parking lot. She walked—ran—across the bridge, glancing down at the rocky riverbed that held the snaking, gurgling ink of water. She jumped up several stairs and through the empty parking lot until she reached a *rue* that followed the railway tracks, holding itself tight between the grassed embankment and the graffitied rear walls of crumbling buildings.

It was only when she arrived at Avenue Rambert that she realized where she was. Somehow she'd missed the main *rue* that climbed up the hill to Châtelard, but no matter. From here she could cut through Cimetiere de Clarens and up through the vineyards to the fortress and her studio.

Rachel hurried toward the ornate gate of the cemetery. Two massive angels rose on either side of the swirling wrought iron—muscled bodies and flowing robes chiseled into botticino marble that glowed in the darkness surrounding them. They each held their right arm forward, thick veins encircling their masculine arms toward upheld hands, urging evil to stay beyond the limits of the hallowed ground. The larger angel held a sword, the other a lance. Only one still possessed his wings. The other's lay shattered below the plinth on which he stood.

Rachel hesitated and stared through the rows of headstones toward the distant vineyard and then back behind her to the *rue*—neither looked particularly inviting as the drizzle continued to soak into her clothing.

On top of the hill, the garden and terrace lights of Châtelard blazed, enticing her forward.

She pulled her jacket tight around her and stepped into the cemetery, the almost invisible moon shadow of the angel's sword slicing across her neck.

Her shoes crunched and sank into the gravel, and rivulets of water coursed across the stones and into her shoes. Tombs hung in the darkness on either side of her, some plain and fading into the night, others elaborate with cherubs and angels that guided her journey though the yard. The diffused shadows of moonlight cast themselves deceptively in every direction.

The rain had created a stream that forced her to cross the grass—and graves—over to the next gravel pathway. She climbed through the tombstones, past a father and son killed in battle, a brother whose family would never forget him, and grabbed at iron fencing to stabilize her foothold. She reached for the hand of a deity whose cold, chiseled fist gave little comfort or support, and finally faltered as she sunk into the grass and mud to tumble toward the bordering path.

A crunch of footsteps running through the gravel approached from behind.

Rachel turned.

"Hello?" she called, an instant before deciding she needed to run. She slipped from the grass down onto the gravel, undecided about whether to run back toward the *rue* or forward through the cemetery toward the vineyard. She jumped up from the wet stones and ran toward the vineyard and its trails that would lead her up to Châtelard. Her heart thumped harder and harder, compounding the roar of blood coursing through her head, behind her eyes, through her legs, making her run faster and more erratically than she . . .

. . . she couldn't think of anything but running.

The heavy, repetitive crunch of gravel grew closer.

She didn't know what the danger was, just *that* it was, and that she had to run. She was in the wrong place, had put herself in the wrong place. The police had made it so she was in the wrong place. And now she was going to be hurt and probably die. Yes, she was probably going to die unless she could keep running.

Of course she'd seen all the horror movies of her teenage years, knew that one should never go through a cemetery, especially after midnight, on a rainy night, as a woman—a girl—alone. She was certain to be slaughtered among the headstones. And yet she was here, and she needed to run and keep running until she was either dead or safe in the arms of a loved one. Isn't that what was supposed to happen? Yes, she was certain—either death or love.

Rachel kept running.

There was an angry grunt behind her. An animal? A man—the most dangerous of animals.

She dare not look but she needed to look, to confirm what she already knew.

Was it him?

She couldn't tell. She didn't know. Of course it wasn't him.

She peered over her shoulder, running blind along the gravel as she attempted to discern who followed her through the darkness.

He was tall. His shadow flicked and loomed large across tombstones.

He appeared lithe. Too skinny to be him. Or was that a trick of the light, a trick of the shadows that seemed to envelope and caress him? Maybe it was him—maybe she didn't need to run.

She needed to run.

He was probably skinny.

It probably wasn't him. But he was dangerous.

Was he dangerous?

Was it him?

She had to keep running.

It was painful to breathe as the rain now beat down upon her face, but she took several quick, shallow breaths, attempting to gain the courage and the air to scream for help. She took a third breath and then a fourth, each new gasp further expanding her lungs as she ran between honed marble, careful not to slip upon the groomed gravel that twisted and cut through the manicured grass and topiary.

Blood coursed through her veins.

She was ready to scream.

Her chest expanded, her mouth opened wide, she forced the air from her lungs up through her windpipe toward her vocal chords . . .

But the wind was knocked from her with little more than a pathetic grunt, and she was slammed to the ground. She landed on the gravel and rolled onto the grass with the full weight of her pursuer upon her. His body was hard and bruising as it hit her, pushed her into the gravel and grass, pressed her face into the sod.

Strong arms and hands encircled her chest.

Muscular legs entwined with hers and twisted her body.

She saw the flash of a tattoo as the palm of a hand covered her mouth. Fingers pressed into her cheek and against her eye.

The hand smelled of pig. No . . . rabbit. No, pig.

Rachel squirmed in his grip, trying to see his face in the dark. She glimpsed the cleanly shaven chin but then saw only the chunk of marble, the tips of fingers spread around it, gripping it to ensure it met its target.

The marble was pure, no vein or speck to blemish the clean white stone.

In the moment the rock bore down upon her, Rachel wondered where it had come from.

Whose tombstone had been cracked?

Whose grave had been desecrated?

Whose epitaph would kill her?

CHAPTER FORTY-SIX

The night darkened a deeper black than Mary had ever known.
 It had been at least two hours since Polidori had bid her *adieu* on the terrace that he might find solace in his suite upstairs with his like-minded companion. Mary had stayed on alone in the warming coziness of the cushioned lounge, isolating her own comfort in the dead of night, in the darkness that surrounded her, that enamored her.
 All visual sense was null, inked out by the complete absence of light on the terrace, in the garden, upon the lake, along the surrounding shores. So, too, was there little to hear other than the distant murmur of gentle waves and an even gentler rainfall far off upon the water.
 Mary remained perfectly still, filled with wonderment that she was in a space she knew well and felt safe in, but that she could see or hear none of it. Whether her eyes were opened or closed, there was no distinction.
 She wondered if that was what it would be like if she were dead—if she had fallen asleep on the lounge and dropped further into unconsciousness and then into death. Would the house staff find her body on the terrace in the morning and wake her from her repose? From her passing?
 Mary felt a rush of excitement as she allowed the lack of perception to engulf her. She would let it take her, do with her what it wanted, give her an awareness of things no one she knew was aware of.
 Would it allow her to feel, to see, to hear, to smell the things that those she had created or killed had felt, seen, heard, smelled before she had placed her quill to parchment and scratched their lives into existence?
 Or out of existence?
 How she hoped it would—that she might know each of her creations as intimately as she knew herself, as intimately as she knew her darling Percy. Would it also allow her to know once more those she had lost, those who had slipped through her fingers but never from her thoughts?
 The minutest resonance of a breeze amongst the shrubbery seemed to mimic the blood coursing through her veins, pumping through her heart and around her body. The sound of it in her own head filled her with a euphoria

that seemed to extinguish all doubt. She knew she was alive. But more than that, she was a creature of her own doing, her own creation and, as such, she could write her own story as she saw fit.

The breeze touched her face.

Her heartbeat slowed, and her breathing mellowed. She felt as if she were floating in the darkness, becoming one with the night.

Neither alive nor dead.

Yet aware of whom she was and the power she held over herself and her creatures.

CHAPTER FORTY-SEVEN

Several *gendarmes* clustered around her body in the Cimetiere de Clarens.
 She possessed the pallor and rigor of death. She was cold to the touch.
 She was dead.
 She had been moved several paces from where the initial attack had occurred—the location delineated by large fragments of skull. Drag marks were evident in the ground, still soggy from the night's rainfall. Now the body lay displayed upon the marble slab of a grave. Her clothing was awry, as if disturbed post mortem.
 "The cemetery watchman came to secure the gates just after one and noticed a man huddled among the tombstones," a *gendarme* told the detective. "Initially he thought it was a grieving villager come to visit a loved one, however he became suspicious due to the man's movements. He called out to him, and the man rose from the grave, stared toward him, then turned and ran toward the vineyard and then in the direction of Sonzier."
 The detective approached the body, nodding to the *gendarme*. The blood from the head wound had spread across the slab, its edges smattered and fragmented by the rainfall. Letters chiseled into the stone had partially filled, detailing a story of sorrow and loss in brilliant black-red blood.
 In loving memory.
 Beloved daughter.
 "The watchman discovered the body upon the gravestone and determined, due to the amount of blood, that the *mademoiselle* was dead. By the time the *gendarmes* were led to the scene, the rain had stopped and they thought it best to not disturb the body any further—to place a guard at each gate and call for your investigation."
 Hunkering down by the grave, the detective caressed a strand of hair away from the *mademoiselle's* face with his gloved hand.
 "We have discovered a shard of marble, which is most likely the weapon of murder. It is covered in blood, tissue, and strands of hair that match the color of the *mademoiselle's*."
 The detective glanced at the stone indicated by the *gendarme* and nodded

in agreement. He stood and walked around the grave, reviewing the body from every direction, noting the shape of the imprint the weapon had left on the front and side of the skull, cracking the cheek and brow to push them sickeningly in.

"We have not yet determined identity."

The detective looked up at the *gendarme* then back to the body—the beautiful curve of the intact chin, the slender lips and nose.

"I am aware of the *mademoiselle's* particulars. She is known to myself and a number of our investigators."

The *gendarme* nodded and handed his notebook to the detective.

"Please bring the watchman to me." The detective surveyed the cemetery in the morning light. Every surface, every gravestone and tomb, every tree, shrub, and blade of grass glistened from the overnight rainfall. The gravel was sodden. The gutters of the walkways still ran with water from the surrounding hills and mountains. On the far side of a rambling wall, a vintner whistled for his dog to keep up. A large, multi-colored Swissy bound up between the rows of vines to join its master and bark at his heels.

The detective walked to the end of the gravel path and peered through the wrought iron fencing that separated the cemetery from the vineyard. He studied the fluted spearheads that lined the top of the border and followed their course to the nearest gate. Though nowhere near as ornate as the main entrance to Cimetiere de Clarens, the one leading into the laneways and vineyards of Châtelard was ensconced with gargoyles meant to keep evil at bay. Slicked by rain, they seemed to leer and smirk at those who had entered the hallowed ground this morning.

"*Monsieur?*"

The detective turned, gave the watchman a cursory glance before continuing his surveillance of the grounds. "Tell me in detail about the man you saw."

"Yes, of course, *monsieur*. He was a large man. Very broad and strong to my eyes. Arms and legs thick with muscle. Much larger than any man I have ever seen in Clarens or Montreux. Even with the tourists who frequent our area, I have seen none who compare in stature."

The detective studied the grand family tombs that took prime position along the cemetery's far boundary—columns and domes sculpted from Italian marble, statues sitting demurely, dancing gaily, or striding forth heroically in stone.

The doors and grates of each tomb were locked, each protecting the dead, each keeping them from being forgotten, from leaving, from being taken. He looked once more over to the *mademoiselle* who lay dead upon the gravestone.

She didn't belong here.

Perhaps that was why she was now dead.

"How did this man move? Was he agile?"

The watchman hesitated as he thought back to the middle of the night. "I would say he was agile but also mention there was an uncertainty in his movements, as if he was not used to how his legs worked under such circumstances, if that makes any sense. I am not sure what I mean, but it was as if he had never run before, had never needed to run before, but now found he could run and the more he ran, the faster he became."

The detective stared into the watchman's eyes. "I do understand what you mean. Thank you." He walked across the gravel, leaving the watchman behind him, passing grave after grave, angel after angel, until he was again beside her, hunkering down to caress her cheek with the backs of his fingers.

"I am sorry, *mademoiselle*. I am afraid I have failed in my duty to protect you while I had the chance."

Two *gendarmes* arrived at the marble slab with the investigating physician, and the detective rose to give him leeway and observe his actions. The physician touched the deceased's throat. With proficiency and humility, he ran his hands down the arms and legs and around the back of the torso to confirm any other areas of damage or absence before concentrating on the victim's skull. He removed an instrument from his bag and used it to urge the hair back from the wound. A *gendarme* indicated the skull fragments three gravestones distant, and the physician went to view them, noted their size and shape, then returned to the deceased. He extracted several small shards of skull from the hole made by the attack and peered at the remaining matter, poking and nudging it to enhance his examination.

After he stopped his probing, he stared not at the wound but at the marble on which the girl lay, at the blood that had coursed along letter after letter of epitaph. He looked back toward the girl's face, touched her cheek just as the detective had, then stood from his work.

The detective placed his hand on the physician's back, urging him to walk with him toward the entrance gate.

"What can you tell me, doctor?"

"I am unable to determine whether it was the blunt force from the piece of marble or strangulation that killed her. The bruising is just starting to appear about her throat. The attack with the rock may have occurred either before or after the strangulation. Either way, its true purpose was as a crude means to gain access to her brain."

"What do you mean, 'gain access to her brain'?"

"There is a substantial portion of her brain missing."

"Missing."

"Yes. I am also of two minds about whether this murder was committed by the same person as the previous attacks. This assault is crude, cumbersome, almost passionate. The previous desecrations and murders were precise and particular, the incisions exact and professional. By comparison, this one was animalistic, naïve, obsessive. Emotional. As if he had a personal connection with her."

"And yet a portion of her is now gone, in the same way the other bodies were missing a part of themselves. These deaths must be linked. The portion of brain—how was it removed? In a crude or professional manner?"

"That, detective, is precisely the anomaly with this body. The entrance by stone was crude. The detachment of the frontal lobe was, however, precise—with extreme prejudice toward a professional surgeon."

"Yet you still believe it was another?"

"Yes, one who is still learning, one whose knowledge is not great but who avidly digests and uses that knowledge with precision. One who himself is still searching for his own identity, his own way to carry out what he feels he must."

They stopped under the shadow of the main entrance gate to Cimetiere de Clarens. Above them, the two angels lifted their weapons, their pristine, white marble wings rising high in majestic arcs.

"Thank you, Doctor Polidori. Your observations are very helpful in this matter."

CHAPTER FORTY-EIGHT

The chunk of marble shattered on the grave beside Rachel's face as she continued to squirm and fight. She clawed at the man, attempted to bite him, flung her arms and hands uselessly, tried to kick him.

A heavy hand slapped against the side of her face and then he was pulling at her satchel. The strap was caught around her shoulder, but he continued yanking at it with frightening strength.

He said several words in a thick French accent that she couldn't decipher.

He was young—perhaps twenty—with hazel eyes and a nose hooked and broken. His jawline shaven but with the shadow of a persistent, heavy beard.

The leather strap of her satchel jerked roughly down her arm, twisting the skin of her forearm before it was wrenched free.

"My laptop!"

Rachel attempted to rise from the grave, but he placed a broad hand on her chest and shoved her back down onto the slab, winding her so she felt her lungs had collapsed.

She struggled for breath as she lay in aching pain, unable to move. From the corner of her eye, she watched the dark-haired, hazel-eyed, broken-nosed youth with his hands smelling of pig as he ran off with her satchel.

With her laptop and her notes.

With the manuscript she'd spent three years of her life researching and writing.

Rachel remained flat on the slab for how long she would never know. The moonlight and rain poured down upon her. The dead of night surrounded her. The dead of Clarens lay beneath her. She felt no grief. What use were tears when the rain had soaked her so completely, had rinsed and washed her eyes of all she had seen so clearly? What use the shudder of grief, which would only exacerbate the aches and pains that already wracked her body?

She felt almost as one with the slab of marble at her back. The force with which she'd been thrown against it had molded her body to its flat solidity.

Any slight movement she made would break the seal between them, releasing pain and excruciating tenderness. It was best to lie still, there in the rain, in the moonlight, in the cemetery. She wondered who lay beneath her. Envy crept in, that she was on the wrong side of the slab, that everything would be so much easier if the marble encased her instead of separating her from the cold comfort of earth, soil, perhaps velvet and wood, a nice embroidered pillow on which to rest her head.

She pushed herself up and rolled her legs and feet onto the grass. Her entire body ached—every bone, muscle, and organ demanding her attention and pity. Sudden panic struck her as she thought of her keys, her wallet. She patted the pockets of her jeans, comforted by the shape and bulge of the items through the worn denim. But her relief was soon overridden by fear that the youth would find no money in the satchel and return to maul her body once more for the few francs she had with her. She could see no movement about the graveyard, could hear no indication of the youth's return, but she moved as quickly and quietly as she could through the gravestones and out the gate to the Châtelard vineyards.

She gave shadows a wide berth and listened for any noise of possible danger. The rain continued but the clouds parted a little more, allowing the moon to light the rows of vines clinging to the slope without disruption. Rachel climbed the hill between the twisting and curling vines. Mud splattered her jeans and stuck to her shoes. By the time she reached the steps to Châtelard's Terrasse d'Honneur, her shoes were large clumps of mud and twig. She scraped them against the metal balustrade then began to climb. As she finally strode across the rain-splashed terrace and around the fortress toward the outbuildings that contained her studio, she felt safe. She passed under the shadow of the *porte cochère*.

He was sitting huddled on her stoop.

Just like Rachel, he was sodden to the bone by the rain and splattered in mud from walking through the fields. He was a sorry, miserable-looking mess.

And she loved him for it.

He saw her, rose to his feet, and ran across the courtyard in silence so as to not wake the other residents of the fortress apartments. His arms encircled her.

"Rachel, what happened? Where have you been? I've been so worried." He didn't seem to require an answer as he lifted her off the ground, tightened his arms, and pressed his lips into hers. Rachel burst into tears in sudden relief. He slid his hand under her legs and pulled her fully up into his arms to cradle her against his chest as he leaned against the ancient stone of Châtelard. The imposing *porte cochère* afforded protection from the rain, but still the night poured down on either side of them, becoming heavier still as the heavens split further open. Rachel pushed into his bulk, glad to have his body encompassing hers, glad to have his lips and soothing whispers at her ear.

* * * *

He walked to the fridge in her kitchenette, freshly bathed, a towel wrapped around his waist, his bare feet padding across the tiles, the Y incision scar that cut up between his abs and slashed across his chest blossoming a raw pink from the heat of the shower.

"I wish you would come and stay with me. After what's happened, it worries me that you're here alone, walking the lanes by yourself when this monster is about."

"Please. I'm from Manhattan. Muggings come with the territory. Besides, I'm fine."

He looked at her, horrified. "Rachel, this is Montreux, not New York."

She shrugged as she dried her hair with a towel.

He poured two glasses of wine and came to sit beside her on the bed. "Please consider my request." They both took sips of sauvignon. "What about all your work? Your book on Mary?"

Rachel sighed as she recalled everything in her satchel. "I'm just glad I gave the letter from *Monsieur* Aldini to Detective Baertschi. At least it hasn't been lost to that ignorant pig in the cemetery—and I'm certain the Chillon Archives Directeur will be able to retrieve it." She pulled her bathrobe around her and took another taste of wine. "Everything from the laptop is backed up on a memory stick here, plus I e-mailed the most recent draft of the book to New York last Monday."

He nodded, pulling her close. "That's good. I'm glad you're okay." He kissed her on the forehead, touched her gently on the throat, and ran the backs of his fingers across her cheek.

She jumped back and yelped. "Why did you do that?" She brought her hand to her cheek.

He looked shocked. "I'm sorry. I didn't mean to hurt you. Did I hurt you? I always try to be so careful when I'm with you."

"No, of course not. It wasn't you. I know it wasn't you."

He narrowed his eyes. "What do you mean?"

"No, no." She shook her head and reached out to touch his hair, feeling the prickle of the buzz cut beneath her fingers. "Please, can we just drop it? I'm okay. There's nothing to worry about. I'll report it to the police tomorrow, and I promise I won't walk alone so late again."

"I know you won't. I will personally ensure you're at home in bed long before midnight from now on."

"Which home?" Rachel chuckled.

He smiled. "Yours or mine, *mon chéri*, yours or mine?" He lay down on the bed, propped up against the headboard, wine glass held to his lips, and his legs hanging over the end of the mattress and down onto the floor. Rachel leaned into his shoulder, into the tree of life that scrolled across his flesh—its branches, roots, and tendrils reaching out to touch her, to caress her skin, to attach themselves and entrap her with their subtle and beguiling force. She ran her finger along one of the branches and wondered where it would lead her.

"Will you tell me something if I ask?"

He nodded. "I have no reason not to, Rachel." He lifted his arm to pull her body in close to his. She rested her cheek against his pectoral, and her fingers traced the scar across his chest and down his belly, stopping in the wave of hair that surged up from beneath the bath sheet.

"Tell me about the men . . . the photos of the men in the back of *Paradise Lost*."

He turned the wineglass in his loose grip, sliding the rim between his upper and lower lip. He pulled the glass away from his mouth to set it on his chest, fingers continuing to spin it upon his flesh. The wine swirled around the bowl.

"Why do you ask? They're just pictures of my family."

"Your family?" Rachel whispered, thinking of the photo of Jack the detective showed her, and thinking—knowing—she'd find the same picture in the back of *Paradise Lost* if she looked again. She thought of Jack's blond, tussled hair, his muscled arms, his ornate tattoos—the tree of life, the tree of knowledge. She could feel the tree of life creeping along the arm behind her, could see the tree of knowledge on the other side of the massive chest—exact duplicates of Jack's tattoos.

"Yes, my family."

Rachel let those words sink in. She continued to study his chest as it rose and fell with his every breath. The scarring had faded as his body had cooled from the hot shower, no longer emphasizing the drastic incisions that had once been carved across it in an attempt to give him life—to stop him losing his life. Now only his nipples were pink against the pristine, white flesh that stretched across his torso.

"They are my fathers." His explanation was touched by innocence.

Rachel felt an underlying shaking deep within his body. Almost imperceptible. Definitely unnoticeable if she hadn't been so close to his flesh. Was he nervous? Upset?

"What do you mean, 'they are your fathers'? Do you mean like a football team adopting an orphan?" Rachel immediately regretted her words, knowing his memories were hazy and that his life before the motorbike accident had become confused, muddled—forgotten. He tensed up beside her and held his breath. His grip around her became tighter, more encapsulating. His chest shuddered and Rachel sensed he was attempting to hold back his emotions, his tears, but still she pressed. "All those men would be similar in age to yourself, a few of them even younger."

He pulled his arm from around her and sat up on the end of the bed. After placing the wineglass on the floor between his feet, he held his hands to his head as if one of his migraines was threatening to assault him.

"How can you know this? You don't know those people. You haven't met my fathers."

"I met Jack. And I think one of your photos might be of him."

He was quiet, his fingers working against his temples to keep the headache at bay. "Your Jack?"

"Yes." She moved to the end of the bed to sit beside him, to wrap her arms around his shaking bicep and rub his flesh to comfort him.

"Which one?"

"You don't know? Jack had blond tussled hair, very white skin." Rachel looked up at the tears that had surfaced in his eyes, then down across the muscled flesh that was as blemish-free as Jack's, the smooth expanse of skin etched with the same tattoos, the single brown freckle on his bicep, encircled by a stylized tendril from the tree of life—a freckle she'd known and loved since long before she'd met him, since long before she'd lost Jack.

He pulled his leg up onto the mattress and rubbed at the scarring around his ankle as if it, too, ached with the loss of memory.

"He was your Jack?" He appeared to be recalling the picture and attaching the name to all he'd thought whenever studying it in the solitude of his hovel. "Your Jack, who had the same tattoos as me?" He looked down at his arm and his eyes widened as if he were seeing it and the tree of life for the first time. It dug into his flesh and took root in his muscle to flourish across his skin. He ran his thumb along the groove of scar tissue that delineated the arm from his torso, studying the fresh ink that covered the thin, shallow crease and spread the leaves of life further onto his shoulder and the top of his pectoral.

Rachel placed her hand on his, stopping its movement along the scar line, and wrapped her fingers around his.

He bent his neck to rub his cheek against her hand and closed his eyes. "I must have admired . . . I must have loved Jack very much to have copied his tattoos."

Rachel glanced at the freckle. "Yes, he was a gentle and lovely man."

He picked up his wineglass, took another two gulps to finish it off, and placed it back on the floor. Rachel crawled up to kneel on the bed behind him, massaging his shoulders and neck, rubbing his temples, and gently scratching her nails through the cropped hair covering his skull. He rolled his neck and head, appreciative of the tender touch.

"I was told they were my 'fathers,' that they had assisted my recovery after the accident."

Rachel thought perhaps he meant as blood or organ donors but didn't want to push the point in case he meant something different and wasn't really aware of their paternal function. She wondered if he even knew they were all dead.

"I search for their faces whenever I walk the streets of Montreux, but so far I haven't recognized even one."

Rachel was glad she was at his back and he couldn't see the anguish that crossed her face at his naiveté.

"I would have liked to have known Jack. But then, I guess if he were still alive, I wouldn't have been able to be with you." He turned to her. "I'm sorry for how things have turned out."

Rachel hugged him from behind and pushed her lips into his neck, to smell his masculine aroma, to smell Jack.

CHAPTER FORTY-NINE

"A few days ago, I felt the longer this case went on, the less likely it was to be solved."

Polidori escorted Mary along the lakeside promenade. "But now I feel our assailant has become sloppy, is invoked more by the heat of passion than by necessity and requirement."

"You suspect he will make a mistake? That he will give away his identity or hiding place by some slip?"

"I do."

"I trust your instincts, Doctor Polidori. Will you be surprised if the culprit turns out to be a man of means and respect—one society looks up to and admires?"

"Oh, Mrs. Shelley, I have no doubt that is exactly who we will establish as the origin of these vile occurrences. I also believe, however, that he is followed on his course by a lesser, more naïve being who willingly or unwillingly also carries out these despicable deeds for the greater architect."

With each word Mary felt Polidori's arm flex under the sleeve of his frock coat as he guided her along the walk. "So your observations have recognized a second involved in the crimes?"

"Yes, but the second has clearly been influenced, manipulated."

"Created?"

"Yes . . . created by the first to continue the original's desecration and disregard for life."

"Do you surmise the second man knows he is being molded in the image of his . . . in the image of his 'father'? That he is being shaped by whatever subterfuge or device to carry out the elder's wishes?"

"That I do not know. How can one tell what another man is thinking? His words may indicate one direction while his thoughts travel another. His hand may be beguiling, but it may also strangle the life from those who meet his needs."

"I see what you mean." They continued their constitutional around the bay, a large magnolia on the promontory their intended destination. "I cannot but think of the people who associate or converse with these wretches on a daily basis—spouses, parents, servants, acquaintances. Lovers. There must be those who ignore the clues being continually thrust before them. Yet they are oblivious that their loved one has the most evil of intentions. They push all indications aside, disregard obvious signals and suggestions of malevolence. They may be aware of conspicuous truths, and yet they are blinded."

"They are unaware of what they are aware of."

"That is my thesis, precisely. It is a superficial awareness they dare not look at too closely in case the true horror of fact should surface and become unavoidable."

They came to the magnolia, its magnificence stunted by the miserable summer weather. Its flowers had failed to bloom, and instead it was covered in desiccated buds that had not even the energy to fall to the ground. They sat upon a bench beneath the tree's broad canopy for many minutes, gazing out at the water, nodding to the other tourists who had followed their route.

"Does the creature in your story follow this supposition? And the girl, what of her? Will she become aware of his true objectives and survive to your last drop of ink?"

Mary stood with a mischievous but thoughtful smile.

"Come, Polidori. We must find a salon to take tea."

CHAPTER FIFTY

A harsh knock sounded on the front door of the studio.

Rachel pushed the twisted sheet from her body in sleepy confusion, wondering what time it was. She wasn't expecting anyone, and she tried to recall if she'd yet paid her rent to month-end. The morning sun shone in through the terrace doors. She checked the clock: 6:15 a.m.

"Coming." She was annoyed as she picked up her bathrobe off the floor, slipped her arms into the sleeves, wrapped the material around herself, and tied the sash. She ran her fingers through her hair and looked back at him on the bed. He was still fast asleep, with one foot and one hand flopped onto the floor. The flimsy sheet did little to disguise his nakedness. She wanted to crawl back in with him.

The knock sounded against the wooden door frame a second time. "*Pardonnez-moi—un moment,*" Rachel called as she picked up several items of clothing and threw them out of view from the entrance. She pulled her fingers through her hair again, then stepped forward and opened the heavy oak door a few inches.

Detective Baertschi stood outside with both feet planted on the marble stoop and hands clasped behind him. A ripple of relief crossed his face, soon replaced by a sternness and a narrowing of the eyes. A *gendarme* rushed across the internal courtyard toward the studio, and a second stood under the *porte cochère* with the manager of Châtelard. They stopped their conversation to look toward Rachel's studio.

"*Mademoiselle* Walton." The detective looked Rachel up and down through the slim view that the partially opened door allowed. "I see you have survived the night."

"What?"

"Though your cheek and right hand are bruised." He was silent for several seconds, watching her movements and expression as she looked down at her hand and then raised it to her cheek, still tender from the assault last night. "I think you need to let me in so that I might hear your side of the story."

"I'm sorry, but this isn't a convenient time."

"No, *mademoiselle*, it is I who am sorry, as I did not make myself clear. Please open the door and step back into the apartment." He motioned with his hand to the *gendarme*, who ran to the far end of the courtyard and around the building, presumably to the terrace on the outer side of the studio.

"Please, just a moment, let me get ready." Rachel started to close the door.

The detective stuck a heavy riding boot between the door and the jamb. He slapped his hand against the oak and pushed it forcefully open. Rachel fell back into the small entrance corridor of her studio as the door slammed against the wall, and the detective strode past her and into the main room. Her bed was in disarray, clothes lay scattered across the floor, and dirty plates and glasses littered the kitchenette.

But the room was empty—he wasn't there.

Baertschi jerked his head back and forth as he surveyed the scene. He took the two steps to the bathroom and kicked the door open. It banged into the side of the bath.

The tiled space echoed in emptiness.

The *gendarme* who had been with the manager rushed into the studio, unclasping the holster of his firearm. He raced toward the door to the private side courtyard. The detective stepped to the other edge of the door and flipped the lock. He threw the door open and the *gendarme* lunged through it, his firearm drawn. It took less than an instant to see the court was empty.

A third *gendarme* now appeared at the terrace doors. He peered through the glass, caught the detective's eye, and then marched to look over the edge of the terrace. He stood there for a long time, peering down into the vineyards and presumably toward the close proximity of Cimetiere de Clarens.

Rachel followed the detective and *gendarme* into the main room of the studio, afraid and confused and angry. She wondered where he'd gone, and why. She looked at the clothes strewn across the tiles—his were no longer among them. She looked to the dresser where he liked to place his Patek Philippe when he took it off. The space was bare.

"What are you doing? Why are you doing this?"

Detective Baertschi stepped to the center of the room and looked down at the sheets, crumpled and thrown from the bed onto the floor. He took two short, sharp sniffs of the air.

"Were you alone before we arrived, *Mademoiselle* Walton?"

"Umm . . . yes." Rachel was hesitant, still looking around, uncertain.

The detective then ignored her as he moved around the room, inspecting every item, rubbing his hand against his chin and mouth, his attention flicking from glass to shirt to plate to sheet to trunk . . . to terrace doors.

The doors were locked from the inside, as had been the door to the private court. He strode over to the bathroom once more and looked inside. He looked through the room's window and into the courtyard, then up the ivy covered walls that enclosed it.

"You are certain you were alone before we arrived, *mademoiselle*?"

She cleared her throat. "Yes."

"You had no . . . er . . . guest at any time during the night?"

"No."

Again he studied the bed, then peered at Rachel blankly. "May I see your passport?"

Rachel picked up her jacket off the kitchen table and extracted the passport from the zipper pocket. The detective flipped through its pages, glancing at her when he saw her photo, then flipped through the rest of the pages and turned the passport to and fro to read the stamps.

"You haven't been to Germany? To Ingolstadt?"

"May I ask what this is about?"

"Please, just answer my questions." He motioned for her to sit down at the table.

"No, I haven't been to Ingolstadt. I have never been to Germany."

"Never?" The detective placed the passport in his breast pocket. "This will be returned to you when I am satisfied you are not involved." He patted the lump the document made.

"Involved in what?" Confusion, fear, and anger warred within her. "What is going on?" Rachel couldn't look away from his breast pocket, knowing her right to leave the country was secured beneath the weave.

"*Mademoiselle*, this situation will become clearer if you tell me your movements since you left the police station this morning. Tell me exactly—but take care, as I do know when you are lying." He thumped his open palm down onto the table. Rachel saw, or imagined she saw, the flash of a smile across the face of the *gendarme* who monitored her conversation with the detective.

"I was mugged. I was going to come into the station this morning to report it. A man in the cemetery—he pushed me down and stole my bag. I got a good look at him."

The *gendarme* shrugged a slim, black leather backpack from his shoulders and pulled the zipper open to fish out a large plastic envelope. "This bag?" He set the envelope onto the dining table and Rachel stared at it. Her satchel was inside. She let out a sigh of relief.

"My laptop is still in there," she said, knowing it was by the way the bag sat. She reached toward the plastic but the silence in the room stopped her. She withdrew her hands and pressed them into her lap, suddenly very nervous.

"His name was Juergen Epple."

"He was a pig," Rachel said.

"Was?"

Rachel furrowed her brow as the detective pulled his phone from his pocket. "Is this the man who attacked you?" He turned his phone around so she could see the photo on its screen.

Dark-haired, hazel-eyed, broken-nosed. She could smell his hands—the smell of pig. "Good, you caught him." She continued to stare at the photo, and the image burned into her eyes until she became aware what she was looking at.

His cheeks were bruised and bloody.

His once-broken nose was broken again—crushed—irreparable.

The skin was ripped from his chin.

His eyes stared, not in the frozen flash of a photo but in response to an unexpected end, awaiting the respectful touch of a coroner to close them.

"He's dead." Even Rachel wasn't able to discern whether she'd uttered a statement or a question.

Detective Baertschi glanced at the photo before placing the phone back into his pocket. "I will ask you one last time, *mademoiselle*. Think about your answer very, very carefully—very carefully. During this night just passed, was there another in your company?" He placed his hand upon the lid of the walnut trunk.

Rachel kept her eyes on the detective's chin, not daring to look away in case her gaze drifted toward the bed, toward the rumpled sheets, toward the trunk and the secrets it held, toward his large muddy boots that lay askew behind the front door.

She could sense him in the room, sense his hands, mouth, and tongue upon her. She could smell him—his sweet, heady fragrance of musk and sweat. She could taste him on her lips. She could feel him within her, one with her.

"No, detective," she said at last. "I was alone."

CHAPTER FIFTY-ONE

Mister Percy Bysshe Shelley
The Hotel de l'Union
Chamonix-Mont-Blanc
France   *July 1816*

My darling romantic; my lyric Bysshe,
I was so pleased to receive your correspondence this morning, just as I have been every morning since our parting. I trust your adventures in the Alps continue to be thrilling and that Lord Byron is not enticing you into too much danger. Please give our regards to George and remind him daily that you are mine. (Please also hint to him to write more often to Doctor Polidori. Though they are both men of the world and traveling their own paths, John is never more happy than when he holds the prose of Lord Byron in his hands, his lips caressing their eloquent beauty.)
Your previous letter detailing the climb to Mont Blanc's summit has been enjoyed immensely by all who reside here at the villa. We've been thrilled by the vivid descriptions of the Alps and valleys, the cathedrals of nature soaring higher and with more majesty than man could possibly construct, encrusted with the wind-chiseled drifts of snow and ancient frozen glacial waters that creep from the Mont's summit down through crevice and crag to the valley floor and the environs of Chamonix itself! I read your words aloud after supper last evening, then handed the letter around so that all might see your splendid handwriting and envision your escapade over their port and cigars. The younger men have all vowed to follow your footsteps up that glacial terrain. I am so proud of you, my darling.
Polidori continues to work with the gendarmerie on the situation here. His schedule is quite erratic. Often he is with me throughout the day with no word from the authorities, only to be disturbed from his bedchamber in the middle of the night and taken to inspect and report on some poor soul found in a desolate lane, muddy gutter, or decaying outbuilding. Other times I have gone a complete day without his company, relying on Willmouse,

Claire, and my books and writing for entertainment. (My ghost story has progressed well in Montreux—a few short days more and it will be complete.)

I was able to catch a brief conversation with Polidori this morning. It seems the gendarmerie have been alerted to a chalet up in the Hauts-de-Montreux. There are suspicions that it is intimately involved with the score of desecrations and murders of the past months. I am hoping John returns to the villa before I retire this evening—it would be comforting to know the wretch behind these deeds has been secured and is no longer a threat to this otherwise peacefully beautiful Riviera town.

Now, my darling, a conversation with Polidori from last night has me thoughtful and intrigued. I will relay it to you here in full as best my memory serves me, as I value your opinion on these matters.

It started at the supper table. The chef had just scraped ample portions of raclette onto our plates, and the sommelier had poured an exquisite Savoie wine. Claire was engaged in an important tête-à-tête of her own while I was between a matron, who prefers no conversation while she eats, and Polidori, who seemed particularly silent and fidgety. He drummed his fingers against the tablecloth, then stroked the stem of his glass, then realigned the cutlery so it was all exact.

"Doctor Polidori?" I whispered. "You seem worried."

He glanced sideways as he skewered his potato and cut it precisely and efficiently, almost surgically, into small bite-sized chunks. Before he lifted his fork to his mouth, he said, "I keep thinking about the girl."

"The woman found in—"

"Yes, that girl." He cut me off as he caught the eye of the matron beside me. "I cannot fathom how she fits into this . . . this story." He gave the matron a courteous nod.

Sensing she was extremely interested in a conversation that had not even started, I followed Polidori's premise so as not to alarm the matron with the details of the girl found murdered in the cemetery and the horrors that are a part of our everyday deliberations. "Perhaps the . . . author's vision could no longer be satisfied solely by male . . . characters."

"But logically," Polidori said, "if you and I are to continue on our original conjecture—that the parts of the many will make up the one—the single perfect one—then why would the woman be required? Surely the author's lust would have been satiated by the bodies of the men, and therefore no woman would be necessary."

The matron let out a short, sharp, shrill gasp that caught the attention of all at the dining table. I turned and fanned her with my napkin as she had turned a bright scarlet—definitely from our conversation, and not the gherkin she avidly blamed afterward. The sommelier poured her more wine, and she imbibed it in a hefty gulp. She patted her abundant décolletage and assured us all of her good health, begging everyone to return to their supper and conversation. I noted how she moved her chair a few inches closer to mine as she resettled herself and asked the chef to scrape more raclette onto her plate.

"Do you not think, Polidori, that any good story must have both strong male and female protagonists to come to a successful conclusion?" I asked.

"Perhaps. I do not know. I myself would have remained more than satisfied if only men had been involved." A fork clattered to the floor beside me, and the matron made several apologetic noises. I could not suppress a slight smile, but then Polidori went on. "Bringing a woman into the story at this stage can have but one purpose . . ."

It was three hours and several courses, followed by my reading of your letter and the consumption of port and cigars, before it was convenient for Polidori to complete his sentence. We had strolled about the garden and now sat on the edge of the Diana fountain.

". . . and that is sexual."

I thought about the context. "The girl found in the cemetery—she was strangled and bludgeoned?" I asked in confirmation of a previous conversation. Polidori nodded. "And what was missing again?"

"The frontal lobes of her brain had been incised and removed."

"And what else?" He shook his head, but I now know our gentle friend too well—it was easy to see he was withholding. "There is something more, isn't there?" I asked as softly as I was able. He began to fidget. He pulled a cigar from his frock coat, clipped off the end, and lit it. His cheeks puffed out as he took a drag, his mouth filling with the pungent smoke. The smoke escaped his lips to curl about the statue of Diana and wisp into the foliage at her back. "What else, John?" I repeated as he mellowed before me.

"I am afraid there are events in this case that I have not told even you, Mary."

"That is understandable, given the horror of these circumstances."

"I have only told you about the first woman."

"The first?" I suddenly realized the genre of our dialogue, but not the plot.

"Yes, there have been four in total over the last three days."

"Oh my." My mind went blank, but then I knew. "He needs a companion—he needs a bride. Of course he does," I muttered, more to myself than to Polidori, as my thoughts turned toward my ghost story and not the events sapping the life from Montreux. "Polidori, these women . . . please tell me of them. I think I must know their circumstances—not only to comfort you and the anguish I see in your demeanor, but also to know and protect myself. Please tell me."

"Very well. The first in the cemetery you know of. Victoria was petite and pretty, but it was not the external presentation that drew our adversary toward her. The detective in charge of the case informed me that she was thought of as intelligent, well read in the sciences, and astute in the management of a residence. All her sisters had married well and kept their intellectual husbands amused and under control. As you know, a portion of her brain was removed.

"The second was Adelaide, a governess recently arrived from Zurich to tend to the children of a wealthy merchant whose wife had died with the birth of their last child. Investigation discovered that Adelaide had trained for over a decade in ballet. She was lithe and very, very strong. This young girl's legs and arms were cut from her torso, her body discarded on the rocky shore of Lake Geneva.

"Which brings us to last night. I was again woken from my slumber by a hand pressed upon my chest. At first I thought it a dream and was quite content to allow it to play out, but then caught the pleasant waft of breath and knew someone was truly with me in my chamber and not some apparition of sleepy imaginings. I opened my eyes to see the young Gendarme Jaecar who has escorted me these last weeks. He led me down to the porte cochère where we mounted steeds and rode off into the night, as he expected the terrain would not be adequate for a carriage. We ventured up through the Haut and deep into the forestation covering the lower Alps. I did not understand the gendarme's pronunciation of the hamlet name, but suffice to say it was a quaint situation of no more than five chalets, where all occupants were related by one manner or another. The lights of the chalets blazed and I could see people milling about through the unshuttered windows, wringing their hands in worry or sobbing against a relation's breast. I myself was choked by a sob without being aware of the cause.

"The gendarme led me to the chalet on the farthest edge of the hamlet. He placed one hand on the door and another on my shoulder as he whispered, 'Docteur Polidori, ils étaient des jumeaux. They were twins—twin girls.'

"I could see the dread in his eyes, could feel the shake that passed from his hand to my shoulder. I grasped his hand in empathy and nodded my understanding before proceeding into the small wooden abode.

"The inside of the home was brightly lit, though there was no sign of parents, spouses, or siblings—just the detective and gendarmes on the case. I surmised the family members had been moved to a nearby chalet to grieve their loss. The home was one large room—barn-like—with sleeping alcoves curtained off below, and a loft above reached by a simple ladder. The detective leaned over the edge of the upper level and motioned for me to accompany him. I climbed the ladder with my bag, wary of what I would soon confront. The higher I climbed, the more aware I was that the twins were up there, the sweet smell of fresh blood almost overpowering my senses.

"I could never, however, be prepared for what I was to see. As my eyeline rose to the upper floor I saw a bare foot—elegant, diminutive, and attractive. Then a second. A third. A fourth. Their legs lay askew across the mattress on the floor, devoid of connecting torso.

"Next I was aware of arms—gracefully slender arms, hands, and fingers—excised and stacked neatly in the corner between two large beams that held the roof aloft.

"One torso had been removed from the room completely, no sign of it within the chalet. The other had been sliced open, major organs stolen, skin peeled back from the redundant muscle and absconded with.

"Their heads . . . well . . . I will not hide that the detective and myself shared many tears as we crouched in the loft amongst the remains of the twins. The girls had once been very beautiful. Strangely . . . they still were."

Polidori puffed on his cigar. I sat beside him upon the fountainhead and watched in silence as his succor glowed in the darkness, as it inched less and less, the radiant head moving closer and closer to his lips. There was no way I would disturb his reverie, the subtle solace in the thickness and heat he held between his lips and teeth. We sat, both lost within our own thoughts, even after the parlor light was extinguished and we were left in the comforting darkness of night.

My dear Percy, I agree with Polidori's observation that the purpose of these latest murders can only be sexual. No matter how deviant, to desecrate or kill someone of the same sex is one matter. But to then transfer those desires and actions to the opposite sex, to so avidly touch the flesh of another gender in such an intimate fashion, to explore and choose, select and maneuver, cut and take . . . there is something immorally inspired, something obscenely sexual in this most basic, physical urge toward creativity, toward survival by whatever means possible.

I must finish now, my darling, that my letter might make the morning service to Chamonix. We will continue our discussion tomorrow.

Love, as always,

Your Mary

(Kisses from Willmouse.)

Post Script: There is a grand supper to be held at Château de Chillon this coming Saturday. Polidori has agreed to escort me in your stead. Don't be jealous, my dear. (George, however, is allowed to be.)

CHAPTER FIFTY-TWO

Rachel pulled her bathrobe tighter around her, uncomfortable that the detective and *gendarme* were still in her studio, surreptitiously looking around for indication that anyone, that he, had been there.

"*Mademoiselle* Walton, I am surprised at the calmness with which you accept this information."

"Am I supposed to feel sorry that this pig received his just deserts? He must associate with his own kind, and they decided his time had come."

"I think you may speak too hastily. I think perhaps you are ignorant of what you are involved in."

"I'm not involved in anything."

"Are you not?"

"No."

Detective Baertschi walked over to the French doors, removed a handkerchief from his pocket, and wiped it across one of the panes. He peered out over the terrace at the *gendarme* who continued to walk the pavement and make notes in his notebook. "*Mademoiselle*, do you recall the photos I presented to you at the station late last evening?"

Rachel nodded at the reflection of his face in the windowpane.

"I know you were acquainted with *Monsieur* Jack, and there were at least two others you knew by sight, if not in person." He turned to see her response, but she gave none. "The others you might also know by acquaintance—not as individuals in themselves, but perhaps by a means no other would recognize them."

"Look, I've already guessed they must have been organ donors."

The detective's eyebrows arched. "Organ donors? *Mademoiselle*, the very word donor implies giving—donating."

"Yes. So?"

"None of those men gave away what was rightfully theirs. In every case it was taken—*taken, mademoiselle*—without prior request or approval. Most appear to have been robbed while they lay in the morgues throughout the Vaud and the Valais. But in at least three cases the men were alive when the 'donation' was made. One of these gentlemen, just a boy of nineteen . . ." The detective looked thoughtfully out the terrace door. "His name was Rique Pascal. A promising athlete whose skill in rugby had caught the attention of the Stade Lausanne Rugby Club. Rique was a massively built youth whose dreams were ended by strangulation." He returned to sit opposite Rachel, who now visibly shook. She clutched both her hands together in her lap, attempting to stop the shudder.

"He had been practicing alone at night. It was not until the next morning that his body was discovered in the club changing rooms. The entire musculature and epidermis of his head and face, plus the inner workings of the jaw and tongue, had been surgically scalped from the skull and facial bones."

Rachel's mind flashed to the photos falling from the back of his book of Milton. One of the photos had made her smile—the young man's scruff of hair sticking up at an odd angle. He'd been handsome, though. Another in a striped rugby shirt had reminded her of him. He'd had the same thick facial features, but gray eyes. A brother, she'd guessed. *No, not a brother,* she now thought.

The detective's words cut through her, jamming shards of Mary Shelley's creation into her mind, slicing precious portions of muscle and bone from the world she'd built while in Montreux, stripping the unblemished flesh from the face and body of the one she loved to reveal what lay beneath, incising and hacking parts of *Frankenstein* from the nineteenth century and transplanting them into her own.

And then she could only think of him.

Her thoughts skimmed along his skin, followed the curve and ripple of muscle, hesitated on smatterings of body hair—gold here, brown there, darker above the neckline—lingered at the finely crafted web of scarification that circled every joint. Some parts of his skin were so pure, so unblemished, so beautiful it didn't seem real, as it stretched across his pectoral muscles, as it clung to the recesses of his abdominals and fullness of his buttocks, as it crept beneath the golden hair covering his forearms and up to his biceps with the serifing ink of . . .

"Jack!" Rachel blinked and brought the detective back into focus. "Was Jack murdered? Did someone kill him?"

Detective Baertschi's face softened. He started to reach across the table but then stopped, dropping his hand to the surface between them. A broad gold wedding ring on his finger shone from years of affectionate rubbing. "We were alerted to the case of *Monsieur* Jack by the Chicago Coroner's office. As is their policy regarding deceased Americans returned home from abroad, the body was quarantined and autopsied, his identification confirmed. The cadaver was severely damaged due to the motorcycle accident, however when they compared their findings to those of the Vaud Morgue, they discovered a substantial discrepancy."

Rachel's view of the detective was blurred by tears. She reached out and grasped his hand, comforted by the solidity of the wedding band beneath her loose grip.

"*Monsieur* Jack's arms had been removed at some point between the original autopsy here in Montreux and his arrival in the United States."

The detective's words blurred until they were unrecognizable. Rachel thought of hugging Jack as tight as she could as they sped along the autoroutes of the Valais, of pressing her cheek into the warmth of his leather jacket, of afternoons sipping wine on the shores of Lake Geneva, of the nights and weekends lying naked in his arms. His arms—the magnificent art of the tattoos that scrolled about his biceps: the tree of life, the tree of knowledge. *"I must have admired . . . I must have loved Jack very much to copy his tattoos,"* he had said. Yes, that was what he had said. But he hadn't copied them. He'd only added to them, had only allowed the branches of the trees to grow further, to cover and entangle with the lines that had created him, to become one with the surgical lineage of creativity . . . of life, of knowledge.

"So, Jack wasn't murdered. It was an accident. It was after the first autopsy that his arms were removed to create . . . that they were removed for whatever reason?"

The detective nodded. "We have kept the file open in case of further information during our investigation, but it does seem unlikely that *Monsieur* Jack's death was anything but an accident." He placed his other hand over Rachel's. "If you will forgive me my questioning, I see that you are still upset by the death of your friend, but you seem less than perturbed regarding the desecration of his body."

Rachel was silent for many moments, the memories of the last year overlaying each other, twisting, entwining, melding into one.

"I lost Jack on a road up in the Alps. I lost someone who was much more to me than the sum of his body parts. If you must know, Detective Baertschi, I loved Jack and I still do. And I'm certain he would be more than glad to know that, even in death, he was able to assist the life of another."

CHAPTER FIFTY-THREE

Mary pulled her document trunk across the desk to better view its contents by the light of the window. The clear morning promised a pleasant day ahead. If Polidori was not called off by the *gendarmerie*, she was determined to rent a cabriolet and explore the hamlets of the Haut above Montreux.

She extracted the skeleton key from the carved filigree emblem of the trunk and inserted its bow into the slim gap above with an audible click. She turned the shaft until it fell free and the two smaller keys were exposed, then inserted them into the almost invisible holes in the top front corners. Mary felt the click-click-click of the lock's inner workings, as the bolts jerked across distinct furrows within their wooden and metal casings.

And then both keys would turn no more.

Mary placed her fingers on either side of the trunk lid and urged it open. It moved without a sound.

The inside of the lid was covered in brilliant red, raw silk. The inner tray held several pieces of unused paper she kept for her letters to Percy. She ran her fingertips over the parchment and sniffed at the scent of lavender rising into the air. After lifting the tray and setting it onto the desktop, she flipped through the envelopes of correspondence from recent weeks and lay them against the front face of the trunk. She opened the small wooden box containing her quills and nibs to confirm she would not need to order more from Geneva and then, satisfied, she turned her attention to the second that had lain hidden beneath her letters.

The rosewood box had been a gift from her mother, and Mary had long imagined the Far East-style carving on the lid to be the scales of a dragon who lay otherwise unseen, its intentions unknown. She slipped her nail under the clasp.

"Mary, darling, I hope you don't mind if I do not breakfast with you and Polidori this morning. I have promised Mrs. Porter-Smith I would accompany her daughters to a petite salon in Clarens—a lovely garden terrace on the lakeside, not more than a few minutes' stroll along the lake walk. Word is, they have the best breakfast baguettes and crepes." Claire swished through the suite to the front door, pulling her shawl about her shoulders and giving a cursory glance into each of the three mirrors along the way to ensure her ribbons were even, her hair neat, and her white morning dress fell perfectly from her shoulders to her ankles. "Do I not look like a Grecian goddess, my dear sister?"

"Nothing less than Zeus's creation of Pandora. Do let me know if you cross paths with Prometheus."

"Prometheus? Was he that handsome young man in the green frock coat last evening?"

Mary smiled. "Never mind. Will you join Polidori and myself on our tour of the lower Alps if the weather holds?"

"No, no, no. Please go without me. I have way too much conversation to consume before my head is allowed to rest upon my pillow this evening. Plus, I am determined to teach at least three nursery rhymes to Willmouse." The suite door closed and Claire was gone.

Mary's thoughts returned to the contents of the rosewood box: a single envelope with a letter within, words ripping across the parchment, heavy dots and slashes scratched by an emotional hand. She held the box a moment more before flipping the clasp closed and placing it back into the bottom of her trunk. She spread her correspondence over it until it was again hidden from view.

The letter horrified her beyond anything she had ever known or even imagined in the worst of her nightmares or waking dreams.

* * * *

Polidori flicked the reins as they approached the steeper incline of the lane. The mare obediently increased her pace, pulling the cabriolet up the rise and onto the next plateau toward a small hamlet of chalets.

"They are so wonderful, Polidori. So rustic," Mary said. The chalets angled about them, their wooden exteriors dark with age; their shutters brightly painted red, blue, and green; their tiled roofs heavy with lichen and small flowering plants. "Look at the shape of tulips cut into the balustrade. Such a beautiful hamlet. Such a magnificent country." She placed a hand on his arm to draw his attention from his inner thoughts toward the beauty about them.

Polidori nodded in subdued happiness as he nudged the mare and cabriolet along graveled lanes, through magnolia groves, across streams bubbling with the melted snows from the upper reaches of the Diablerettes, and through fields wild with flowers. Their cabriolet crested a hill to expose the valley embracing Villard-Sur-Chamby. It was intimate, surrounded by steep hillsides still topped by a smattering of snow and covered by clouds that promised another deluge of rain by late evening. The cabriolet wove down through laneway after laneway, passing hundreds of cattle and antique barns that must have sheltered their ancestors for many generations. As the morning and noon wore on, they ambled their way into the deep valleys above the Hauts-de-Montreux.

Mary motioned toward the valet who balanced on the rear platform. The doctor pulled the cab onto the curb by a tavern. The rambling building seemed to anchor a score of fine chalets, barns, and determined hovels. He gave the valet several francs and said, "My good man, have yourself a hearty lunch and ale. I will be taking the lady about the village and nearby fields so she might view its pleasures. We shall luncheon within the hour at the hotel salon. You may attend to your animal and cabriolet at that time."

The valet nodded and jumped over the mud, onto a clump of grass, and through the door of the tavern.

Polidori took the cabriolet on a roundabout course through the wooded trails of Foret de Jor. They passed estates that sparked the romantic, meandered through groves and along streams that enchanted the imagination, stopped amongst herds of cattle to be enamored by the symphony of their bells.

They came to a stop in a lane that at first appeared isolated but that, Mary concluded, was perhaps a single minute's stroll from the center of Les Avants. Immense trees lurched from either side to create a canopy that would halt even a torrential rain. Light shone into the graveled tunnel from both ends to create a space that was surreal. Mary smiled at Polidori as she became lost within the sublime landscape.

But then she noticed Polidori's sad, lifeless eyes. He did not return her smile but instead looked through her. She followed his line of sight to a neat lane, a tidy gate, a drive that went no more than two paces before it turned into a circle around pleasantly clipped shrubbery. Beyond was a two-storey villa, perhaps a little dilapidated but still pretty and comfortable. All the shutters were pulled to, except for a single window downstairs on the left. The main door was shut, the stoop and front stairs scattered with leaves.

A *gendarme* wandered from the side of the villa and took his position by the front step. He peered out at the cabriolet in the laneway containing Doctor Polidori and Mary. He must have recognized the doctor, for he tipped his hat in their direction before making himself comfortable beneath the cover of the entrance porch.

"Is this where you came last evening, Polidori?"

"Yes, it is the chalet . . . the villa."

The outer walls were covered from foundation to eave by broad wooden planks turned black by their history.

"It is connected to the murders?"

"Of that we have no doubt."

A dozen chimneys punctured the slate roof. Smoke fell from one, like the entrails of a slaughtered animal.

"Then you have located the fiend responsible?"

"No, not exactly."

A pergola covered with thick, twisted, ancient vines hung from one side of the building. It created a corridor that led toward darkness.

"I think I see someone looking out from the downstairs window."

"That would be the housekeeper. It was she who alerted the authorities."

The shrubbery in the center of the drive now appeared tortured. The gravel seemed cold, hard, and stained.

"Strange how a scene can appear one moment quite wonderful and the next foreboding. I am certain this may once have been a very happy place, but the thought of what has occurred here lodges a lump in my throat to constrict my breathing. And yet I do not know what occurred here. How odd." Mary could not look away from the murder house, eager to devour every intricate detail of its construction and ambiance, even as Polidori cleared his throat to relay his story.

"When I arrived with the *gendarmerie*, the ground floor and entry were ablaze with light. Lanterns had been placed along the drive and the garden, lighting every aspect of the grounds and buildings. All appeared as a phantom-white apparition in the otherwise pitch-blackness of the surrounding wood. Officers searched through shrub and foliage, two following dogs that pulled tight on their leads. I was escorted into the entrance lobby. A grand stair climbed beside a paneled wall to the balcony above. The walls, floor, and ceiling were of a dark, heavy wood. Even the chandelier was of the same weighty timber, its candles burnt down to black stubs. Two large oil paintings that adorned the walls had obviously gone many decades without a professional cleaning, the faces of past residents camouflaged beneath layers of tar. They were as black as the surrounding walls.

"Three senior officers and the detective in charge were listening to the housekeeper, *Madame* Ballard, in the study. She explained that one of the suites had been let for the last several months with rent paid for several months still to come. The tenant had recently been called away to attend to urgent personal matters in Geneva, but no correspondence or indication had been received of his intended date of return. *Madame* Ballard had been under strict instructions not to enter the rooms, as they contained valuable samples and equipment that might be damaged if she attended to her normal duties of dusting and cleaning. The tenant assured her he would maintain the continued civility of the rooms.

"Two nights past, *Madame* Ballard was awoken from her slumber by the scrape of furniture from the suite upstairs. She lay awake in her bedchamber for a repeat of the noise, but none occurred in the few minutes it took her to drift back to sleep. But then, a second sharp sound echoed throughout the house, and this time she jumped out of bed, pulled on her gown, and ignited her candle from the kitchen fire to climb the stairs and investigate. She pressed her ear to the door of the tenant's empty suite but could hear nothing. She squinted through the keyhole and, though she had a good view of the first chamber, there was no sign of movement.

"*Madame* Ballard was about to return to her own chamber when again she heard sounds from within. Again she peered through the keyhole and this time, she declared, she saw a ghost of beastly proportions lumbering through the room. The shutters had been closed, but a sliver of moonlight shone just so and struck across the beast's face, delineating a fractured grotesque that all but made her heart stop. She could only think such a wretch was a demon, a specter, a ghost, and immediately she ran down the stairs and through the kitchen and bolted herself into her chamber, where she spent a sleepless night in terror."

"Oh, the poor dear," Mary said.

"*Madame* Ballard did not unbolt her door until the sun had risen almost to noon. She had heard no noise for many hours, but still she imagined the horror to be standing in a dark recess or sitting behind her chair, ready for her to drop her guard. She lingered in the kitchen for almost an hour, not daring to move or breathe, willing only to listen, to silently sense, to enhance her awareness of any other who might be with her in the chalet, by the stair, outside the back door, in the entrance lobby, or waiting for her in the study.

"When she could bear it no longer, she ran from the kitchen into the rear garden, through a break in the back hedgerow, and across the field to the neighboring residence, where she banged on the doors and windows, yelling and pleading for entrance and protection.

"*Madame* Ballard was in a sorry state for much of the afternoon, talking in an incoherent gibberish that would not leave her until her terror had subsided. The neighbors called the local doctor and *gendarme* to attend to her distress. As the doctor administered the necessary salts and opiates, *Gendarme* Visser, who had maintained the peace in the village for more than forty years, took it upon himself to inspect the villa.

"The *gendarme* retraced *Madame* Ballard's steps through the field and hedgerow and into the kitchen. He halted there for several minutes, much as the housekeeper had, listening for any indication of the intruder. Though it was now mid-afternoon, the interior of the residence was still in darkness, the morning chore of pulling back the curtains and opening the shutters not attended to on this day. The kitchen fire, also lacking its usual attention, had almost extinguished but it did however allow the *gendarme* to light the wick of a lantern. He progressed through the downstairs rooms and corridors as silently as he was able, observing every situation and noting in his own interview, later on, that nothing seemed out of place.

"It was at the bottom of the stair, just as he was placing his boot on the first tread to climb, that he heard a ghoulish moan from the upper suites. 'Who goes there?' he called. The noise repeated—a distressing utterance, one of total bereftness and sadness, grief, fear, and loneliness. 'Show yourself!' *Gendarme* Visser demanded as he climbed the stairs, wary that his lantern could not reach into the darker recesses of the upstairs gallery.

He stopped on the seventh step from the top landing, his line of sight at floorboard level. The rug had been disturbed—twisted and rolled up at the corner to lie back upon itself—but none of the doors, chairs, tables, or pedestals seemed amiss.

"There was a heavy thud against the inside of the suite door closest to him. He climbed the remaining steps and could hear the fractured breathing of the wretch on the other side of the door—a deep and guttural breathing akin to a large animal, a beast. Visser was reminded of a bull, once vital and valiant in battle but that now lay defeated in the dust of the auditorium, the matador's spears thrust into its carcass and now shivering and jolting in its last movements of agony.

"Visser took another step, and the floorboard creaked.

"The wretch yanked the door open in a shattering tug and jumped upon him, enormous in stature, impressive in strength. He flung Visser into the air like a rag doll. Enveloped in the foul stench of decay, Visser glimpsed the utter misery of sunken, watery-yellow eyes, the gangrenous pallor of skin long tortured by grotesque scars, festering wounds, and coarse, bloody stitching. As the *gendarme* hit the floor, the fiend leapt over the balustrade to land in the downstairs lobby with a hefty thud. Visser heard the racket of the escape even as he slipped into an unconsciousness brought about by the pain of his injuries."

Polidori looked toward the sky. "Best we attend to luncheon so that we might complete our tour before the clouds burst." He nudged the reins, and the cabriolet pitched forward under the horse's strength.

"Yes, of course, doctor." Mary craned her neck to catch one last glimpse of the murder house. "How does the *gendarme* fare?"

"*Gendarme* Visser will recuperate. No broken bones."

"That is good. But what of this wretch, this intruder? How is he involved with the recent acts?"

The cabriolet pulled out of the canopied tunnel and into the open fields once more. Though the village was close, they would need to take a circuitous course of laneways to reach the promised luncheon. Mary was indifferent to the delay, as she hungered more for the ending of Polidori's story.

"The detective in charge and I remained by the mantle of the unusually-squat fireplace for a good hour, listening to the interviews of the housekeeper and *gendarme*. At last they were excused and the detective led me through the lobby and up the main stair, where I could not help but recall the *gendarme's* story and fix my eyes upon that terrible door—now a shattered ruin of wood. We stepped over the debris and into the room, and immediately the stench of death assaulted our nostrils. I will admit that, even with my training and what I have beheld over the last weeks, the odor was repugnant, vile, abhorrent in every sense of the word. We held our cravats to our noses as we progressed through the rooms, but the acrid bile of sickness hung about my throat and threatened to expunge any respect I may have garnered with the detective.

"And then we entered a second room through a door that hung askew from a ripped hinge. Instruments, vials, and jars of glass lay obliterated around the chamber. They had been struck to the ground in a rage, their chemicals and organic contents flung about and damaged. The detective motioned toward the detritus at our feet. A forearm with its hand closed in a loose grip lay beside my heel. A foot, partially dissected, lay broken beneath the shattered remains of the jar that once held it. A face, a second, a complete pelvis with its masculinity intact, a heart, liver, bladder, lung, brain, several eyes, another heart. I counted the souls: at least thirty-five separate and unique human beings—men and women—littered the floorboards, rugs, and furniture in varying stages of dissection and decay."

Mary placed her hand upon Polidori's in comfort. She noticed his did not quiver—he had somehow steeled himself against the dreadfulness of his current occupation. He gripped the reins, his strength giving her comfort. The cabriolet slowed to a stop at the side of the Les Avants Hotel, where the valet rushed toward them and slipped his hand under the horse's bridle. The doctor climbed from the carriage and then assisted Mrs. Shelley onto the pavement beside him. Mary stood a moment, arranging the folds of her gown and pulling her shawl about her as the cabriolet and horse were led to the livery at the rear of the hotel.

"Tell me, Doctor Polidori, for I feel I know this villa we have just viewed, that I am acquainted with the layout of the rooms and the contents contained therein. Tell me, was the suite you described tenanted by Doctor Victor Frankenstein?"

Polidori was incredulous. "Why yes, it was. But how could you know?"

CHAPTER FIFTY-FOUR

Rachel felt trapped within her studio despite the detective's assurances she was free to roam Montreux as she pleased.

She wanted nothing more than to go to the hovel in Sonzier and see him, to talk to him. To see if he'd hurt that pig who had attacked her. To confirm and reconfirm what he recalled about his past, about his life before . . . Jack's accident.

Why had he run away this morning and left her alone to confront the *gendarmes*? Didn't he trust her?

When the detective had left her sitting in her disheveled bathrobe at the small dining table, he'd said she needed to trust him and the other *gendarmes*.

And no one else.

For many hours she'd sat there, confused, her thoughts and memories of the last several months playing over in her head, becoming one with her research into Mary Shelley, her own story no longer hers alone but intermingled with the very subject of her passion. Or was it just her imagination? Just as Mary had created her monster through keen observation of the world around her, surely Rachel's own thoughts and conclusions had been tarnished, pushed toward the absurd, toward something that could only be possible in fiction. Science fiction. Science . . . fact?

Did Mary open the box that would lead to the future Rachel now believed was hers?

It made her head ache.

She stepped out onto her terrace to let the breeze from the lake hit her face, but withdrew inside again when she saw the distinctive color of a *gendarme* uniform at the corner of the building. She glanced out the front door of her studio, urged it open less than a finger's width, and spotted the second *gendarme* on the far side of the *porte cochère*, wandering the Terrasse d'Honneur. She closed the door and went to sit at the table once more. She sat there, her bathrobe no longer held tight around her but allowed to fall as it might, while her thoughts dove deeper and deeper. When she next became aware of her surroundings, she was in the bathtub looking down at her body through the luxuriant warm water, the skin fresh and freckled, no sign of scar or even wrinkle where hand met forearm, where arm met shoulder, where thigh met pelvis. She ran her hands through the water, across her skin, sensing how alive she felt, and how dead she would feel if she lost him.

The faucet dripped, and a fat, cold drop of water fell into the tub.

She thought of him hunkered down, naked in his shower, covered in blood, holding his head in the agony of one of his migraines. The showerhead spraying him, blasting drops of water against his skin, splashing the blood away to reveal the pure flesh beneath. She recalled his frantic efforts to expunge the blood from himself, flicking and scrubbing it from his body to be washed down the drain with all it intimated.

"It was a rabbit," he'd said.

"It was a rabbit," Rachel had told herself again and again.

Once, while they'd shopped the Saturday markets in Montreux, he'd let go of her hand and grasped his head so forcefully she knew a migraine had struck him like a shock of electricity. Pain contorted his face, made the veins at his temples flush fat with blood, tinting his skin blue. She had rushed into an apothecary to buy him some remedy, but when she'd returned he was gone. It was several moments before she'd found him again, sitting on a bench, looking at the swans floating on the lake. He'd seemed confused when she'd offered him the painkillers—the migraine and the last few minutes of their morning cut from his mind.

She'd held his hand.

She'd thought about the rabbit.

And now, in the warmth of her tub, she thought about the youth whose hands smelled like pig.

When she had made it back to Châtelard after the attack last evening, he'd been there, drenched and muddy, on her stoop. But not bloody.

But he'd been there.

Long after all heat had left the bathwater, Rachel soaped and scrubbed and touched herself in a way she hadn't done in many years. She was fascinated by her body and the fact that she was alive. The fact that she was aware she was alive. And whether, by accident or evil, she might lose a foot, a leg, a hand, an arm, or a kidney, she would be no less alive and no less aware of who she was.

She wondered who he was.

For a moment it made her sad, for she knew he didn't know, that he was searching for something perhaps he would never find.

Rachel thought of the letters still unread in Mary's trunk. She wondered if they held the answer, some datum that might assist her . . . and him in his search. She pulled herself up out of the tub, wrapped herself in the bath sheet, and walked, dripping, out into the main room. She drew the sheers closed across the terrace doors and then sat before the trunk, patting her hands dry and slipping on protective gloves before she inserted the two secondary keys into their dual locks.

Click-click-click.

She dug through the letters she'd already documented.

The next was unaddressed. Unopened.

The sealing wax was melted and smeared without the indent of a seal. Closer review showed the original seal had been broken, the letter opened and then resealed in apparent haste.

Rachel extracted the envelope from the gaping maw of the ancient trunk and opened it as carefully as she could.

CHAPTER FIFTY-FIVE

July 1816
I know you write about me, about my life, about my creation.
I have heard your whispers, noted your observations, been aware of your gaze.
I know what you are thinking.
But I speculate whether you will learn the lessons that I have failed to.
I have read many books and studied with exceptional clarity to make my way in the world in which I live—in which we both live. I have trod in the footsteps of those who came before me but who refused to acknowledge the direction we walked. I have laughed in happiness and cried in despair. I have been tormented by worry, been driven mad by the unexpected, by the abhorrent.
By the wonderful.
I have seen the lightning play upon the summit of Mont Blanc. I have seen the vast sheets of fire that cross the night sky and plunge into the turrets of the fortress that floats upon the lake—such a beautiful, terrific tempest.
I have lost friends and family who have been very dear to me.
I have seen the figures of our history, of our own creation, supplicate in shame, lament their own existence and yearnings, fearful they desire that which their own creator says He did not create.
And yet their desires exist.
They are real.
Surely the creator of all is just that—the creator of all that we may desire, that we may yearn for.
Who is He to create an ache and then relegate those who long for it to a hell that He also must have created? Should not the creator be the one called evil, or is He good because He is the first, because He is the author who writes the rules by which all must follow?

To create a thought, a society, a world where a woman does not have the same rights as a man, and not all men hold the same rights as those who deem themselves above him . . . Whether fashioned by procreation, by science, by society, by wonder, or by ink, is not every woman a woman and every man a man? Regardless of how they recognize themselves by origin, gender, intelligence, or inclination, are they not deserving of whatever they settle their minds upon, whatever they create for themselves?

I have created something and let it loose upon the world.
Whether it was my right to do so or not, I cannot say. At times I am filled with love for my creation. At others I am filled with regret and horror.
But it is done. It has been created.
Mankind's judgement of me is now beyond my control—it has been thrown to the wind of discourse and conjecture.
You may argue that my creation is evil, a horror against the original author's integrity. But was it not driven to this conclusion?
Did it not start out pure, unadulterated, and willing to love and be loved? And yet, was it not shunned and vilified?
In all its beauty, in the beauty of any newborn, it was spurned and treated with hostility.
Of some of my actions toward my creation, I am remorseful, and at times I wish to seek it out, to follow its footsteps to the end of the earth, across the seas and ice fields to the very Arctic and beyond, if I must—to kill it, to dissolve it, to erase it from the pages of existence.
And yet I am unable to, for I know it now has a life of its own.
Beyond my own scientific tinkerings, meanderings, and writings, it has a life that will outlive mine by many generations—perhaps centuries.
And for that I am horrified, but also very, very glad.

CHAPTER FIFTY-SIX

Rachel read the letter a single time.
 She did not know who it was from, or who it was to.
 She would never read it again.

CHAPTER FIFTY-SEVEN

The luncheon salon within Les Avants-Sur-Montreux Hotel was wonderfully quaint. Blue and green wallpaper covered the rooms in a style so antiquated it appeared to Mary as revolutionary, a slap against the trends, a refreshing assault of the rational. It made her happy. The salon also afforded a view of the entire village and valley beyond. Streams fed into forestation, and Mary's mind wandered to discern their final destination. Herds of cattle meandered across the vista, bringing the simplistic joys of existence into a conversation too long reserved for the harsher elements of life and survival in this modern world.

Both Mary and Polidori had opted for the *Emince de Veau a la Crème*, but neither had expected the heady rush of shallots, garlic, and cream to consume both the tender cuts of veal and their senses so completely. Mary cut her veal into small succulent morsels with mature flavors, she surmised, that dear old England might never dare to experience, to taste, to hunger for.

Polidori licked his lips, savoring the dish that was only available upon the continent. He sat for many moments, eyes closed, attentive toward his food and innermost thoughts.

Mary watched and rejoiced in her friend's ecstasy, happy he was able to be who he was within her company—that he could be himself in this world so far from that which they dutifully, but perhaps regrettably, called home.

But the meal was a diversion, a much needed distraction from the horror that lingered nearby.

When the last of the cream and mushrooms had been devoured and Polidori's eyes had opened once more to view the real world, he asked his friend, "What do you know of Doctor Frankenstein?"

Mary was thoughtful as she settled her knife and fork upon her empty plate and lifted the small glass of kirsche to warm in her hands. She sniffed at the brandy liqueur as it matured in her grip, breathing and exulting in the succulence of cherries. She recalled the times she had seen Doctor Frankenstein—firstly in the bookshop and then in the salon and on the terrace of Châtelard. She reminisced on the words of *Monsieur* Aldini's eloquent correspondence, recollecting his horror and sadness as he invoked the tale of his friend: the sad news of the doctor's murdered young sibling; the strangulation of his dearest and most devoted friend, Mr. Henry Clerval.

She brought the glass to her lips and upturned it. Heat flowed across her tongue and down her throat in a luxurious exuberance.

"I have known of Doctor Frankenstein only by mutual acquaintance since my arrival here in Montreux. He appeared a pleasant, intelligent, and well-mannered gentleman, and I will admit I did seek to have dialogue with him, but circumstances did not permit."

Polidori emptied his own kirsche before indicating to the waiter to refill both their glasses.

"At first I was intrigued by his physical demeanor and confidence," Mary continued. "He held himself as any gentleman should and showed interest in the subjects I myself have studied. From my understanding, he was well respected by those both within and outside his circle. But there was more I did not understand . . . I detected a desire within him, or perhaps obsession is a more appropriate word. An obsession to pluck the apple from the tree of knowledge. To eat and consume that which was forbidden."

"The tree of knowledge of good and evil," Polidori reminded Mary.

"Of *good and evil*."

"Exactly. His attentiveness at *Monsieur* Aldini's lecture struck me as frenetic. Later observations confided to me by the *monsieur* served to compound my theory of the doctor's mania. But despite my assumptions, he at no time struck me as a man who would kill—only as one who was dedicated to an unknown cause. Intensely dedicated."

Polidori relaxed into the cushioned dining chair, his eyes closing so his thick lashes brushed against the tops of his cheeks, made ruddy by the kirsche. "The detective believes Doctor Frankenstein was more than capable of these recent events. The doctor was most definitely responsible for the desecration of those who were already dead. Evidence of that abounds within the rooms of the chalet. But because the man studied and worked so intimately with flesh that was already deceased, that could serve no further purpose than to be devoured by worms and maggots, it does not follow that he is capable of killing another. A doctor's purpose is to maintain life, and in my heart I believe that was the subject of his studies. However, he has doubtless led a life surrounded by death, which has thus placed him under much scrutiny from the authorities."

"Then he was suspect in the deaths of his brother and his friend, Mr. Henry Clerval?"

"No, not his young sibling—the doctor was here in Montreux at the time. He was, however, suspect in the murder of Mr. Clerval for several hours, but again it was proved without reservation that he was not in the vicinity. Both of the deceased were nevertheless murdered in the same manner—strangulation."

Polidori opened his eyes, shifted in his chair to correct his posture, then leaned forward to grasp Mary's hand upon the table. "The detective in charge has also informed me that a further murder has been perpetrated. This past week, Frankenstein married his sweetheart. On the night of their union, situated in a residence in Evian, just across the lake from here, his bride was taken from him and strangled."

"Oh! Dear Lord. That such calamity could plague one man to make his life such a misery."

"Witnesses confirmed the doctor's innocence again, but none could decipher his ramblings. He spoke as a madman as he described the wretch he said was responsible: uncouth in structure; misshapen in countenance; size, strength, agility, and speed far exceeding that of any mortal man."

"Exceeding mortal? Could this brute be the same that terrorized Frankenstein's housekeeper? Could he be responsible for the epidemic of murders surrounding the doctor and the environs of Montreux?"

Polidori furrowed his brow. "I do not know, Mrs. Shelley. All we are aware of is that Frankenstein swore vengeance and has not been seen since that night."

Mary studied the impeccably white tablecloth. Within its purity she saw the demon strangling Frankenstein's brother, his friend, and his bride, before she turned back to Polidori in horror to repeat his earlier words.

"The tree of knowledge of good and evil."

He held her gaze. " 'And as they had dared eat of its fruit, they were banished from the garden in shame and denied the tree of life.' "

CHAPTER FIFTY-EIGHT

Rachel placed the unaddressed letter back into the depths of the trunk. Her fingernails scraped across the indented details of the small rosewood box beneath, and for a moment she was intrigued at the design, which looked like the scales of a dragon.

She slipped her nail under the clasp that secured the lid but then stopped, uncertain, and let the box drop onto the layers of envelopes.

There was no doubt that the contents of the trunk belonged to Mary Shelley—that the correspondence, the fragile nibs in their case, the beautiful shawl with its empire design, all belonged to Mary. Rachel leaned over until her face hung within the plush, red silk confines of the trunk.

She could smell the faint sweetness of lavender.

For almost two hundred years the contents of this box had lain with little disturbance. Now she was severing its mysteries, dissecting its contents, categorizing its dispatches, shaping a being from the scattered remains of a life that could never truly be known and which, she surmised, could never be as vital as the original.

Did she have the right to completely expose, to desecrate the contents of the trunk? Or should some items within remain unread and unknown?

She sat at her dining table staring at the trunk for many hours until, finally, she crept into her bed and cuddled into the sheets.

She could smell him.

The room sank into darkness as the sun retreated to the west. It was pitch-black when next she stirred. The studio was an inky, indiscernible place, the ornate walnut trunk no more than a shadow within shadows. It, too, it seemed, had deserted her. She felt around in the dark and pulled on her jeans and top. It took several minutes to find her shoes, but soon she pulled them on and stood by the terrace doors, peering out into the night.

At the far end of the pavement, a cigarette glowed. The *gendarme* stood there for an interminable amount of time, the cigarette burning bright each time he drew on it. Eventually, he flicked it to the ground and stamped it out, only to follow by flaring up his lighter to start another. Rachel stood in silence, watching his every move through the glass pane.

He raised his hand as if acknowledging another and strode toward the end of the building and out of sight. It was all the time Rachel needed to undo the latch, slip through the door, and rush the full length of the terrace and down the stairs at its end. Crouching on the cold stone of the garden stairs, she looked back across the terrace. The *gendarme* returned around the corner of the fortress outbuilding, this time with another. They talked in whispers and smoked their cigarettes.

Rachel crept down the stairs to the lower garden and the path that would lead her to Sonzier.

That would lead her to him.

CHAPTER FIFTY-NINE

Polidori held out his hand to assist Mary up into the cabriolet. She placed her slipper onto the step, held tight to his grip, and lifted herself up onto the platform. Instead of sitting on the bench, she remained standing and tightened her grasp of Polidori's hand, staring at the vista.

The afternoon sun was far from setting; it had, however, fallen below the Alps surrounding the valley to throw it into deep green and purple variegated shadows. The pasture across the lane had been turned, the pungent aroma of cultivated soil overpowering and brilliant. Further afield, succulent grasses grew high to fringe the tops of ancient, ramshackle stone walls that had been built and rebuilt by farmers and vintners and landlords over the centuries. Mary suspected the valley had changed little since the time of the Savoys. The same stones, the same family lines, crops begetting crops, cattle begetting cattle. The buildings and chalets were perhaps more grand but still contained the remnants of the original homes and shelters at their very core.

Where the Alps thrust themselves up from the ground to define the valley's side, thickets of undergrowth and magnificent woods sprouted. The pleasant light that rippled across the valley floor and against the steep inclines toward the east dared not intrude into the woods, which enveloped themselves in a self-made blackness—a wooded blackness so impenetrable Mary felt a sudden shiver run through her body. Stories of wolves, of little Red Cap, of monsters, filled her mind.

"He's still here, isn't he?"

"You are referring to Doctor Frankenstein?"

"No. I am talking about the wretch, the demon. The creature who has tormented his creator and who is undoubtedly capable of the murders we believe the doctor is not."

"Mary, such a fiend would find it hard to hide from civilization and the authorities."

"He would find sanctuary within these woods. Secreted into some forgotten hovel, he may discover solace."

"Until the urge to kill comes once more."

Mary turned toward the copse of trees that snaked from the valley's edge to devour the nearby Frankenstein residence. The highest chimney pots were visible above the thick canopy. Her eye and imagination followed the magnolia- and wolf-filled wood down the valley to Sonzier and that pig sty, that disgusting hovel, that place of murder and desecration where the bodies of the young men had been subjected to unbearable horrors.

She thought of him huddled within its muddy confinement, his sad, watery-yellow eyes sinking deep into pale skin as decay, gradually but inevitably, ate away any semblance of physical beauty or mental integrity he might once have possessed.

Mary felt faint and had to sit upon the bench. Polidori jumped up into the cabriolet to steady her. "Mary?"

She gave an embarrassed smile. "I am fine, John. Too much kirsche. But still, my mind wanders, and I cannot help but think someone even now is being groomed and courted by the one who holds the apple of destruction before her."

CHAPTER SIXTY

Within fifty minutes Rachel had crossed the vineyards of Châtelard and the autoroute, climbed higher into the Haut along the *rues* of Chernex and Sonzier, and was now on the route that meandered toward his property. While walking the village streets, she had met the kind eyes of strangers and heard the soft melodies of simple life as people readied their suppers and evening entertainment.

Rachel had repeatedly looked over her shoulder, hesitated at intersections, and anticipated the flash of blue light or the sound of siren. When there'd been none, she'd run across the almost deserted roadways, slipped down alleys between chalets and shops, and walked through muddy pastures when a gravel road would have afforded a more direct course.

Heading deeper into the valley past Sonzier, she was now surrounded by open pasture on her left and dense forest on her right. She stopped at a water reservoir and sat upon its rustic wall. Staring into a glen filled with foliage and shadows, she wondered what she was doing. Why hadn't she told the detective about him? Why hadn't she been truthful? Surely there was nothing to hide, no evil to regret, nothing that she—or he—could be held accountable for. Does one blame the child for the sins of the father, blame the masterpiece for the indiscretions of its artist, or author, or creator?

A vast sheet of fire, of lightning, streaked across the sky. The clap of thunder almost instantaneous, the air taking on the taste of metal. The sky was darkening and stars were disappearing.

Rachel needed to hurry.

The route plunged into thick undergrowth so the few remaining stars were now obliterated from view. The lane became tight, the forest rising at an unclimbable angle on her left and falling away to the right. The drop was so sheer that the slim metal balustrading at the lane edge did nothing to alleviate her fear of falling into the stream far below.

She passed a small pasture that had been cut into the undergrowth. A single cow reviewed her movement. Its bell clanked once before the cow chose to ignore her in favor of chewing on its cud. Within several paces, she was at his gate. She climbed the wooden beams and jumped to the far side before running to the protection of undergrowth where the path twisted around its first corner. For several minutes she waited there for any indication of *gendarme*, for the knowing smile of Detective Baertschi. But all was quiet.

The night sky was soon pitch-black, lit by intermittent fragments of lightning and tossed by a gusting wind. Rachel was almost blind as she followed the drive around the edge of his pasture. She felt her way more by memory than by sight, knowing she was moving closer to his home, closer to his arms with every step. She imagined the glow emanating from the rear of his hovel and knew somehow they would work it all out, that they'd unravel the confusion.

She came to the tree that all but blocked the entrance door. She placed her hand upon its trunk, happy to see the crack of light beneath his door.

And then she smelled it.

She didn't move as she inhaled, allowing her sense of smell to determine all around her. She breathed silently but deeply, letting the salty sweetness envelope her.

The clouds above hadn't unleashed their threat of rain, and yet Rachel sensed her hand was wet and that the trunk of the tree was sodden.

Lightning lit the sky.

The tree trunk was saturated in blood.

The front door was saturated in blood.

Her hand was saturated in blood—blood that began to drip and ooze down her forearm.

A scream threatened to rip from her gut, but she bit her tongue and clasped her hands across her mouth to stifle the noise. She gasped, realizing she'd smeared blood across her mouth, across her face. Again she strangled the primordial shriek determined to engulf her.

"Stop it, stop it, stop it . . . Stop it!"

She wiped her hand against her jeans, her face wincing to halt the flow of tears.

"*Stop it.*"

Lightning flashed and again illuminated the blood. One line of splatter arced across the entire front of the hovel.

There was no sign of rabbit—no sign of the traps that usually hung on the wall.

And then the rain fell in a torrent. She was instantly soaked to the skin.

She pushed into his front door, determined to see that he was okay, that he was alive, that he was innocent.

Sauvignon blanc and rabbit stew. That was what she wanted, what she needed.

She swung the door open, knowing she would get neither.

CHAPTER SIXTY-ONE

Lightning struck across the full length of the Les Avants valley, coursing from the top of the Alps right down to Montreux and zigzagging about the lake to plunge into an unknown destination.

Twilight had been blotted out and it now seemed as if it were the middle of night.

"How quickly the darkest hour comes." Mary pulled her shawl about her and unfolded the carriage blanket to place upon her and Polidori's knees.

The valet pushed the hood of the cabriolet up and over the doctor and Mrs. Shelley before upturning his collar against the approaching inclement weather.

Polidori whistled and the cabriolet lurched forward into the darkness.

CHAPTER SIXTY-TWO

At first the lights would not switch on, and the interior of the hovel was left in a darkness barely lit by the glistening light of the kerosene lantern out on the deck. Rachel flicked the toggle up and down until the kitchen lights buzzed and flashed on. One of them blew with a loud pop. She looked around, her eyes wide, her face slackening in shame.

The shelves that ran the entire length of the studio had been ripped from the wall and now lay in pieces. One shelf had been smashed against the fireplace, shards of botticino marble broken from the mantle and scattered across the floor. Another had been splintered over his enormous bed, which itself had been upturned, the sheets pulled from it, the mattress cut open as if with a knife. The hundreds of books from the shelves lay strewn about the room, some of them open, their pages wrenched from their covers, others torn in half, their spines no match for the force that took them. Classics were scattered—*HAL* and *Emma*, ripped by the same hands that had shredded *Tess of the d'Urbervilles* and *Winston Smith*, *Tom Sawyer* and *Jesus*, *Othello* and *Mohammad*.

Rachel closed and locked the entrance door behind her and leaned against it, wanting but unable to close her eyes against the desecration.

Utensils, crockery, and wine glasses had been shattered against the kitchen floor. The contents of the pantry and fridges had likewise been searched and thrown to the ground—lettuce, onions, steaks, bratwurst. A dozen apples lay crushed among the sticky spread of milk and wine—red. Fragments of broken glass glistened.

No sign of rabbit.

Rachel moved nervously, her breathing labored, her attention flicking around his home. The gleaming blade of a knife caught her eye . . . the knife he'd placed on top of the shelf when he'd first brought her here.

She crouched to pick it up and gripped it firmly without knowing why, but knowing it was best she did. She brought it close to her chest and clambered around the shelves and over his lounge and bed toward the deck.

His smell pervaded the space—his musky, masculine, independent odor that told her without a doubt he was innocent of the detective's suspicions. That he was innocent of hers.

And then she saw him.

He was outside, past the deck, on the far side of the glen within the dense foliage of the surrounding wood. He was soaking wet from the rain. His shirt and jeans clung to him as if they were no more than his own flesh. The severe military cut of his hair shone and glistened. His chest heaved. His fists were clenched.

The branches and leaves above him fluoresced a pale tinge of blue, and then the sirens of the *gendarme* sounded in the distance, as if they reverberated down the lane, across the field, and through the wood.

He appeared angry and confused, standing among the foliage, glancing left and right.

Rachel's gaze locked onto his, and she wondered if this was all her fault.

The doors to the deck were open. The rain fell hard against the roof, and she stepped forward to balance on a bookcase, her hand pressing against the glass to stop her falling.

The repetitive blue flashing of the canopy above him became brighter still. He held out his hand. His skin shone in the rain.

"Rachel!" he shouted. "Do you trust me now?"

Without hesitation, Rachel screamed, "Yes! Yes, I do trust you!"

She scrambled over the wreckage and out onto the deck just as the heavy thud of a shoulder hit the front door of the hovel. At the same moment, the kerosene lantern fell from its branch and smashed to the deck, throwing liquid and flame across the wood and into the studio. Rachel stifled a scream as the flame leapt around her and across the literature and furnishings. Fire reflected in glass and shot through precious memories to consume days, weeks, and months of innocent happiness.

Strong arms embraced her from behind and lifted her from the deck, branches of trees brushing past her vision, the glimpse of blue *gendarme* uniforms at the far end of the studio, behind the escalating inferno. Flame exploded across the deck, reaching out into the glen to sizzle in the rain.

Her fierce horror faded into the undergrowth as he carried her tight within his arms, deep into the wood. But every branch, every trunk, every leaf reflected the glow of the intense fire they were leaving behind.

CHAPTER SIXTY-THREE

The cabriolet pulled over the ridge to the outskirts of Sonzier. The rain poured relentlessly and, despite the blanket and hood, both Mary and Polidori were thoroughly drenched. The empire shawl clung to Mary's arms as she attempted to pull it up to cover her dishevelled bangs.

"Would you care to take the comfort of rooms here, Mrs. Shelley?" Polidori wiped the water from his face. "We may wait out the torrent or, if need be, secure a residence for the night."

"No, John. We are almost home. Willmouse will be waiting and I would much prefer the warmth of my own bath and robe before the evening is . . ."

Mary squinted toward a fire in the wood not far from their transport. Giant flames leapt into the air, making the drops of precipitation sparkle a yellow halo around the heat of the source.

Polidori kept the cabriolet at as fast a speed as he dared in the wet conditions but he, along with Mary and the valet, craned their necks in wonder at the bristling glow in the woods. They passed the wagon of the fire brigade, the *gendarmerie,* and two score of robust men on horseback carrying torches that hissed and cracked in the rain.

"They will certainly handle it," Polidori said.

"Yes, of course."

But Mary's imagination refused to ignore the truth.

CHAPTER SIXTY-FOUR

He traveled more swiftly than Rachel had thought possible. His massive arms cradled her, and at times he used a single hand to hold her body close to his chest as the other pushed branches and dense brush from their route. He ran down forested ravines, leapt across brooks, and climbed steep hills, all without effort. His shirt smelled brilliantly pungent of rain and sweat. She could feel the blood coursing through his body as he ran, the thickening veins that crisscrossed the musculature stretching his skin to almost complete transparency. The increasing strength of his heartbeat appeared to make his flesh ripple, creating a hot, rhythmic energy that vibrated throughout Rachel's body.

He sidestepped a tree, passing her from one arm to the other with ease, before clambering up an almost vertical path. She wrapped her arms around his neck and pressed her face into the hollow below his jaw. He was breathing so heavily she knew she breathed only the air that had already passed through his lungs. She inhaled, holding him within her, savoring the moisture and warmth of his very being. She could taste him in her mouth, upon her tongue. Her lips were pressed against the skin of his neck. It was as smooth as it had always been, but now, slicked by sweat and emanating an almost scorching heat, it seemed utterly permeable.

Rachel felt she could melt into him and be a part of that which she loved more than she'd realized.

They broke into a clearing in the wood and he fell to the ground, gasping for breath, and rolled onto his back, pulling her fully into his arms and on top of him, his massive chest heaving beneath her body.

His eyes were gleaming. His mouth, opened wide to suck in as much air as possible, turned up at the edges in an exhilarated grin.

The excitement of the chase had made his entire body buzz electric. His skin prickled. Rachel ran her hand across his forearm and up over his wet sleeve before pushing her face once more into his neck and holding him as tight as she could. She lay there, her body rising and falling with his every breath, clinging to him as she attempted to make sense of what had just happened. His breathing slowed, and he ran his hands over her shoulders and down her spine to the small of her back.

"Are you okay?" he whispered.

Rachel pushed her lips close to his ear. "Yes, I'm good." She pulled back to stare into his eyes, into his soul.

"Good."

The rain beat down upon them both as they lay in the grass, surrounded by woods but paces from the cover of any tree. No matter. The rain was warm, luxuriant. It came in bursts, at once fierce, hard, and urgent and then gentle, caressing them with a lover's touch. It subsided until it was no more than placid, subtle drops, and then showered them with excruciatingly pleasurable force, driving them further into each other's arms. Their thoughts and lips touched, the faintest brush of their souls and flesh.

"Don't ever leave me," he whispered.

She exhaled, her eyes locked on his. The conversation needed no further words.

He rose from the grass and pulled her up and into the tight grip of his arms to move deeper into the forest than either had ever been.

And again he was running, down a steep drop and through a rocky streambed that soaked them no more than the incessant rain before. He jumped, barefooted, from rock to rock, at one point bounding over ten feet down through a falling stream, into waters cascading across boulders and fallen trees. Not once did he lose his footing.

Rachel could never question his inhuman strength and agility, as she had studied his origin for many months, many years, before she'd even met him, as she'd prepared to research, compile, and write the biography of Mary Wollstonecraft Godwin Shelley and her wretched creation. He was who he was. No matter his immediate creator, he was the offspring of none other than Mary herself—of the imagination, the concept, and the story she'd dared release from the box. Mary was the true modern Prometheus.

It must have been just before midnight.

The gully they'd been traversing now plunged under the broad concrete overpass of the Autoroute du Leman. Above them, cars and trucks sped past. Below them, the lights of Montreux sparkled.

"We should follow the autoroute. We should leave Montreux."

Rachel nodded up at the pylons that held the roadway high above them. The sides of the valley climbed to where the roadway shot into the Tunnel de Glion. Rachel tightened her grip around his neck and back, pressing her arms into his muscle, her fingers gripping the stretched material of his T-shirt.

He climbed the steep embankment, his feet and fingers digging deep into the dirt. They made it halfway up to the roadway before he fell face-first into the soil and foliage. Rachel was thrown with him, and the full weight of his body pushed her deep into the mud. He hefted his bulk outward and pulled her free before getting to his feet, his free hand grabbing at the branches of errant plants.

He lugged her to the roadway and lifted her over the barrier to place her onto the autoroute.

Vehicles shot toward them through the tunnel. Rachel clung to the soldered balustrade of the overpass as he pulled his torso and legs over and onto the roadway. She helped him to his feet, knowing she did little more than touch his skin as he lifted himself to his full height.

"Come on," he said, grabbing her hand.

They ran into the tunnel, sticking close to the side. The concave wall was painted white and slipped up into total blackness where it curved across the roof—except for the intermittent slash of fluorescent lighting that followed the full length of the tunnel. Car after car after truck flashed past them, their headlights blinding, their drivers bashing hard on their horns at the unexpected sight of pedestrians on the roadway where they had no right to be.

He kept his hand flat against her chest, pressing her close to the wall of the tunnel. They moved as fast as they could, stopping so he could protect her with his full body when convoys of trucks thundered by.

For several minutes they caught their breath within the confines of an exit door. She placed her hand upon the handle, but he shook his head, and she knew it was best not to take it in case it raised some kind of alarm.

Instead they continued, stopping at each safety door, wondering when they would reach the other end. They ran along the tunnel as it arced to the right for hundreds of yards until they passed the concrete embankment out into the open air.

Conifers and cliffs loomed on their left. To their right, a second autoroute held speeding traffic, and beyond that was the lake. It rippled in the torrential rain and glowed beneath the moonlight.

Beside it rose the battlements and turrets of Château de Chillon.

Streaking fire shot across the sky. It dazzled the water before turning back on itself and plunging into the highest turret of Chillon. The thunder followed, immediate and deafening. Both Rachel and he held their hands to their ears, crouching as the amalgamation of blinding light and horrendous clap surrounded them.

The air vibrated.

They ran another hundred yards before the elevated roadway was low enough to the ground for them to jump onto the steep, wooded incline. They slid down the hillside and under the autoroute, through brush and mud. They came to a skidding stop at the base of the pylon, where there stood a small, dilapidated wooden structure surrounded by dense undergrowth. He stared into one of its windows before walking around to the far side and nudging the door open with his shoulder. He placed his hand on her back and ushered her inside.

The shack had no furnishings. One wall held some kind of electrical box covered with knobs and dials, but it looked dead—inactive for many years.

He arched his eyebrows as if seeking permission, and she nodded. He crouched to sit on the concrete floor, his back against the rear wall, his bare feet against the front. He held out his arms and Rachel sat between his legs, relaxing against his torso, her head against his pectoral.

The rain clattered on the metal roof.

Rachel's entire body ached.

CHAPTER SIXTY-FIVE

The night in the shed passed slowly. He did not move from his position beneath her, and yet she knew he was awake by the uneven rhythm of his breathing, the almost imperceptible caress of his fingertips upon her thigh, and the subtle sounds of his tongue wetting his lips in the nervous habit that accompanied his deepest thoughts. His body was very warm. Though his jeans were still damp, his T-shirt had long been dry.

Rachel lay motionless in his arms, attempting to make sense of her own thoughts before beginning to contemplate his. No matter where her reflections ventured, she inevitably came to the same conclusion.

She stretched and shifted, thankful for the comfortable contour of his flesh. He lifted his hand as she moved and returned it to her thigh once she'd settled.

"I did not destroy my home." His voice echoed in the darkness, the beating of his heart quickening. "When I returned to my hovel, the blood was already splattered over the tree and front door. My traps had been moved, and I feared someone had gotten caught in them. Perhaps an intruder. I didn't know at that point. All I knew was that it wasn't you. The door was open, and the inside . . . I can't describe the sadness. My life has been short—I mean that my memory has been truncated to the last several months—but those were the objects that were helping me find myself and determine who I am, or could be.

"I . . ." His voice broke. "I don't know how I even came to own those things. They were just there and so was I, and they were mine. They'd been placed there to help me. And now they're gone."

Rachel grabbed his hand and pulled it up close to her heart.

"I don't think someone wanted to rob me of my belongings—just that I've been taught a lesson by those who believed I was theirs. And that now I've been abandoned, I'm on my own."

Rachel turned to look at him—a sliver of moonlight defined his nose and lips in the dark. "What do you mean?"

"I see them in my nightmares, Rachel. I see them when the migraines rip through my skull and threaten to drive me insane. They wear their white coats. Their mouths and noses are hidden by surgical masks. They make notes on their clipboards. They fill syringe after syringe with glistening, yellow liquid and inject it into my arms, my legs, my chest, my spine, my . . . They turn me and shock me and rotate me. They force tubes down my throat and into my nostrils to pump food and water and gasses and more of the yellow liquid into me. They shine lights into my eyes, blast noise into my ears, wipe tastes into my mouth, and waft smells into my nostrils. They rub and caress and touch and hit and slap and punch and cut and suture to cause sensation after excruciating sensation. They make my body tremble. They make it hurt. They make my heart beat until it feels like it will break. It's like they don't know I'm alive—they don't know I'm a living, feeling human being."

Rachel stared into the darkness. She could think of no words to comfort him.

The inside of the shed glowed white as the reflection of lightning struck through the window. The rumbling shudder of thunder soon followed. Another strike and rumble. Then another. The shed vibrated.

"I know what I am, Rachel. And I know that you know, too."

"Yes." The word hardly left Rachel's lips.

They lay in silence for the remainder of the night. Eventually sleep overtook him, and his breathing slowed. The shallow movement of his chest and abdomen soon lulled Rachel into a mutilated, dream-filled slumber.

* * * *

The rain was still falling when she woke, but it was light outside and her watch said it was almost noon.

"We should stay here for today, at least until it's dark again," he said. "Perhaps it'll stop raining."

Rachel sat up between his legs, turning so she could lean against the wall opposite him. Her arms and hands rested on his shins, her feet dug into the warmth of his inner thigh.

"Why are we running? We haven't done anything wrong."

He stared at her and clasped both her feet in his hands. His eyes seemed to change hue.

"I know in my heart I have never harmed another. But wasn't Frankenstein's monster also innocent when he was created? And yet he was shunned, ridiculed, and attacked. He was provoked for no reason other than that he existed."

"But the creature wasn't the true monster of Mary's novel—of that I'm certain."

He looked up at the ceiling in search of his thoughts. He stretched his neck side to side to work out the kinks of an uncomfortable sleep, the scars on his collarbone and under his jawline flushing pale pink against the whiteness of his skin. "Still, he'd be blamed for the crime of his own creation, and that would lead inevitably to his debasement and eventual demise."

"But you are intelligent—beautiful. Mary's wretch was an outcast that society rejected, whereas you've thrived in Montreux without consequence."

"He was intelligent, too. He found his way around Europe with no assistance, learned to walk, speak, recognize words, read, and study. His depth of knowledge was profound. And as for whether or not he was beautiful . . . can you tell me, Rachel, was the original Adam beautiful? Was Eve?"

"I get it. And now, whether we're responsible or not, we're burdened with the consequences."

"In the long run, we're dependent upon the *gendarmerie*. That detective . . ."

"Detective Baertschi."

"Yes. We're dependent upon him to locate the true monster—or monsters —that instigated the need for his investigation in the first place. Then perhaps . . ." His face darkened to crimson, one side contorting, and he let go of her feet to push the palms of his hands against each side of his head. "Then perhaps . . ." His voice grated in palpable pain. "Perhaps they will leave . . . us . . . alone." He balled his hands into fists and slammed them into the walls on either side of his torso. He clenched his arms and hit a second time with a force that made the entire shelter shudder and rattle.

Rachel leaned back, knowing his migraine would soon pass, knowing she wasn't in danger. His face darkened further. The muscles of his legs tensed around her. The veins that swept down his biceps and through his tattoos swelled thick and hard with blood and anger. His fists thudded into the wall again with the sound of splintering wood and the screech of loosening nails.

The glass window above him cracked, a fracture traversing the dirty pane from one side to the other.

His anger shattered and fell until it was no more. He crouched in silence, his eyes squeezed shut, his shaking body the only indication of the upset. He lifted his hand once more to his temple and dug in the pad of his thumb to relieve the pain.

Rachel drew herself close to sit on his lap. She held his head in her hands, her fingers and palms massaging the musculature too tightly woven around his skull, neck, and shoulders. "We'll leave it for Detective Baertschi to handle, okay? We'll leave it to him and the *gendarmes*. Perhaps we can help his investigation. I have his card. We can e-mail him everything we suspect . . . everything you know . . . anything you can remember that might assist him."

"But wouldn't he know where you were e-mailing from? Couldn't he track us down?"

"It would take him days to work that out. By then we could be anywhere."

"Okay." He bit his lower lip and studied her face. "Where do we find a computer?"

Rachel reached into her jeans pocket and pulled out her access card for Chillon.

Lightning blanched across the cracked windowpane.

CHAPTER SIXTY-SIX

"I have but one chapter to write and my ghost story will be complete," Mary said, as Polidori escorted her down the main stair of the villa and across the lobby toward the *porte cochère*. She had spent the entire day in her suite at her Maggiolini, inscribing all that had filled her mind since she had last allowed her fingers to caress her quill. Young Willmouse had gurgled and laughed in the crook of her arm, but still her mind and words had leapt across the parchment.

"Well done to you, Mrs. Shelley. Will your creature, your monster, cross paths once more with the one who created him?"

"Perhaps . . . you will see."

The doorman held the villa entrance door open wide and bowed as Mary and Polidori passed to the outside landing. They waited patiently for their carriage to arrive from the livery. Lanterns lit the marble columns and thick expanse of white gravel. The paths and gardens glimmered in the moonlit drizzle of early evening.

"And would it be his intention to strangle her . . . I mean . . . him? To cast his maker to the ground despite all his noble mutterings and confidences?"

"Could you blame him if he did? Do any of us know for certain what our actions would be when confronted by the thing that has abandoned us, that most fills us with dread and shame, that has been so thoroughly disgusted by our very creation and continued existence upon this landscape because we did not do what it wanted?"

"But all of us have created something that, perhaps, we are not so proud of, that we would rather hide or relegate to the gutter or scrap heap."

"True, but when that creation is a life unto itself, surely we cannot determine to keep it in check, demand it do our will, threaten it with vengeance for any disregard for our imagined authority or, indeed, hide it from ourselves with upheld hand because the sight of it is not as we had envisioned?"

The four-in-hand pulled under the *porte cochère*, all of the horses slick from rain that had fallen all day and now continued without sign of abatement. Polidori assisted Mary into the enclosed carriage before climbing in beside her. The valet presented a blanket, which Polidori accepted and cast across their knees.

"Yes, I expect you are right," he said at last. "The creator of any morsel or magnificence can never merit complete omnipotence over his charge, especially when that charge is another living being."

The carriage heaved out into the darkness of the garden drive, past the gatehouse and along graveled laneways until it lurched up onto the cobbles of Avenue Des Alpes. Mary peered out the carriage window, always entranced by the ever-changing vistas and moods of the village. The rain had now become more a pleasant mist rather than the uncomfortable torrent of the previous day and evening.

They passed the cluster of businesses in central Montreux—apothecaries, grocers, meat merchants, and traders of books, cloth, millinery, haberdashery, and other fine goods. All had shutters drawn, with merely a suggestion of light seeping through from the private apartments at the rear of each store. Street lanterns flickered to light otherwise deserted avenues. Water rushed down the gutters. The carriage clattered past the bookstore in which Mary had first spied the intriguing figure of Doctor Frankenstein.

She was about to ask Polidori a question when she became distracted by a shadow that slipped into an alley just ahead of them. The illumination of a lantern threw the shadow up onto the wall, distorting and elongating its shape. Though its source was not apparent, the representation was splendid and horrible in size. Its movements were cumbersome, but with an agility belying the surprising capacity of the imagined brute. The shadow stopped, the deformed head turning to gaze in the direction from which it had come, as if waiting for their carriage to catch up, to follow its course through the village and along the lake's edge toward Chillon.

Mary stared at the shadow, willing the carriage to come upon the alley more quickly, wiping her hand continually across the pane to keep the condensation from ruining her vision. She pressed her soft nose against the glass as they at last came level with the alley, but no sooner had they turned the corner than the shadow dissolved from the wall, falling off into the darkness of the night.

Mary sunk back into the cushioned interior of the carriage and let out an exasperated sigh.

"Do not fret, Mrs. Shelley. We shall arrive at the Château de Chillon in good time for this night's supper and festivities."

She smiled. "I am afraid, Polidori, that my thoughts are still very much with the wretch that has invaded this territory with no regard for the life of those who live here."

"We will be safe at the château. He would never dare approach such a populated arena. The *gendarmerie* are also circumspect and apprised of all matters. They have become aware of the trail Doctor Frankenstein now travels in his quest for vengeance, and I am certain that, while the doctor may think he follows the wretch who has destroyed his life, it is actually the wretch who is following him."

"So you believe neither is in this vicinity—that there is no reason to be concerned, despite the recent sighting at the Frankenstein residence up in the Haut?"

Polidori hesitated. "We must always take care, Mrs. Shelley."

He looked past Mary and out the carriage window. She followed his gaze. The four-in-hand had passed Bon Port and was now traveling along the laneway that clung to the lake's edge. The water was dark and churning, the Alps beyond iridescent. The moon hung low in the sky to delineate the battlements, embrasures, and turrets of their destination. Storm clouds that had been crouching in the Valais now flung themselves across the sky toward the château at enormous speed, blotting out the Alps, the moon, Chillon, so that all appeared enveloped in a black heaving mass without edge.

Many miles to the west—as far as Geneva—the sky illuminated in a blinding brightness. The sheet of lightning, of fire, appeared as wide as the lake itself and coursed its full length within several blinks of the eye, dragging a terrific rolling thunder in its wake. Mary and Polidori watched in abject horror as the lightning threw their surroundings into blinding tones of white on white before converging on the highest turret of the château with a horrendous clamor that reverberated across the lake.

The château fluoresced in the darkness.

CHAPTER SIXTY-SEVEN

It struck up from the shallows of Lake Geneva. Ancient masonry shimmered obsidian in the rain, the Cross of the Savoy a dark red gash across the stonework. Turrets and battlements glowed as they fed upon the repeated strikes of lightning, licking it from the sky to devour without satiation.

Bonfires burned on the landside. Flames popped and sizzled.

Rachel ran up the walkway from Chillon's pebbled beach and along the rim of the natural moat toward the fortress's entrance. He was behind her, his breath on her neck, holding himself low to the ground, wary whenever the bonfires cast his shadow up across the building. They stopped under the protection of a magnolia.

"This place is pretty ominous at night," he whispered.

"Even in the daylight, if you ask me—especially in its passages and caverns."

The moat was less than a few yards wide, but the water at the bottom of the steep and slippery descent rippled with unease, shards of rock now and then exposed amongst the waves, murkiness suggesting the presence of something best not disturbed within its depths. The stone on the far side was unclimbable, worn smooth by time and slick with algae. Rachel wondered how many had lost their lives in that ditch or on the shore where they now stood—whether by arrow or oil, stone or axe, sword or strangulation.

He rested his hand upon her shoulder, his thick fingers touching the curve of her neck. She peered at the battlements high above, pierced by defensive slits and topped by holes that at one time would have spewed burning oil onto attacking hoards. Rachel shuddered.

She stared at the moat. "There's only one way in."

Ahead of them, three dozen or more people hurried from the roadway, through the rain, and across the drawbridge into the tight confines of Chillon's entrance, only visible as silhouettes behind the glare of the bonfires. The babble of excitement drifted through the night.

"I, um, thought the château would be deserted," he said.

"I'm afraid not. There were often visitors here at night while I was doing my research—conferences, dinners, celebrations, that sort of thing. It's probably better for us that the place isn't empty."

He nodded, but still his eyebrows furrowed.

They remained under the magnolia for many minutes, scrutinizing the arrivals, undecided whether to slip in among them or wait for them to enter first. Several individuals sought cover from the rain under the expansive canopies of other great trees. They smoked and laughed. They pointed toward the entrance, ready to make their own dash once the initial crowd had retreated into the stone. The men sported top hats and wore long coats against the weather. Cigars glowed.

"A wedding?" he guessed, standing behind her, his hands on her shoulders as they waited beneath the tree. They were sheltered from the rain but still Rachel felt damp. She was glad to have his warmth at her back. She was glad to have him.

"Come on, let's go." She grabbed him by the elbow as the entrance cleared and the group beneath the far tree seemed distracted by conversation, the approaching high-pitched neigh of horses, and the rattling percussion of a carriage. They ran over the grass and gravel and across the bridge that spanned the moat and stopped at the massive arch before plunging through the dimly lit foyer and sidling around the crowd that had gathered under the awnings of the first courtyard.

* * * *

The four-in-hand pulled off the main roadway and into the gardens of the château. Mary wrapped her shawl about her shoulders as she stared out her window at the bonfires and the light they cast upon the stone.

"Polidori, it's magnificent. Look. See how the light plays—"

The carriage curved around the drive and jolted up onto the grass to stop beneath a tree. Several men, who had been taking advantage of the cover, called out when they recognized Doctor Polidori climbing down the step. Plumes of cigar smoke surrounded them, the musky fragrance mixing with that of wet earth and foliage. Polidori held the carriage door open as Mary leaned out, sniffing at the air to take in its pleasure and nodding toward the men.

"Remember that you are my escort tonight, John." Mary smiled as she took Polidori's offered hand and stepped to the ground. She was dressed for the occasion at Chillon in an extravagantly trimmed, high-waisted, flowing gown of periwinkle blue that cut low across her breasts. Long white gloves crumpled just above her wrists to expose her smooth and fair arms. A dark velvet mantle trimmed with swan down draped across her shoulders and fell to her ankles as defense against the evening breeze and drizzle. She adjusted her cashmere shawl beneath the mantle before placing her hand upon Polidori's extended forearm.

"Time to go in and see where the evening takes us, Mrs. Shelley."

They hurried across the grass. The metal pattens secured to their shoes held them an inch or two above the soggy squelch of ground, but still Mary pulled at her mantle and gown so they would not become wet at the trim. They made it to the covered drawbridge without being struck by a single spot of rain. Almost immediately they were amongst the congregation of tourists, local dignitaries, and ancient Montreux families that clustered in the first court of the fortress.

Both Mary and Polidori recognized many in the crowd as acquaintances they had made in their weeks on the shores of Lake Geneva, either at suppers, lectures, and excursions, or during the passing niceties of any constitutional the weather had allowed. Polidori appeared to know most of the men—at least the ones close to his twenty-three years of age. There was much shaking of hands and patting of backs as he guided Mary through the high-class milieu.

* * * *

Rachel felt uncomfortable as she pressed between the well-dressed crowd and the damp stone of the fortress. Both she and he wore only T-shirts and still-damp blue jeans. His feet were bare, in contrast to the high-polished boots of the men and the silk or leather slippers of the women. She was aware of the momentary flashes of curiosity thrown their way as they passed through the tunnel from the first court toward the second. He was crouching now, so his head was in line with the others instead of two feet above. He kept his massive hand at the small of her back—not to push or guide but merely to follow, as if he were afraid of losing her.

The tunnel opened out into the second courtyard. The yard was lit by torches and lanterns, the smell of burning oil rags lending an archaic feel to the scene. A score of windows and doorways punched through the thick stonework, and high wooden walkways clung to the walls to link otherwise unattainable openings. Deep timber awnings offered protection from rain, stone projectiles, arrows, and falling bodies.

The crowd had thinned, allowing faster movement into the third court. For a moment, he dropped his hand from Rachel's back. She turned to reassure herself he was still there, but her eyes were met by one of the well-dressed party. A handsome man with pale skin; dark, clipped, curling hair; and mutton chops extending along a defined jawline. Yes, very handsome. His attention flicked down to her shirt and jeans before averting, embarrassed and flustered. He glanced again at Rachel's face and gave a polite nod before moving off into the crowd. The lady on his arm craned her neck to see what had disrupted her escort's movement toward the banqueting hall.

Her eyes glimmered.

I know you, Rachel thought.

* * *

"How very odd. I can only assume she works in the stables but, still, to be seen in little more than a chemise and breeches is quite awkward for all." Mary giggled. "I wish I were so daring."

Polidori, always the gentleman, said nothing of the girl's attire. "Did you notice the man that crouched in her wake?"

"I did—a man of gigantic proportions."

"And a strikingly pleasant countenance."

"Yes. I agree."

Polidori led Mary up the slick stone steps that ran up the side of the crooked space. On the top landing, they paused to look upon the guests that followed. The view was dominated by top hats, ornamented coifs, and ribboned bonnets. Fans flared and flicked in excited conversation.

They took one last look at the night sky. The stars were invisible. Darkness roiled upon darkness as storm clouds collided and rumbled. Lightning flared deep in the depths of night, apparent as the black shapes crossing the sky pulsed with an inner purple so dark it pulled the breath from the lungs.

The stable girl, if that was what she was, and her large companion pressed themselves into a doorway on the far side of the yard.

"How intriguing," Mary said to herself as she followed Polidori's lead into the Heraldic Hall. A young girl assisted with slipping the mantle from her shoulders and arms to expose the periwinkle blue of her dress to the room's soft candlelight.

Polidori shrugged off his dark overcoat and hat to hand to a servant. He was fashionably replete in a double-breasted tailcoat with puffed shoulders and turned-back cuffs, with a matching high collar of velvet. Beneath was his best waistcoat and shirt—both brilliantly white in contrast to his subtle chamois-colored pantaloons and the high polish of his Wellington boots. He tugged at his coat and peered into a side mirror to confirm the settlement of his coif. Mary reached up to straighten his white, silk cravat.

"Do not worry, my friend. Do you think I would have allowed you to escort me if I did not know you would eclipse all other gentlemen in the room?"

"Ha! Has your writer's imagination finally elevated me to the realm of Miss Austen's Master of Pemberley?"

Mary laughed.

The window casements of the large hall were set deep into the stonework, allowing views of the outside darkness. The lake vista was all but invisible in the night—the eye only imagining the whip of waves and the crag of Alps that must still be out there. Thick beams cut from ancient forests straddled the space to hold the ceiling high. Murals of heraldry covered the walls, documenting the history of families, conquests, and vanquishments dating back hundreds, if not thousands, of years. The soft tones of a fortepiano echoed the latest sonata by *Herr* Beethoven.

"An inspiring room—so grand." Mary accepted champagne from a waiter, and touched glasses with Polidori. "I have heard rumor that tonight's banquet will contain over one hundred and twenty courses."

"I have heard the same—a French chef by the name of Marie Antonin Carême. His culinary works are said to be without equal. I will admit in confidence that I even had my man lace my corset a little loose this evening, so I am not restricted in tonight's gastronomic adventure." Polidori held out his forearm. "Shall we stroll about the room, Mrs. Shelley?"

"Always a pleasure, Doctor Polidori."

* * * *

The rain had started to fall heavily again and now pounded with deafening noise against the cobbles of Chillon's courtyards. All the guests had made it up the steps and into the opulent shelter of the fortress, but Rachel pressed into the doorway on the far side of the yard, completely drenched. He stood over her in attempt to cover but without any success. Their jeans squelched, their T-shirts clung. Except for them, the yard was deserted.

Rachel hesitated as she noticed a shadow pass across the roof of the tunnel they'd come through, but when no one appeared, she ran across the yard and up the stairs. He followed close behind, assisting when she almost lost her footing, his bare feet padding against the rain-soaked cobbles and steps up into the foyer. They turned from the grand hall, now bustling with the warmth of festivity, and instead entered a small salon and closed the door behind them.

The room was full of brightly painted furnishings, sumptuous chairs and bedding, ornate, decorated tables, and shelves filled with glass decanters and pewterware. Tapestries hung from the walls. A wooden candelabrum dangled from the ceiling on a swooping chain. On the far side a door opened into a second foyer, which offered several directions to try. Rachel squeezed down a slim corridor of rough-hewn masonry.

"Rachel." His voice skimmed against the stonework in an urgent whisper.

She turned to see him wedged into the tight confines of the passage. Even sideways the bulk of his chest wouldn't fit. His head was lowered and his neck bent, but his massive thighs and the length of his legs stopped any progress.

"I'll wait in this last salon. Okay? I can't think of anything else I didn't tell you last night. You know who I am. You know what to write."

"Okay. I'm just in this next room. I won't be long." She held her key card against the small plastic dot set into the wall aside the solid oak doorframe. The lock clicked and she pushed the door open to enter the archives.

Ignoring the floor-to-ceiling shelves crammed with books and boxes, she ran to the far end of the room and sat at the computer. She hit enter and the machine purred to life, the screen filling the room with its dull blue ambient light.

* * * *

Polidori engaged in polite conversation with several young men whom Mary thought only mildly interesting. Still she smiled and nodded as required, studying their mannerisms and gestures, the lines of their faces, the trim of their chops, the sweetness of their attentiveness toward her escort.

And then she saw him again.

The huge Gothic window reflected him clearly as he stood in the shadows of a doorway. Through the window's reflection, she saw him peer almost directly at her, his eyes just below the lintel of the doorway. His bulk was perhaps the size of two or three men amalgamated. Mary's heartbeat quickened as she likened him to her own creation—her own beautifully horrible wretch. His face was clean-shaven, absent of the facial adornments affected by all the men she had ever known. The smooth skin of his jaw made him appear yet a boy, an innocent who was unaware of his strength and masculinity.

The reflection flared as lightning cut across the sky outside, the tall arched window filled with the garish vista of torrid waves and the Alps beyond. Mary held one hand to her eyes to block the blinding glare and placed the other on Polidori's forearm. There was a general exclamation throughout the room as the light shone into the hall and hushed all conversation before the chatter sparked again with renewed vigor.

"Undoubtedly a festivity to remember." Polidori chuckled, beckoning the waiter to refresh their glasses.

"Yes, certainly." Once her eyes had readjusted to the ambient light, Mary peered once more into the reflection of the Gothic window to seek out he who had held her interest, but he was gone.

The dinner gong sounded.

As the guests wandered toward the banqueting hall, Mary caught Polidori's sleeve. "I think he is here, Polidori."

"Whom do you mean?"

"As you know, when I first arrived here at Montreux, I attended the lecture by *Monsieur* Aldini up at Le Château du Châtelard."

"The lecture on Galvanism, 'animal electricity,' and attempts to give life to inanimate flesh—to corpses," the doctor recalled.

"Yes, precisely." Mary pulled her friend into a broad alcove as the other guests moved past them. They both nodded in salutation toward acquaintances as she continued their quiet conversation. "At the lecture's end, everyone retired out onto the Terrasse d'Honneur for cocktails and discussion of the evening's events. Doctor Frankenstein was there, though distant from the attendees of the lecture, preferring to find solitude at the edge of the terrace where he studied his notes. During *Monsieur* Aldini's explanatory discourse, I noted that the doctor held conversation with a young man—an exceedingly beautiful young man of extraordinary stature."

They took slow steps out of the alcove and followed the crowd toward the red velvet curtain that gave entrance to the banqueting hall.

"And do you think, Mrs. Shelley, that the young man with Doctor Frankenstein is the same man we saw in the courtyard this evening?"

"Perhaps not the same man, but I am certain he is of the same ilk."

"Do you suspect he is dangerous—that I should alert the *gendarmerie*?"

Mary hesitated. "Oh." She thought of the recent spate of murders and desecrations for which Doctor Frankenstein was no longer completely suspect. She thought of the creature Frankenstein claimed was killing his friends and acquaintances, his bride, for naught but revenge. Could the young man she saw on the Terrasse d'Honneur be the one who killed in the dead of night—who sought retribution for the perceived wrong dealt against him? Could a creature so physically pleasant be guilty of such abominable acts? Or had the apparent beauty she had witnessed at Châtelard now decayed and putrefied into the grotesque that tortured the region on its own rampage, fueled by fear and revenge?

And now this second man, this second beautiful creature—was he also implicated in an exceedingly unpleasant narrative?

Of the same ilk, but possibly not of the same intention, Mary thought to herself. She surveyed the all-but-empty Heraldic Hall behind them. An elderly gentleman sat at the fortepiano looking through his music sheets; a waiter collected champagne glasses from the tables and ledges. "Perhaps I am mistaken, Polidori. Forgive my alarmist ramblings—the notions of a fledgling author. I am certain they will amount to nothing."

Polidori escorted Mary through the velvet curtain and into the banqueting hall. Almost immediately, she began to second-guess her assumptions about the man who lurked nearby in the corridors of the château—who had invaded her mind and creative thoughts for so many weeks. Could he have tricked even her, beguiling her into a sense of security when he was in fact capable of the most heinous of crimes?

* * * *

The computer was infuriatingly slow as Rachel clicked through several Internet screens to access her e-mail. She pulled out Detective Baertschi's card—sodden, ripped, and smudged from being in her jeans—typed his e-mail address into the "to" field, and started writing. She let the words flow, neglecting spelling, syntax, and grammar, just wanting to get her thoughts across as best she knew how. She conveyed his story, or at least the parts he'd communicated to her, piecing together the conversations they'd had, the fears he'd revealed during their most intimate moments, his dreams that made up who he thought he might be—who they both knew he was.

As she jogged her memory, she thought of the youth who'd attacked her in the cemetery, whose hands had smelled like pig.

The pig who was now dead.

The dark-haired, hazel-eyed, broken-nosed youth who'd pushed and hurt her as no man had before.

The detective's phone had captured a photo of cheeks bruised and bloody, a once-broken nose, broken again—crushed—and skin ripped from a crooked chin, jawbone exposed.

Eyes staring blank in the horror of unexpected death.

He had said he didn't do it, and she'd believed him. And yet she wondered whether he truly knew what he had done, what he was capable of, what he had exacted during the moments of his migraines . . . the moments he could never remember.

She loved him, and yet the uncertainty of his memory scared her, made *her* uncertain.

Rachel jumped up from the chair, needing to see him and reassure herself. She ran to the door of the archive and pulled it open to peer down the corridor.

He wasn't there.

She called out for him but he didn't answer.

She stood and waited, called a second time, waited.

Nothing.

She returned to the computer to finish the e-mail. When she sat down, she felt confused. The message had gone. It had been sent. She thought about what else she had wanted to convey but, looking over her shoulder toward the door and down the empty corridor, she recognized that there was nothing more she could add.

* * * *

The banqueting hall of Chillon was nothing short of spectacular. Medieval in atmosphere, its massive stone columns rose from the floor to support overarching wooden beams. The ceiling itself was a thatch of beam upon beam upon beam, discolored by centuries of festivity and defense. The walls were muraled with horizontal zigzags of red and white, and the broad, blackened, stone fireplace was huge enough to shelter a cabriolet and horse. Its mantle was held high by more columns, its fire roaring, the White Cross of the Swiss Confederation emblazoned across the hood. Ornate tapestries hung from ceiling to floor. The wall opposite the fireplace was pierced by the same large Gothic windows as the Heraldic Hall, the pitch blackness of the evening outside resolving them to a mirrored reflection of the internal celebrations and carousing.

Polidori and Mary proceeded the length of the room, stopping before the fireplace as the *maitre d'hôtel* consulted his book to confirm their seating. Mary waved acknowledgement toward an acquaintance as they waited. The room was filled with excited conversation.

An elaborate construction of marzipan and sugar ruins dominated the center of each dining table. Crumbling, sweet-smelling Corinthian columns and edible statuary lay across the tablecloths in a display surpassing Lord Elgin's Marbles. Trestles along the hall walls held uncountable dishes, though Mary was able to determine at least eight different pottages before the sheer number of courses began to overwhelm her.

Mary and Polidori were seated at a table with a dozen others who were more than happy to continue consuming champagne and wait for the rush to subside before perusing the menu.

Corks were popped and glasses refreshed. Boisterous conversation ensued. Mary was glad to see Polidori at ease and smiling. He had suffered much at the atrocities he had witnessed, but now perhaps they were over. Perhaps. With word that Doctor Frankenstein and his adversary were many leagues distant, it was likely Montreux could now settle back into its quiet, beautiful existence.

The ladies of the table rose as one with much flouncing and preening of gowns. Mary felt duty-bound to align herself with them as they made their way toward the buffet. She winked at Polidori as he continued his courting of the men. They hung on his every word.

Mary passed one of the thick central columns—it felt cold to the touch, reaching up from the very core of the ancient fortress. She strolled toward a large salmon and, as she accepted a small plate from a steward, she was distracted by a movement at the periphery of her vision. Through the flux of the banquet room, her gaze was drawn to the opening into the deserted Heraldic Hall and straight across to the stone archway leading from the entrance foyer.

He stood there, staring at her.

Yes, he was definitely staring at her.

Did he know her? As well as she thought she knew him?

Mary looked down at the salmon, placed her plate next to its dead eyes, and then peered back at him.

His feet were bare. He wore blue breeches, dark with saturation. His dirty, white chemise clung to his torso. Mary blushed at how massively masculine he appeared.

And then she noticed his countenance. His expression seemed at first pleasant, but as she studied it more closely, she noted the ripple of his brow, the curl of his lip, the glimmer in his eye. He pushed his palm against the side of his head—dug the pad of his thumb into his temple—as if he were besieged by head pain.

She recognized anger.

No . . . hatred. Intense hatred and confusion—the pent up emotion of one who had never been true to himself or acknowledged his true temptations and provocations, his true fears and desires.

They locked eyes on each other for several moments and then he turned away. He hesitated, glanced once more into her eyes as if he wanted her to follow him, then passed back through the foyer where she could no longer see him.

* * *

Rachel paused a moment, looking back toward the computer as it purred and buzzed, and then, without thought, hurried toward the entrance of the archives. She rushed through the oak door and along the tight confines of the corridor. She ran across the small salon, past the brightly painted ornate furnishings, and out into the foyer.

* *

Mary paused a moment, looking back at Polidori still deep in conversation, and then without thought hurried toward the entrance of the banquet hall. She rushed through the opening, brushing past the velvet curtains. She ran across the Heraldic Hall, past the fortepiano, and out into the foyer.

*

Her heart skipped a beat. The foyer was deserted.

She looked around, confused—as if she had been turned about.

Steadying herself against the jamb of the entrance door, she held a hand to her chest and stared down the glistening stone stairway out into the rain-soaked courtyard. All but one of the flaming torches had extinguished in the downpour. The cobbled ground shimmered under a layer of water. The central ditch was a torrent that fed through the main tunnel to be jettisoned out a grate into the surrounding moat. The sheer noise of it all was deafening.

But he was not there—no one was.

He must have gone deeper into the fortress.

She ran beyond the foyer into a small suite of interconnecting rooms and stopped dead in the center of the sitting room. The substantial oak door closed behind her with a thud, the latch clicking into place as if of its own accord. There was not the slightest hint of noise except the incessant slap of rain against the sliver of glass set into the loophole. The thick masonry of the walls blocked all other sound, even the boisterous festivities of the banqueting hall. She dared not move, fearing even to breathe, as her heart pound in her chest. She felt cold, though there was no hint of a draft.

The room was plunged into utter darkness, the loophole offering nothing from outside to light the way. She could see nothing as the heaviness of black on black consumed her. She could feel nothing but the floor beneath her shoes. She could not move, would not, lest she touch something . . . something warm in this cold space. The hair on her arms rose and her skin pricked as a breeze manifested from nowhere. Had a door been opened?

Something passed beside her without a sound, apparent by the soft caress of the very ends of the upright hairs on her arms. She wanted to pull her arms close to her body, away from the touch of the unknown, but still she held rigid, unwilling to give any indication of fear to whoever—whatever—might now share the room with her. At last the sensation ceased, and she knew she was once more alone.

The loophole flared with lightning. The crack of thunder followed. The room was fleetingly lit before again subsiding into darkness. But it had been adequate to give her her bearings among the furniture, to see the farthest doorway, and to feel her way across the room toward it.

The corridor beyond was a twisting encasement of solid stone. Taking tentative steps, she felt her way through the darkness, aware the surface beneath her was rising higher inside the battlements of the fortress. Ahead was an almost imagined glow. She stumbled over an unexpected step in the middle of the corridor and fell to her hands and knees in the cold, stone passage. With her face close to the ground, she inhaled in fright. The space smelled of dampness and mildew. She thought of the men who must have run up this ramp, crossbows and longbows in hand, to defend their families and land, their freedom. It smelled of leather and sweat, of loss and casualty, of death and decay. Perhaps the dead and dying were removed from the ramparts via this passage—the corpses of heroes dragged into the depths of the fortress.

A door banged somewhere above and echoed down the passage. There was the momentary piercing noise of wind and rain, and then the door banged again to deaden the sound. She climbed to her feet, her hands pressed against the wall of the corridor. As she moved forward, her eyes adjusted to the gloom and she was able to discern a stairwell. The stairs curved up and to the right, becoming brighter toward the top from an unseen light. She crept up the treads one at a time, knowing he had passed this way, able to sense the warmth of his handprint upon the curving stone, becoming more and more aware of his smell as it hung in the air.

She perceived the warm, sweet moisture of his breath permeating the space as she reached the top. The door on the landing was jammed shut. The latch was free, so she leaned her full body weight against the wood and shoved. It scraped open, jerk after screeching jerk. The increasing gap allowed wind to blow into the well. Rain seeped over the threshold and around her feet. A gust pulled the door from her grip and flung it open to expose the upper fortifications on the land-side of Chillon. Vast sheets of stone followed the curving walkway between the dominating, conical-roofed defense towers. A massive wall, punctured by loopholes and crenulations, followed the bend. The keep rose majestically higher still in the center of the fortress and shone against the night sky. Though all was shattered and indistinct in the darkness and continuing torrent of rain, she saw him on the far side of the battlement, crouching beneath a protective overhang.

His head jerked in her direction, both hands held to his temples, his face twisted by pain.

"Why do you follow me?" he yelled. "Surely your life would be less complicated without me in it. Just let me go. Forget I exist."

She hesitated as he moved uneasily in the shadows of the tower. He placed a hand against the awning above him, his flexing bicep enormous beside his head.

"I need . . ." Her voice didn't carry the distance in this weather. "Wait!" she yelled with all her might before running out into the deluge. The rain pelted her with unexpected force, and she shielded her face with her hands to stop the stinging pain. She was not even halfway across the battlements when lightning struck the top of Chillon's keep. Less than several yards away, the strike was blinding, the smell and taste of metal all-consuming, the clap of thunder so instant and so loud that it seemed to vibrate throughout her body and paralyze her from top to toe. She was thrown to the ground, her hip, shoulder, and head hitting the flagstones with a bruising thud. Unable to breathe, unable to will her body up and out of the open, she began to shake uncontrollably.

The smooth stone, glossed by water, reflected the battlements and turrets in hallucinogenic splendor. Shapes shifted in the water, lit by the fire. A hand slipped around her waist and under her buttock, the other skimmed past her breast and around to her back. She was pulled into him, her face into the crook of his neck, her breast against the warmth of his heaving chest, her thighs against unexpected heat.

She stared at the underside of his chin as he passed from the open battlements and through a doorway. He drew her more tightly against his flesh. Her body jolted as he jumped down the stairs—three, five, eight at a time. In less than a moment they were again in the entrance courtyard, but instead of heading toward the main arch he ran along an inner wall and leapt down several more steps. One hand left her body for an instant to punch into a low door and send it flying open. He ducked and ran through into a flickering, gray-gold, torchlit cavern. The door slammed closed behind them.

The floor and the walls were raw rock, molded by nothing but Mother Earth. He ran past Gothic columns that held an ornate stone-arched ceiling high above the rough. His grunts echoed throughout the space until finally he stopped, his chest heaving, the sound of his breath reverberating against the stone.

He lowered her onto the rough before stepping off into the darkness.

Stone arches crisscrossed the ceiling. Column after column, arch after arch marched along, forcing a medieval order upon the decaying crumble of rock. It was as if the order grew from nothing, sprouting from unwanted rubble into something of magnificence. Something ordered, structured, and beautiful.

Heavy metal rings were secured to the stonework. Chains, collars, and irons were scattered about the floor. A battered and stained stock stood nearby.

The debris tumbled down the slope of the natural floor of the cavern toward the outer walls of the fortress, into a wide ditch where the lake surged in through a grated entrance. Waves, ripples, and fish dared to intrude into the horrid gloom of Chillon's dungeon, where little other than misery and dripping water had echoed for centuries. A moaning wind moved timidly through the cavern, hiding behind columns, creeping through damp crevices, reminiscing in low echoing tones of those who had been imprisoned and tortured in this space.

She pulled herself up against the column and looked around. He sat several feet away. Rippled light skewed through the lake entrance onto his legs and chest, but his face was invisible in the dark. His breath was heavy, and his right hand flicked and clenched in obvious agitation.

"You will be okay down here," he said. The deep echo of his voice made him seem like he belonged in there.

She remained silent, waiting for her eyes to adjust to the gloom.

"Please move into the light," she finally said.

He eased away from the wall to sit on his haunches and crossed legs in the middle of the raw rock. A slight glow drew the lines of his face from the darkness. He was at once horrible and beautiful to behold, as the undulating light cut across his features.

"Tell me," she said.

"You know all there is to know."

"But why do you run from me?"

"Because you, as much as anyone, are my creator. I am only that which those around me have allowed me to be."

She studied the shadows of his face and frame. "No, that isn't true. With or without me, you would still exist. No matter your creator, you are yourself and no other. You create your own emotions, your own desires, and your own dreams and future."

"Perhaps . . . But what of those who have died so I might live?"

Water dripped from the ceiling, echoing hollowly as it splashed against the rock.

"They are dead. But you did not kill them. And in you, they are still alive."

He was silent for many minutes. "Shouldn't I seek vengeance?"

"You have not been wronged. You have been given life."

"But . . ."

"Those responsible will find their own end. They are not your concern. This is your story, not theirs."

"And you? Why do you follow me? Why have you allowed me into your world?"

She was hesitant, at first unsure of how to answer but gladdened as the words resolved down to a very few.

"I follow you because I love you and I need you to exist."

Again he was silent, his breathing settling into an easy rhythm that soon became imperceptible beneath the ambient noise of the dungeon. He placed both his knuckles onto the rock on either side of his crossed legs and pushed himself up to his full height, his awesome bulk a silhouette against walls well-accustomed to death and misery, pain and sorrow, murder and loss. He approached her and knelt without a word to press his palms against either side of her slender neck. His skin was cold. His grip trembled as it tensed to hold her immobile. The mere caress of his fingertip against her earlobe made her shiver as she was engulfed by his shadow.

He leaned forward and pressed his lips against her forehead in a soft, warm kiss. He skimmed his lips over her cheek toward her ear and whispered a few words meant only for her. As they burned deep into her heart, he pulled back and stood, releasing his gentle grip from her neck and grasping her hands to draw her to her feet. He brushed the pad of his thumb across her cheek and then turned to walk over to the ditch where the lake entered the dungeon.

The water lapped and eddied as he waded in up to his shoulders. The crossed grate barring the way rose high above, and the waves thrashed about him with increasing vigor. The muscles of his shoulders flexed repeatedly, his strength apparently working the metal bars below the waterline. A dull thud resonated throughout the subterranean space, and he ducked beneath the waves. She held her breath, watching the surface where he had disappeared.

Interminable minutes passed. The water continued to swell and rip and foam, both inside and outside the cavern, until finally his head and torso rose from the wake outside. He drew a deep gasp of air into his lungs that reverberated through the grate. She took a breath, and her heart unclenched.

He took one last glance at her and disappeared.

She shuffled closer to the edge of the ditch and stared out the barred entrance into the darkened night.

Lightning flashed.

He was gone.

CHAPTER SIXTY-EIGHT

1851

Mary mused that life needed to be taken advantage of whenever possible.

Her first three children had died before they were aware of who they were, something that could never be reconciled and which was still beyond any capacity for her to confront. But her fourth, Percy Florence, had matured into a sensible young man who gripped his life with much vigor, promise, and imagination, and ventured off into the world to make it his own. He reminded Mary of her husband and perhaps a little of herself, when they were both much younger than he.

She recalled, with a reflective smile, the summer of 1816—her exploits with her friends and acquaintances, the creation of something that meant more to her than she could ever have thought possible.

Such happy times.

But for almost thirty years now she had been alone, bereft of the company of her closest friends. Her beloved husband, Percy, had drowned off the rugged shores of Cinque Terre when he was but twenty-nine. Their dear acquaintance Lord Byron followed soon after at the age of thirty-six, when he threw himself gallantly into the salvation of Greece against the Ottoman might. Both men had died in endeavors of love and valor. Both had died happy.

Mary brushed at an obstinate tear and looked out the window of the train. Time spent in Edinburgh would do her good, she thought as the moors swept past in their beautiful undulating bleakness. She caught her own reflection in the glass, noting how the passage of time had altered her face but still feeling as vibrant as the eighteen-year-old girl who had once wandered the streets of Montreux and dared release the demon from the box.

Her vision blurred with tears.

Perhaps the greatest sadness was the useless loss of Polidori. A trustworthy and gentle man who had found a freedom on the continent not available in the empire he called home. The life he longed for—love, happiness with the companion of his choosing—was disdained, ridiculed, accused of being unnatural and evil, thought wretched and monstrous, a hideous creation that needed to be relegated to an ice-covered hell far from civilization. He was found dead at twenty-six, broken by depression, unable to live in a society that could not accept him for who he truly was: a trustworthy and gentle man.

Mary extracted a silver cigarette case from her travel bag, selected one of the long slender sticks, placed it between her lips, and lit it. The moors passed by with repetitive reassurance, each mound and dip as predictable as the sound of the locomotive that pulled her closer and closer toward the city. Languorous ribbons of smoke curled in the confines of her compartment, attempted to occlude her vision of the moors and the reflection of her aged countenance in the window.

The door of the compartment rattled and creaked, and Mary smiled when she saw him. He had found her once more.

"Welcome, old friend," she said. His immensity was still shocking even to her, even after all these years.

She patted the leather of the bench beside her. "Come. Sit with me for the rest of my journey."

CHAPTER SIXTY-NINE

Rachel had been sitting for the best part of the morning on the top deck of the South Street Seaport, the *New York Times* folded in her lap. She'd made her way through signing a few dozen copies of *FIRE ON THE WATER: A Companion to Mary Shelley's Frankenstein*, and now she pressed the rim of a satisfying cup of coffee to her lips as she looked out over the East River and the sweeping magnificence of the Brooklyn Bridge.

She was content to sit and study the beautiful construction that had risen from the river at a time when many had thought it impossibile. For something so massive and beautiful to be conceived and built and then endure was one of the great wonders of the world.

She glanced down at the paper in her lap, skimming over the words buried deep in the international news section:

Modern-day Frankenstein—Montreux, Switzerland: This week just passed, the local gendarmerie raided a château in the village of Les Avants, just minutes from the opulent Swiss Riviera resort town of Montreux. The antique château has for the past five years been utilized by the F- Medical Research Institute for advanced studies in the areas of genetic, aesthetic, and reconstructive surgery. The staff is at this time assisting the gendarmes in their ongoing investigation into reports of corpse mutilations, unauthorized procurement and use of human organs, and performance of unethical medical procedures strictly banned by the World Health Organization.
Detective Gendarme Chevalier Baertschi released a statement indicating they are interested in talking with the head doctor of the Institute, whose current whereabouts are unknown, in relation to the unauthorized use of body parts and also several recent murders in the region. Baertschi had been led to the château by an anonymous informant who continues to assist with the investigation.

"Hello," he said. His tongue was Swiss, possibly more German-Swiss than French. Rachel still had never heard a voice more masculine, more . . .

"Any sane person would think I was following you, or you me." He sat down on the deckchair beside hers. She had no time to answer before he leaned into her, and she knew there was no more need for words.

He kissed her slowly and passionately, their tongues exploring their love for each other as his hand caressed the burgeoning belly that held their own creation.

THE END

Acknowledgments

A novel is never really written by one person, especially when the writer is surrounded by a life, family, and friends he loves very much. And so it is with *Fire on the Water: A Companion to Mary Shelley's Frankenstein*. Even after *The End* has been typed on the last line of the manuscript, it is only the beginning, as there are more friends to be made through the editing and publishing process. Words and sentences are polished to give life to something that conveys some kind of joy to those willing to allow the creation into their own lives.

P.J.

About the Author

P.J. Parker was born and raised in rural Australia. With a Bachelor of Science in architecture from the University of New South Wales, he has traveled and lived extensively around the world, focusing on cultures of historic interest and buildings of architectural significance before transitioning into a career as a fraud analyst and programmer with a leading international financial institution. An avid reader and researcher, P.J. undertakes his writing with a passionate and exacting attention to detail.

CPSIA information can be obtained at www.ICGtesting.com
Printed in the USA
LVOW05s2336201213

366021LV00001B/30/P